A
HANGING
AT *Cinder*
BOTTOM

Also by Glenn Taylor

The Ballad of Trenchmouth Taggart
The Marrowbone Marble Company

A
HANGING
AT *Cinder*
BOTTOM

GLENN TAYLOR

b

THE BOROUGH PRESS

The Borough Press
An imprint of HarperCollins*Publishers*
1 London Bridge Street
London SE1 9GF

www.harpercollins.co.uk

Published by HarperCollins*Publishers* 2015

1

A catalogue record for this book
is available from the British Library

ISBN: 978-0-00-810480-1

Set in Perpetua by Palimpsest Book Production Limited, Falkirk, Stirlingshire

Printed and bound in Great Britain by
Clays Ltd, St Ives plc

This one is for the people of McDowell County,
West Virginia, past, present, and future.

Author's Note

Though this novel is an unruly work of fiction, the reader may be best served to know a few truths. First, the last name Baach is pronounced BAY-CH. My wife Margaret's great-great grandfather was Isaiah Lee Baach of Kermit, West Virginia, in Mingo County. He was most likely born in or around Pocahontas, Virginia, where his parents had settled after emigrating from Germany. Though I. Lee Baach was for me a starting point and a fascinating man, it is important to note that he is nowhere indicated or alluded to in the pages that follow (beyond the use of his last name), and that I have taken great liberties in the writing of this novel. Thus, all characters, their actions, and their speech are the product of my imagination and in no way represent any person, living or dead. The reader might also note that Keystone's beginnings and explosive growth occurred slightly later than is depicted herein. Likewise, the layout and geography of the town (including its infamous red-light district, known as Cinder Bottom) was slightly altered for ease of understanding, though Keystone is not a place to be easily understood. It has been many things since its inception. The same could be said of its county, McDowell, a place that is anything but ordinary, a place I have sought to better comprehend through reading the important work listed in the acknowledgments at the end of this novel. McDowell County is a place that is often misrepresented. I invite the reader to find it.

Cook ovens glare red-eyed upon the darkness
And belch their cinders at the fevered days.

—LOUISE McNEILL

A man with a guitar laid flat on his lap
And a pocketknife for a slide
Called a song about old Keystone
Where the strumpets and knaves reside

Come all ye fornicators he sang
Come on Death's Black Train
Ain't no difference 'tween here and hell
'Cept a creek running 'side the lane

He told the tale of the Kid and the Queen
And he told what came before
The years he gave were wide apart
A season apiece made four

1877's Fall and Winter '97
1903 in Spring and Summer 1910
The hell he conjured was so glorious
I found salvation in every sin.

—JENKINJONES CHESTER

Contents

THEIR DAY HAD COME

August 21, 1910

The condemned man wore no shoes. He stood over the drain hole in his cell and hummed the low notes running swollen in his blood. He shed his trousers while he hummed, and his shirt and his undergarments too. Each he folded in a square and set upon the straw tick in the corner. The foul drain at the floor's middle called out to him in the singing voice of his woman down the hall. He answered, a long weary-throated note, a brand of humming borne from a troublesome lot.

He was better than six foot two inches and sturdy despite incarceration. He'd turned thirty in January. Most considered him the handsomest man they'd seen, though he wore a wide scar across his jaw.

At the pith, the condemned man was good, but he'd forever run afoul of temperance and lawmen.

Daylight through the barred window marked his lower half. His feet were pale, and his pecker, in ordinary times a swag-bellied hog of considerable proportion, was, on this morning, contracted. His woman's voice grew louder, and in his mind he could see her, and he hummed to his contracted pecker a snake-charmer tune fetched from a hoochie kootch show, and its furrows protracted, and it was made long and serpentine. And the condemned man imagined then that it grew longer still and mined the drainpipe clear to the cell of his woman, and it whispered to her there, *Keep your temper.* And this thought made him smile.

Down the hall, the condemned woman hummed along. When he crescendoed she did too. When he went so low she couldn't hear him, she sang things like, *There's a hole in his pants, where the crabs and bedbugs dance.*

It was the same snake-charmer melody the Alhambra house band had played seven years prior, on the night the condemned man had lit out of town, the night a big-name magician had levitated a woman on the Alhambra's stage while the melody built. High above, crouched on the fly rig, the man who was now condemned had hummed along, and he'd spat tobacco juice down upon the stage from a height that caused much spatter, and he'd cursed the magician for having not paid the gambling debt he'd owed.

The tunes they hummed to each other down the corridor and through the drainpipes had meanings. They'd worked out a system of codes. The condemned woman knew then from his hum that the morning-shift hall guard had arrived, and that it was nearing time to change into her finery. She took off her underskirt while she sang. She took off her umbrella drawers. Each she folded in a square and set upon the straw tick in the corner.

She was graceful and everywhere arched proportionate. Her skin was tanned despite incarceration, and she stood above the drain hole and hummed some more, waiting for her man.

Young officer Reed would be along shortly with the last meal and fine clothes they'd requested, and she knew he'd not be able to take his eyes off her, for even after a month in the pokey, the condemned woman was the cat's whisker.

Outside, the chief of police, a runt of a man named Rutherford, watched the people come on foot and horseback and great big farm wagons with three families to a bed. The night before, passenger cars on the nine o'clock train had folks pressed to the windows, and more had stuffed themselves into boxcars and empty coal hoppers.

Now it was morning, a Sunday. Rain fell hard after forty days without. On Railroad Avenue, mud ruts made by wagon wheels multiplied and widened. A tied, riderless horse had been made to drink rye whiskey. It fell down buckskinned and got up half brown.

By nine o'clock, three thousand people had gathered at Keystone in order that they might witness a public hanging in the state of West Virginia. There'd not been another in thirteen years, and this one was to be a double.

Chief Rutherford had not expected word to get out as wide and fast as it had. In truth, the impending execution was not intended to be publicly viewed, beyond choice residents of Keystone. It was likewise not in any way legal. Few had even known the pair was incarcerated before Thursday. It was on Wednesday that circuit judge Rufus Beavers—who had no jurisdiction even if the condemned had been given a trial—declared guilt and handed down the sentence too. He said they'd hang just as soon as the big black oak was roped. This he'd proclaimed inside the jailer's office, with exactly seven men present. Rutherford had believed that such actualities would prohibit word's spread, that it would only leak a little on Thursday, when it was decided that a fast gallows would be built. And when it became clear that the date of the hanging was the Sabbath, the God-fearing, he hoped, would keep away. And so it was that all of the police chief's beliefs had proved foolish.

Even the first rain in over a month could not keep the people away.

Rutherford watched them walk in it.

He stuck his head inside the jailhouse to be sure his men looked alive. Six of seven were there. Three rode the bench and three leaned against the block wall. Behind them came humming, singing. More symphonious orchestration from the condemned, each day the same tune. Every law man knew better than his own name by then that there was a place in France where the naked ladies dance and there was a hole in the wall where the men could see it all. On and on it went. The condemned had a repertoire of words a mile long. They stuck those words without cease into the snake-charmer song. There was a place in New York where the hambone chased the pork. There was a place Rutherford prowls where the chickens pork the hoot owls.

It was relatively cool inside the jail. Humid, but no sun to speak of through the small windows facing north. Rutherford looked at an officer who was in particularly bad shape from the previous night's imbibing. "Pick your chin up Reed," he said.

Reed was one of three black men on the police force and the son of Fred Reed, owner and president of the Union Political and Social Club. He was gut-sick, but he nodded and did his best to look alive. "Clothes is patted and stacked," he said. "I'm to fetch the chicken at ten."

"What about my noontime eggs?" Rutherford said. He hadn't yet eaten a thing.

"They'll be ready."

The two of them listened to the condemned woman sing of oiled bed springs and steeple dicks and the devil as the man in the moon. Her voice was high and sweet.

"Last lullaby she'll ever croon," the chief said. He stepped outside again.

In the street, a Chinese man in a stovepipe hat walked along bent, a flat-top trunk on his back. He nearly lost his footing in the mud, then continued until he was square in front of the jailhouse. A leather strap secured the heavy trunk, strung bandolier-style across his chest. He sat down careful and undid himself. Then he stood and pushed the long box onto its side, kicking mud at the mass of ankles passing by. He rigged a tarpaulin to a telegraph pole in order to keep dry. He took off his slicker. His tan three-piece suit was dry. He undid the trunk's latches, hefted out his broken-down Punch and Judy booth, and proceeded to erect it around himself where he stood. It took no more than a minute. Head-high and striped red and white, a curtain up top framed in whittled driftwood to frighten and delight.

The rain slowed. A woman with a baby on her hip stopped to watch, and then a young man did the same. So too did a drunkard with bleared eye and clumsy foot. "What is that contraption?" the drunkard asked, and, as if to answer, a voice erupted from inside the bright booth.

"Good Men and Madames of Keystone!" The greeting cut through the drizzle like a horn. More stopped and waited to be entertained. The street clogged and the rain picked up again. Umbrellas deployed. "I shall send round my bottler," the voice went on, "and if you'll put a coin in the hat, the Great Professor Verjo will furnish you a show!" The Chinese man emerged from the booth and twirled his hat from his head. He maintained a scalp-lock fashion, like an Iroquois warrior, a singular black rope of hair falling to the small of his back, the rest of his head kept bare by straight razor. "Right here, right here," he called, hat brim upturned and waiting on compensation. A nickel hit the bottom, then another. The people were confused by him. Some had never known a Chinese man. Those from Keystone knew only Mr. Wan, and he had never worn a vest-suit in his life. One woman asked another, "Is he Injun or Chinaman?" They wanted to know how he spoke good English. The man calling himself Professor Verjo had long since grown accustomed to such folk, and he was predisposed to answer any question on his origins. He told the truth. He was born in a freight yard at Los Angeles, California.

In front of the Busy Bee Restaurant, a jewelry peddler heard the Punch and Judy man's call. The peddler stuck his fingers in his mouth and whistled so loud that the woman regarding his wares stumbled back. He banged his stand with a cow's bell and called, "Here, here is where your money is wise! Gold watch-chains! Silverware!"

Another man on Bridge Street stuck a fist of rolled paper high over his head and waved. He called, "Only true confession of Goldie and Abe! Here are the words of the Kid and the Queen! The rest are forgeries! Here's your confession!"

The calls carried through the open jailhouse door, down the narrow hall, and into the cells of the condemned man and woman. Abe Baach ceased his humming. He looked upon his bare feet and smiled and spoke to himself. "That's it boys," he said, quiet. "Run em in and run em out."

Goldie Toothman called out a high note and danced a circle around the drain hole.

Their day had come.

In the street, the Punch and Judy man whipped his hook-nosed puppets side to side on their stage above his head, his movements furious and precise. Punch was not Punch on this day, and Judy was not Judy. "How can they string us up Abe, oh how?" she sobbed, her little wooden hands against her red-circled cheeks. "Don't you know by now Goldie," the puppet man answered. "Old Scratch is in Rutherford's skin." And with that, they dropped behind the striped curtain, and in their place the red devil appeared. He was not sanded smooth like them. His jawbones were jagged, his paint job ragged. From each dull horn hung a kite-string noose. His head swiveled slow, surveying the crowd. They waited. They were quiet. The red devil bowed and the nooses swung like earrings. He straightened and said, "Let em dangle."

Some in the crowd clapped their hands and whistled. Others moved on repulsed.

Inside, officer Reed walked into the hall with his arms full. He toted two covered pans balanced atop a stack of pressed clothes. Abe and Goldie had ordered the same last meal—fried chicken, cornbread, and pinto beans. In Reed's pockets, their morning whiskey ration chimed, pint bottle clacking shot glasses. He carried triple portions on account of the unique circumstances.

They'd quit their music-making.

There was a sheen on the stone hallway floor. Reed watched the pans tremble on the stack he hefted. He stopped in front of cell one and excused the tall officer who'd been on watch there for three hours. The man was tired, but he said he'd just as soon stay. "I've got used to the hummin and singin," he said, "and I can watch him with one eye shut." He popped a glass eye from its socket and held it out while shutting his other one tight.

When Reed saw that Abe was naked, he turned his back and set down gingerly his stack.

When he slid the suitclothes through the bars, he kept his eyes on his boots.

Abe said not a word, but took his pressed goods and retreated to the corner. He put on his fresh underclothes. He watched Reed pour a swallow of whiskey and set it on the food ledge where his uncovered chicken steamed. "Thank you," he said. "And maybe a boiled egg if they're ready?"

Reed looked him in the eyes and nodded his head. Then he turned away and bent to regather Goldie's stack. He started down the hall and then stopped. "Preachers is here," he said. "I can bring them to you."

Abe had stepped to the food ledge. He breathed the air of his chicken and said, "By all means."

Reed was clenched tight as he came upon Goldie's cell. When he saw that she too was naked, he did not turn his back to set down the stack. And when he slid her dress through the bars, he did not look at his boots.

She stood with her arms crossed under her breasts. She was still-balanced on one foot. "Morning sunshine," she said.

From down the hall, the tall officer called, "Reed, don't you look too long. She always up to somethin."

At half past ten, chief Rutherford again stood out front of the jail, this time atop a stack of upturned tomato crates. Such a stack was necessary for a man of short stature. "Ladies and gentlemen," he hollered. The crowd didn't listen. "Ladies—" The thin wood split beneath him and he broke through all three crates, clear to the porch boards, so that he was boxed in to the waist. The short drop had caused him to lose his stomach, and for a moment, he considered the long drop awaiting the condemned. What must it be like, he wondered, to free-fall through a door such as that.

The Punch and Judy man ate an apple on break between shows. He was next to the chief as he fell. He stifled a laugh and helped the man to his feet, lifting him at the waist until Rutherford slapped at his hands. A little girl had seen too, and she didn't stifle her own laugh, and she pointed at the lawman where he stood, his face having lost its color. The chief kicked at the splintered wood, regained his composure, and called out: "Ladies and gentlemen, this here hangin is about to come off. We'll start over to the site shortly, and if you want a place to see from, you had better go now." He pointed downriver toward Cinder Bottom, where the hasty gallows stood high. He was nervous. A man had told him that word could go as wide as the governor that very morning.

At eleven, Rutherford walked past the condemned without looking at them. He threw open the door at the end of the jail's hall and stepped into the embalming room.

"I'm liable to faint if I don't get them eggs," he said. Taffy Reed sat on an iron stool and read the newspaper. He pointed to the big steel table, where he'd laid out a soup-plate of a hardboiled dozen.

At a quarter to noon, lawmen toting repeating rifles cleared a path, and two open box wagons rode up to the jail's side door, a black coffin centered on each. Behind them was a long-top surrey. Most of the crowd had started for the gallows, but some remained. They watched the big door swing open, and there stood Abe Baach beside chief Rutherford. The lawman's full height, upon first sight, marked him a boy next to the condemned, though Rutherford was nearly twice his age. Abe was bolt straight in shined shoes and three-piece suit. He wore a high collar and a fine silk necktie. No expression on his face.

"My Lord that fellow is handsome," one woman said.

His hands were shackled in the front, and his steps into the wagon were short and measured for the ankle cuffs. He sat down on the coffin with the chief on one side and a portly preacher on the other. The driver nudged the big bay forward, and the second wagon fell in.

Officer Reed appeared in the doorway, Goldie Toothman's elbow gripped loose in his hand. She'd gotten her plaid dress in line and her hair tidied. The wrist shackles rode tight against purple velvet cuffs. Her eyes were shut. She sang in a whisper.

Reed and the skinny preacher guided her to the coffin bench. She sat down slow. Men astride horses regarded her movements, her magnificent shape, the fine hue of high-cheek skin. The big, beautiful assemblage of her up-tied hair. They looked on with lust in their eyes despite their wives, who rode behind them in the same saddle, pressed uncomfortable against stiff belts and gun grips.

The second driver lashed the haunches of the big black horse, and the wheels spit mud as they pulled away from the jailhouse. The surrey fell in behind. It picked up four lawmen, two reporters, and the court stenographer.

The wind shifted, and thick ash from the coke ovens on the hill began to fall. Light rain started and stopped. The procession was relatively quiet, save for the street peddler calls and the barkers beckoning folks to the three shell tables. In an alley, men were shooting dice. One called, "Come you seven, come eleven!"

Abe Baach smiled where he sat.

Next to him, the portly preacher started up. He shouted, "The Savior comes and walks with me, and sweet communion here have we." The skinny preacher in the wagon behind raised his face to the heavens, and they God-called in unison. When Abe could take it no more, he lifted his shackled hands from his lap, sprung his elbows, and swiveled at the hips, knocking the preacher from the coffin and the wagon too. It was a mighty blow that sent him circling, his backside to the sky before he landed on his belly in the mud. It took his wind from him. Some gasped. Others had a laugh. Two onlookers came to his aid, and when they rolled him to his side, a muddy crater he'd left behind.

The driver held up the horses, but Rutherford said move on. He'd stood from the coffin and put his colossal revolver to Abe's head. "This road is full a ruts," he told him, "and my finger's inside the guard."

Abe shouted at him: "Well go on Admiral Dot and squeeze it!"

Goldie had opened her eyes long enough to see the gun at Abe's head, and when she shut them again, she gathered her air and coiled herself and let out a war cry so full as to ring the ears of the dead. It set the skinny preacher's arm hair on end. It panicked the breath of officer Reed, and it ceased the barking of those hawking corn salve and silver and fixed games of chance.

Rutherford grit his teeth and told the driver to see to his buggy whip.

Abe sat on his coffin and swayed in time with the rusted wagon springs. His head knocked the barrel of the long short gun, but he did not much feel it. His ears caught the echo of his woman's din, but he did not much hear it. His eyes looked ahead to the waiting gallows, but he did not much see it.

The people had amassed there, four thousand strong. Most had traveled from Mingo or from Mercer. They'd caught wind the day before and made haste to see the show. They stood upon a plot northeast of Elkhorn Creek, a flat patch where a house of ill fame had once held sway as the unofficial boundary to Cinder Bottom, Keystone's red-light district. Now the land had been carved and leveled by seventeen mule teams in preparation for a new switchout and tipple. The people filled it up and stood on their wagons. They covered the surrounding hillsides, slipping and lending one another a hand. They waited fifty deep in line for hot roasted peanuts at five cents a bag, and they pressed against the barbed wire fence that circled the scaffold stage.

The gallows platform was wide and high, its ladder bearing thirteen steps and its side-by-side traps triggered by a singular lever. It had been built by a stranger. An Italian master carpenter with the straight-ahead eyes of a clergyman who called himself Signore Buonostirpe. He'd walked into Judge Beavers' office early Thursday morning and proclaimed, "I make catafalco. I make for nothing." He had a letter from George Maledon at Fort Smith Arkansas which read: *This man has a gift from God, and it is to build, completely gratis, the most beautiful killing mechanisms you're likely to see.* Buonostirpe said he believed the guilty should pay with their lives. He wanted only to have his choice of timber and to work in solitude. He was granted both, and in two days' time, he'd built the custom long-drop scaffold. The beams were spruce. The encased bottom, sweetgum. It was costly to panel the high pillars, but encased bottoms were customary since 1901 when Black Jack Tom Ketchum had been decapitated by a long-drop gallows in New Mexico.

Four policemen hopped from the surrey and cleared an entrance at the fence gate. It took some time. The people were thick, and when they parted, they pressed against one another in a ripple. The wagons rolled inside, and the gate was latched behind. Abe and Goldie stood from their coffin tops and waited.

The officers toted stepladders to the rear of each wagon. Rutherford and the skinny preacher descended like the rest. Reed did not. He unhitched a key ring from his belt and bent at Goldie's side.

"What are you doing?" Rutherford called up.

Reed said, "We undo their ankles now. Less you want to carry Baach up that pitch."

Rutherford looked at the stairs awaiting. He mumbled for Reed to hurry on and do it.

A procession toward death commenced as a new vendor began to call out, "Abe and Goldie's picture, twenty cent! Last chance!"

Folks patted their pockets and fished for coins.

"They'll never have another one took," the man called.

They ascended the stairs single file.

The rain picked up again and the beaten ground troughed under the feet of the people. They listened to the rain against their shoulders. They were quiet and uncertain. Those who knew about rain and ground asked how in God's name the earth could be so wet after having been so long dry.

On the platform, the players took their places. Chief Rutherford, officer Reed, news reporter, preacher. The court stenographer was given a straight-back chair too small for her frame, but she took her seat and produced a leather-bound book and fountain pen. She held them at the ready, her fat hand trembling.

Rutherford moved Abe to his spot on the drop door. Reed followed suit, escorting Goldie to her own square. The two ropes dangled behind them, nooses nearly touching the platform floor.

The preacher took his place in front of the condemned and spoke. "These two, convicted of the worst crime, are standing on the line of eternity and time."

A loose conglomerate of horses began to whinny, and babies cried as their mothers held them high to witness.

The preacher preached on. "Their immortal souls are about to enter the unseen world, where the years are as the sands of the sea, as the leaves on the tree."

His hands were crossed over his Bible when he stepped to the back of the platform.

Rutherford nodded to Reed, who in turn nodded to Goldie that she could make her speech.

Rutherford had proclaimed the night before that when it came to hangings, speeches were customary and that ladies spoke before gentlemen.

The people waited for Queen Bee to speak.

It had been said of Goldie that you could ask her what time it was and she'd tell you how to build a clock. She could dress a man down in two sentences. But on this day, upon being asked to speak, she said nothing. She looked at Abe, who looked at the square beneath his polished shoes.

She looked to the sky above. The dark gallows crossbeam split the dirty clouds. She looked back at the people, whose numbers and expanse took her breath. She'd not seen so many together, and when she let her eyes blear, it was as if the people were a wide gray skin on the land. She took note of the mothers in the crowd, the ones holding their fat babies aloft, and how those little ones shut their eyes against the rain and opened them again, looking askance on the world before them, and she said, too quiet to be heard by any but those on the stage, "Children ought not be out in this choke damp rain."

Rutherford told Abe to make his speech.

The stenographer kept a good pace. *Tiny impels condemned to speak*, she wrote.

Abe cleared his throat. "My name is Abe Baach," he said. "I was born right here in Keystone on the ninth of January in the year 1880." The people listened. "Up to April, I had not stepped foot in this place for seven years." He looked at them. "Most of you people know me, even if you act like you don't." His voice carried clear to those in the trees. "My mother is Sallie Hood of the Burke Mountain Hoods. My Daddy is Al Baach." Men from outlying counties yawned and checked their pocketwatches. "Maybe you drank something once upon a time in his saloon on Wyoming Street," Abe said. "I served plenty of you, and so did my brothers Jake and Sam."

Two dogs got into it at the foot of a hillside birch tree. Their throated snarls turned the heads of most in the crowd until a girl kicked their snouts apart and the smaller one ran for cover under a tall horse.

Abe pointed his shackled hands at an old man who stood at the fence with his knotty fingers intwined. "Right down here is ole Warts Wickline," Abe shouted. "When I wasn't but knee-high, I'd set up on the bartop and play dishrag peek-a-boo with this gentleman right here in front of me."

"Handsome baby," Warts Wickline said. His neck was covered in skin tags of varying size and shade. "He done a dance up there, stuck out his little hand for a cent piece." None could hear him but those in proximity, and the crowd along the edges murmured and moved. The old man kept on. "Stuffed your britches with them pennies didn't you," he called up to Abe. "We called you Pretty Boy Baach back then."

Abe nodded his head. "I remember," he said.

The whistle of the westbound noon train came faint on the air. It was nine minutes behind schedule. The rain slowed.

"There's a good many of you that want me to take out my cards and show you a trick or two," Abe called out. "There's a good many more wants to know the truth of who does the killin around here and who fires their gun in defense." He held up his wrists. "It's hard when you're shackled, but I'll oblige." And he opened his clasped hands, and in them he held a fresh deck.

Rutherford's stomach made a watery sound. He didn't know whether to shit or go blind.

Abe split the deck's seal with his thumbnail and said, "At the end of it, if the law is still standing behind me, he can by God yank the handle."

There was a rumble among them then. Some had had enough of this talk from a convicted criminal. "Go on and stretch his neck," somebody called. One woman yelled that Goldie was a whore. Another man advised not to listen to a half-Jew swindler such as Abe. Others leaned to the ones in front and asked what it was that ole Warts Wickline had said, and when told, they passed it on to another who'd inquired, and so it spread, and there were those then uncertain about the hanging of such a beautiful young woman and a handsome man who'd once been a boy who peek-a-booed and danced for a britches penny. Those uncertain knew themselves to be good then, and they leered at those about who were drouthy for spilt blood.

Reed leaned to Rutherford and whispered, "I best put them ankle irons back on." Rutherford nodded, and Reed knelt before Abe and set to work.

"Yank the handle!" a skinny boy said.

An old woman said no. She said the condemned ought to be able to say his piece.

The people were stirring, talking loud over the slacking rain.

Rutherford had seen enough. He bent to the nooses where they hung and gathered their lengths in his fist, and as he did, a tingling commenced in his fingers and toes, and thereupon Abe let loose a booming invocation which carried to the scant trees on the ridge and beyond. "I'll tell the truth before I die," he roared, "or I'll walk out of hell in kerosene drawers and set the world on fire!"

Rutherford was still bent at the waist when he let go the rope lengths. He wobbled, then dropped to his knees. When his face hit the boards, there came from his backside a mighty gust. It escaped him in a long and steady rush, a flatulence known only to the leprous gut, a ragged slap of wind that carried forth without cease for a full fourteen seconds.

When it was finished, Abe said, "Amen."

So short was Rutherford's height that those up close had not seen him go down, for the gallows was a steep-pitched endeavor. But they had heard the call of his marsh gas, and they were confused. Those farther away thought maybe he was fiddling with the shackles, or praying.

The stenographer's hand had ceased to tremble. She wrote in her bound book with furious tranquility: *Tiny falls on face, farts in carefree fashion. Condemned remarks "Amen."*

The rain quit and the people were again quiet.

Abe tossed the deck to Goldie. They played shackled catch as if it were a common game. She winked at him and pulled back the flaps and dropped the wrapper to the boards. The cards wore heavy varnish.

The sun came free of the clouds then, and the people looked skyward, and there was only the north-born sound of the tardy noon train's wheeze. The engine was not yet fully stopped at the station when men began to jump from inside the empty coal hoppers. They hit the hard dirt beside the railbed and rolled and got to their feet quick. They ran on wrenched ankles, headlong into the people staring dumb at the heavens.

FALL
1877

ARE YOU A DRINKING MAN?

September 22, 1877

Al Baach commanded the peddler's wagon from its single broken spring seat. It was an old buckboard, modified to carry wares, and it clanged and slapped and creaked along what had once been a Cherokee trail. Now some called it the Baltimore Turnpike. At the place where Virginia met West Virginia, the roadway was steep and everywhere switchbacked. Al Baach had known hills in Germany, but he'd not piloted a wagonload of wares across them. His forearms were tired. The old horse he steered had quit listening to his commands. She stiff-rumped the britchen and downhill was too swift. Al's reins were dry and taut. Up ahead, Vic Moon rode in a fine saddle, and Al thought momentarily of leaving him and walking south to Tazewell, where he hoped his uncle lived.

The wagon belonged to Vic Moon, who was toting a load of pewter mugs to a man in southern West Virginia. Vic sharpened knives outside the Fell's Point cigar factory where

Al had stripped leaves for two weeks before deciding to leave Baltimore, though he'd only stepped off the steamship at Locust Point two weeks prior. He'd come from Germany, alone. Twenty years old and twenty years late. Only one other in the entire men's steamer compartment had spoken German, and that man was seasick most days—he'd done more vomiting than talking. Only two others in his compartment were Jews, both from Poland. Those in the berths above and below Al had spoken Russian, and so he'd slept as much as he could, a handkerchief plugged up his noseholes. In Baltimore, there were those who would spit at his feet, for he was a foreign man, and some were blaming foreign men for what had happened. A month before his arrival, during the railroad strike, the state militia had shot workers dead on Camden Street. Al did not care for people spitting at his feet. Nor did he care for stripping leaves. His work was repairing boots and shoes. And so it was that when Vic Moon said he needed a traveling companion to McDowell County, West Virginia, Al had looked at a map. He knew his uncle had lived and worked in Tazewell, Virginia, since before Al's birth, and now there were Baaches in Virginia who'd never seen Germany. Al aimed to get to these Baaches and work in their dry goods store. Vic Moon was his chance.

His given name was Arnold Louis Baach. Al was what the Americans called him.

His English was good. He was six feet tall and weighed one hundred and ninety pounds. Across the chest he was big as an iron stove.

Vic Moon had a wife and boy he was leaving behind until he could pay their way to join him. The three of them had come over from Calabria, Italy, the year before. He had told Al Baach, "In southern West Virginia, the people are the finest I have seen." He said the railroad in those parts was just getting started, and there was money to be made, and all you had to do was holler out front of a house and someone would open the door and say, "Get off your horse, come get you something to eat, and stay all night." Fifteen cents got you that. Twenty fetched breakfast and your horse taken care of too. That very scenario had played the night they came down off the mountain to Bluefield. The people of West Virginia laughed easy and looked at you straight when they spoke, and there was something in the closeness of the hills that Al found agreeable.

Now it was their fourteenth day of travel, and Vic Moon said he'd bet on reaching their destination by five.

In truth, it was not Al's turn to pilot the wagon, but he'd done so because Vic Moon was fifteen years his senior and claimed the wagon seat was hell on his hemorrhoids. He rode ahead on his big bay. It was a fine horse, full-rumped, unlike the bone-pointed animal pulling Al along. She was a small old mare who, in the morning hours, farted in time with her gait. Vic Moon had complained three evenings prior of the cart-pulling mare and said he'd not be down-wind again.

He whistled the melody to Yankee Doodle and called back to Al every quarter mile to make haste. He enjoyed the quiet away from towns and cities. He enjoyed the company of the untroubled youngster from Germany.

Two miles out of Keystone, twelve feet up above the road, a man clutched the thick bough of an overhung red oak. Its canopy of leaves hid him well. When Vic Moon passed underneath, the man let go his clutch and dropped, turning mid-air and landing with considerable force upon the head of Vic Moon, snapping his neck and pulling him to the ground at once. It happened so quickly that Al Baach saw only a falling blur. He stood in his seat and watched the holey bottoms of Vic Moon's socks as he was pulled into the stickweeds by the armpits. The waylayer had yanked him from his perch so hard his boots had hung up in the irons, and there they swayed, open-mouthed and foul. So foul were the boots that Al nearly choked when he stepped off the wagon and neared them.

He tied the horses one-handed, pistol drawn. The bay bit at a grass knot like nothing had happened. Al followed the drag trail into the woods, where, a hundred yards in, he found Vic Moon on his back in a scatter of brown pine needles. His pockets were inside out and his forehead was staved in deep and square by an axe butt. His eyes were open, dead to everything.

Al Baach pulled him one-handed by the ankle back to the road, pistol still readied in his other hand should the waylayer return.

He hefted Moon into the wagon, and when he fetched the stirrupped boots, he saw something through a tear in the left sole. He pinched his nose and dug and came up clutching one hundred and twenty-three dollars in folded bills.

He rode into Keystone with the bay tied and trailing, a dead man behind him in the wagon. It was nearing eighty degrees. Hammers called in rhythm and echoed all around, frame houses and buildings springing upward inside the narrowest stretch of creek land Al had seen. Hills rose up on either side like walls, striped empty here and there in clear-cut lines of stumps. Up at the bend, he could see men lining ties and spiking rails.

He stopped at the first place he came to, a frame building that had yet to get its siding or window glass. Two men stood out front in the mud. Al got down, gave his name, and reported the peddler killer to one Henry Trent, a sharp-shouldered man in a tailored suit, and one R. Rutherford, the smallest man Al Baach had ever encountered. Rutherford made some claim to being the law, though there was no official law to be had in those times. He ate a hardboiled egg. Its white had smeared gray from the filth on his hands.

They stepped to the wagon where Trent leaned over the top box to see for himself. Rutherford had to climb the wheel and perch on the hub in order to have a look at the dead man. Vic Moon was stretched lengthwise along the side rail where Al Baach had refashioned crates to make room. Tobacco tins lay scattered across his middle like an offering.

Henry Trent shook his head and took his pipe out. "I believe that's Vic Moon," he said.

Al Baach was caught off guard by this and managed only to nod.

Field crickets signaled louder from the ridge.

Trent struck a match and put it to the bowl and drew, all the while watching Al Baach. "I suspect you were unaware of all his business here?" he said.

Al did not know who or what to look at. He could not speak.

"I summoned Vic Moon. He served me a drink once upon a time in Baltimore." Trent smiled despite the pipe stuck in his teeth. He said, "His price on pewter was competitive."

Al Baach thought a moment and then took the one hundred and twenty-three dollars from his pocket. He held it up. "Mr. Moon has wife and boy in Baltimore," Al told them. "I need to make arrangement."

They were highly accustomed to the sight of paper money.

"What's your accent?" Rutherford asked. He was still perched on the wheel hub, where he picked at the seat of his pants, eyes on the wad of bills.

"I am from Germany." He looked from one to the other. He said, "There is one hundred and twenty-three dollars to arrange this man's family."

Trent nodded at Rutherford and pointed the bit of his pipe at a small building up at the bend. "You had better get things ready," he told him.

Rutherford leaned over for a last look at the dead man.

"You're lucky I'm a undertaker," he said. He jumped off the wheel, cocked his head, and took a good look at Al's broad trunk. "Lucky besides it weren't you." He laughed a little. "You a Jew?" he asked.

"Yes."

"Vic Moon was married to a Jew," Trent said. "I suspect you knew that?"

Al nodded that he did.

"I met his little boy," Trent said. He shook his head. "Half-Jew, half-Italian. I said they ought to have named him Sheeny Dago. It tickled Vic."

Rutherford walked off in the direction of his undertaker's room. He'd only just been trained a month before in the embalmer's ways. He muttered to himself as he strode. Rutherford was a lazy little man, and there was much preparation for the slow work of body draining.

The small building at the bend was half jail, half mortuary. Men in Keystone were already acting up sufficient to be jailed, and in the mines there would always be rock fall and cage drop and white damp and black damp and choke damp and fire.

The hammers quieted and the crickets could be heard again. Trent said, "Vic Moon's real name was Vincenzo Munetti." The pipe waggled while he talked. "He had himself a woman down here too. He tell you about her?"

Al nodded that he hadn't.

Trent let his pipe go out and watched Rutherford in the distance. He laughed and squinted one eye and used his thumb to sight his associate. "Isn't as big as your fist is he?" He turned and squared up on Al Baach. "Tell me your last name again," he said.

"Baach."

"You say you're a Dutchman?"

"I come from Germany."

"You come from one of the big cities?"

"No."

"What are you doing here?"

"My uncle has dry goods store in Tazewell."

"What's his name?"

"Isaac Baach."

"I know of him." This was not true. He worked his jaw muscle, and when he tried to imagine what Germany looked like, he saw nothing but castles and men in funny hats. "Your people live in the hills or on the water?"

"Hills."

In the mud of the lane, they looked each other in the face.

Trent was twenty years older. Trent was three inches shorter and Al Baach outweighed him by thirty pounds. But Henry Trent had eyes only prizefighters possessed and hands like meat mallets too. After the war he was known for a time as the man who went sixty-eight bare-knuckled rounds with Professor Mike Donovan in Mississippi City, Mississippi. He'd lost on a foul.

He found intrigue in the young man. Al Baach wore a brand of confidence that Henry Trent liked to test. "Well Baach," he said, "ole Vic Moon was abandoning his wife and child." This too was not true. "Taking post as Keystone's very first bartender. I had him all fixed up and ready to go." Trent raised his left fist up between them and knocked his pipe hard against the knuckles. Black ash settled in the creases between his fingers. He held his fist there, clenched, and, with his right hand, slipped the pipe back into its pocket. He asked, "Do you know what I used to do about now if I smelled something wrong on a fella?"

"No," Al Baach said.

"I puckered up and blew him a kiss." Trent stepped to the side so that he wouldn't dirty the young German, and then he demonstrated by pursing his lips tight and blowing hard on the pipe ash. It jumped right off his knuckles. He told how his blast of ash blinded a man in a half-second, and how, before another ticked away, he'd have already sent a straight right home to its justifiable place—the smack-dab middle of the lying man's face. "Put him to sleep every time," Trent said. He smiled at the memories. "Give the devil his due."

He told Al Baach he didn't smell a thing wrong on him. There was something he quite liked in the young man. "And if you want to know my mind, you'll make a damn sight more money here than you ever will in Tazewell." He considered the offer he was about to make. "If you think you can do it, I'll make you bartender at the saloon. I'll pay you a better wage than your uncle, I'd imagine."

It was then that Al Baach truly considered the strangeness

of his day. Vic Moon had the good luck to ride the good horse, and the bad luck to be killed. Al had been downwind of a flatulent equine, but he was alive, and now he was looking at a prospect that, in his estimation, would not come along in a dry goods store.

Trent considered further. He said, "I'll wire that money to the Munettis in Baltimore, pay out of my own pocket to embalm ole Vic and put him in a sod-box too." He looked up at the clouds coming purple-black from the west and started toward the frame building. He waved Al to follow. "Hell," he said, "You know what else?" He scraped his boots on the threshold and stepped in the empty doorframe. Al followed suit. "Rutherford can tote Vic up to White Sulphur and have him on the B&O mail train by sundown tomorrow."

"The little man will do this?"

Trent nodded. "He's got a rig for pulling coffins."

Inside, there were two men at the back. One sanded the floorboards on his knees. The other stood on a wobbly split-pole ladder and looked up through the empty rafters.

"Go get supper," Trent said, and the men stood and walked out between two wall studs.

In the center of the room stood the most beautiful table Al Baach had ever seen. It was a great big round table, thick as a headstone at the edges, and it sat atop cast-iron legs. It carried only a stack of fine paper, and next to the paper, a silver inkwell and dip pen. Trent said, "I'll tell you the story of this table." He rubbed its thick lacquer. He ran his finger along its circle rings. He asked, "Are you a drinking man?"

He poured from a hammered flask given to him by his company captain after the war. There were no chairs about, so they stood, each man lifting his glass with considerable frequency.

He told Al how he'd fashioned the table from a white oak tree with a breast circumference of twenty and one-half feet. The tree had been felled in 1867 by his logging crew out of Pumpkintown, South Carolina. "I was high-climber," Trent said. He said he bucked the logs himself and drove a length down the Saluda River to the mill, where he won, on a bet, the thick stump cross-section that now stood before them. He said he'd ridden the log knots up, whistling all the way.

Al listened and drank.

Trent could tell a story, and his whiskey flattered the palette of any sensible man or woman.

He told of how it wasn't long before he bought that timber outfit and it was his name branded on tens of thousands of floating butt cuts. "Everybody called them hot cuts on account of my initials." Oliver was his middle name.

He told of 1875, when he sold the company for four hundred times what he'd paid, and, like so many speculators before him, bought up considerable land tracts in southern West Virginia. Hill land he stripped of timber. Creek bed he built upon. He settled in Keystone and partnered with two local men, the Beavers brothers. Together, they opened a sawmill and a mine.

Dynamited railbeds and opened coal seams had men primed

for a rush on black gold. Clapboard and brick raced upward, and there were, at that time, too many thirsty workers and too few barstools. But Trent said he would keep pace, building two-story tenements and boarding houses and squared-off spaces meant to be saloons. He motioned all around with his hands, gesturing at the air beyond the open wall studs. "Virginia ought not to have given up McDowell County," he told Al Baach, "for this is where fortunes will sprout."

And so it was that on that September day, Al Baach gave over the one hundred and twenty-three dollars to a powerful rich man who vowed he'd wire it to Vic Moon's widow and boy.

Trent picked up the pen and dipped it. He wrote the contract in a fashion that was nearly indecipherable, but his numericals were in order. They were readable and substantial, the kind of numbers that allowed ample room for a man like Al to save in a hurry.

In those numbers, Al Baach could foresee a time close at hand when he'd buy the saloon outright and do as he pleased with it.

He said, "The many men who come here to work, they will need shoe repair."

Trent nodded. "Isn't but one cobbler, and he's missin an eye."

"When there is no man at the bar, I repair boots and shoes for money?"

"You mean to say extra money? Make something on the side for yourself?"

"Yes, on the side."

Trent smiled. "Well hell, by all means." And he held out the pen, and Al took it.

There were words put together in English that he sometimes couldn't follow but that he nonetheless enjoyed for their thick combined sound on the air. *On the side. By all means.* His insides were warm with drink and his head tingled as he signed his name where Trent pointed a finger.

"You are a lucky man, Jew Baach," he said, "for the real money always comes to those who get there first."

He poured the rest of his flask into their glasses and they raised them.

They walked along Elkhorn Creek and toured what would become the saloon. Trent went for more whiskey while Al unloaded Vic Moon's wagon. He opened the crates with a pry bar and saved a wide length of board. Upstairs, he set it on the floor and put down a blanket. He stretched out and closed his eyes. He would soon enough be rid of the memory of his paperboard bed in the cigar factory storeroom, of his foul steamship berth. He sat up on his elbows, and through the open ceiling rafters of what would become his room, Al watched the sun fall behind the hill.

At midnight, drunk, he watched Rutherford trot his horse out of town with a fresh-cut coffin in tow, the rig drawing lines in the dirt.

He stood in the dark with Trent, a lantern on the ground between them.

Rutherford winced at the buggy seat's unforgiving springs. He muttered about there being not enough moonlight to see. He gave a wave as he passed below the balcony veranda of a long-roofed house. The two men perched up there did not wave in return. They leaned in slat-back chairs, their feet propped on the balustrade. They were the Beavers brothers. They liked to think they saw everything from their high covered domicile.

Trent could see their cigar tips glowing. He watched his man pass beneath. He watched Harold Beavers lean sidewise in his chair and take something from a covered basket on the porch floor.

Harold stood up clutching a pair of writhing black rat snakes. He leaned over the rail and aimed and tossed the snakes upon the passing Rutherford.

One landed on his shoulder, the other on the swell of his trail saddle. He screamed as a small child would scream and he pulled free his boots from their stirrups and leapt to the ground, where he clawed at the mud, pulling himself from the scene, panting in the high notes of a woman in labor.

The Beavers brothers laughed as hard as they had in months, and so too did Henry Trent as he watched from afar. When he'd understood what he'd seen, Al Baach followed suit, chuckling uncomfortable at what evidently passed for humor in his new environs.

Rutherford stood up and drew his lengthy sidearm and shot both snakes dead where they'd slithered against the ditch wall.

His horse just stood there, long since gun-broke. Rutherford did not look up at the Beavers brothers where they roared, nor did he turn to regard Henry Trent. He holstered his pistol and climbed back aboard by way of an extra-long fender, and he rode off in the quartermoon dark.

There was nothing in this world Rutherford feared more than serpents. It could not be helped, and it would never change. He only prayed that others would not likewise abuse his phobia.

Trent let his laughter fade slow. "Little loyal Rutherford," he said. He pulled a money roll from his jacket and peeled off three. "Start-up money."

Al took it and said goodnight and returned to the unfinished room above the saloon, where he would live rent-free so long as men drank in droves below him. He unpacked the pewter.

He had not yet gone to sleep when the sun came up over the ridge. It was Sunday, his first in a strange new home. Soon it would be his only day off.

On that morning, he took the first of many Sunday walks up the mountain. He guessed the temperature to be fifty-two degrees. A fog sat wet on the lowland. He followed a switchbacked path through one of the few wide stretches of hardwood left. He came upon a plateau clearing where he encountered Sallie Hood.

She stood on a slant yard shaking out a rug. Her arms were strong. She snapped the square of braided wool like a bullwhip and watched the dust carry.

It seemed to him then that talking to a woman might prove orienting. He was brave on drink and the money in his pocket and lack of sleep and the witnessing of murder. He took off his hat and attempted to slick his hair. "Hello," he called, and he walked straight to her and said who he was and how he'd come to be there. Up close, she was even better-looking than she'd been from afar.

She found him handsome, and he had the eyes of a good man, but when he spoke on the murder of his traveling companion, she backed up a pace toward the porch step where her rifle leaned.

He saw that she was afraid of him. "I'm sorry," he said. He walked back toward the woods.

There was something true in his apology, and something familiar in his walk, that struck her then.

He was only ten yards off when she hollered, "Are you a coffee-drinking man?" When he turned and said that he was, she waved him back and invited him inside the big square house.

They sat at a long oak table and neither was afraid to stare or ask questions about family and homeplace. She told him she came from the Burke Mountain Methodist Hoods and that the Hoods had a plot just up the hollow where they'd buried their people for one hundred years.

He listened close to her every word.

Sallie was two years older than Al. She was possessed of a good singing voice. She had little meat on her bones, but her back was strong from work, and she spoke her mind if need be. She'd recently made the big square place on the hill a boarding house. It offered a bird's eye view of what was coming down below. Her Daddy had built the house in 1851, and in the summers it was made a meeting grounds for the preachers of God's good word. In '75 he was named pastor at the new church in Welch. The rest of the family followed him there. Sallie did not.

Her mother and father and sisters and brothers knew better than to try and persuade Sallie of anything, and so she had watched them go and then she had painted a sign that read:

HOOD HOUSE

SALLIE HOOD, PROPRIETOR

50 CENTS PER DAY OR $3 PER WEEK

She regarded the man across the dining table that morning and found him delightfully unordinary. She knew, in fact, on that very first Sunday morning, that if he could kiss decent, she would marry Al Baach. And so, after a second cup of coffee, she said, "I am going to come around the table and kiss you now."

He smiled.

She got up and came around and kissed him on the mouth, and it was to her liking.

He said, "The people here in southern West Virginia are the finest I have seen."

"Just wait till I cook you supper."

When Sallie made up her mind on something, it could not be unmade.

The twice-a-year preacher came through at Thanksgiving. He wed them at the Marrying Rock at two in the morning. A candlelight service, no witness in earshot but the crickets.

There were those who chattered about the couple, and Sallie's family was among them, but from the start she was unenthralled with such talk. Those who would fault her love for a German Jew could go on and fault themselves silly. She had a boarding house to run.

Inside a year, she had a baby boy to rear, and inside another two she had a second. Her third boy came in '83. There were easy years and hard, and when Hood House had no vacancy, the boys lived over the saloon. Each boy was free and lively and sweet, and each was trouble. The first was Jake and the last was Sam. The middle one they named Abraham.

QUEENS FULL OF FOURS

February 17, 1897

It was Wednesday. Snow had stuck to the mountaintop but not the road. It was the day on which a game of stud poker commenced in Keystone that would last thirteen years. It wasn't intended to last that long. It was intended instead to carry in the kind of money most couldn't tote, and it would do so in a quiet fashion, for the game itself was the only of that day's events not publicized by handbill in the growing town. *You must see the lobby to believe it*, the papers said. *Grand Opening. Alhambra Hotel.* It was Henry Trent's most ambitious project to date, a three-story brick building with four columns in front. He'd built it on the southwest bank of Elkhorn Creek, where the monied folk had moved.

Five men had been invited by courier to sit at the big stakes table. One of the five was Abe Baach, then seventeen years of age. Having already cleaned the pockets of the men at his Daddy's saloon, he had a reputation. Most had quit calling him Pretty Boy Baach in favor of the Keystone Kid.

The Kid whistled that stale February morning as he walked west on Bridge Street with his arm around his girl. Goldie Toothman whistled too, pressed against him tight for heat. She'd bought him a six-dollar gray over-coat for his birthday to match the stiff hat he wore. The coat was long, well-suited for Abe, who'd stretched to six foot two.

They stopped halfway across the bridge, and though his pocketwatch told him he was nearing late, Abe said he needed to spit in the creek. It was superstitious ritual, but neither of them was taking chances. They regarded the water below, rolling black over broken stones. Along the banks, it was frozen. Brittle-edged and thin and the color of rust.

"I'll play quick and clean," Abe said.

"I know you will." She put her hands inside his coat button spaces for warmth. She kissed him at the collarbone and told him, "Don't cross Mr. Trent." She whispered, "Keep your temper."

He locked his hands around her and squeezed. "Liable to freeze out here," he said. Beneath her jacket she wore only an old gown. There had been little time for sleep the night before and no time for proper dressing that morning. Sleep came short and ended abrupt when cards and bottles turned till sunup.

Where the crowd grew thick, Abe and Goldie parted.

Her Daddy had taken ill again, and she'd have to see about his duties. Big Bill Toothman swept up and kept order at Fat Ruth Malindy's, a boardinghouse-turned-whorehouse above which he and Goldie lived. Goldie's mother had died giving birth to her, and Big Bill had raised her alone ever since, with no help from Fat Ruth Malindy, who was his sister-in-law. She was madam of the house and the meanest woman there ever was. So Big Bill got help from the Baaches, whose saloon sat directly across Wyoming Street, where Abe, from his second-story bedroom, had spent his boyhood kneeling at the sill over stolen card decks, knifing seals and opening wrappers like little gifts, shuffling and dealing and laying each suit out to study them. All the while, he waited for Goldie to look back at him from across the lane. From the time he was ten, he'd waited for her, and while he did, he memorized the squeezers from the New York Card Factory, emblazoned in cannons and cherubs and birds of prey and giant fish and satyrs and angelic, half-nude women who fanned themselves with miniature decks of cards. He stole a fine dip pen from his father and began marking them, even recreating their designs on newsprint, down to the tiniest line.

It was Christmas Eve 1892 that Goldie had looked him back.

Now he watched her return to the swinging bridge. He blew hot air into his cupped hands and moved at a fast clip up Railroad Avenue, side-stepping the crowd and walking, without hesitation, between the wide columns and into the kind of establishment only a boomtown could evidence.

The Alhambra's lobby was indeed rich with curvature and girth. Through the right bank of mahogany double doors was a small auditorium, equipped with a fine stage. A purple felt grand drape hung behind it, a narrow row of gas footlights in front. They were lit for an ongoing opening-day tour of the facilities, and the children of the rich danced before their glow with spotlighted teeth, and one girl fell onto her fragile knees and cried.

At the back lobby wall, a man named Talbert recognized Abe and showed him around a card room with fourteen tables. Each one was covered in fine green billiard cloth. Iron pipes striped the high walls, and twenty or more jet burners lit the place with steady little flames that left no wall streaks. Abe was accustomed to the flat wick lamps at A. L. Baach and Sons, where kerosene smut marked every inch. Al Baach wasn't concerned with decor. He was content to merely keep open the saloon he'd bought outright in 1891, for the great panic of '93 had frightened him, and he'd not cleared sufficient money since to renovate.

Abe surveyed the men at their tables, the timid manner in which they moved their wrists and fingers, the slight shiver of their cigar tips.

The smell of good varnish was still on the air.

Talbert asked what his pleasure was.

Abe took the invitation from his pocket and showed it.

Talbert scratched at the mass of greasy hair on his head and squinted at the invitation card. On it was the embossed seal of a round table. "Why didn't you show me this right off?" he asked. "You're late." He told Abe to follow.

They walked across the wide main card room and Talbert tapped five times at Trent's office door before entering. Inside, it was empty. Wall-mounted gas lamps ran hot. He shut the door behind Abe and pointed to a second glass-paned door at the back. He said, "They've already gone through." When Abe didn't move, Talbert said, "Go on in."

When he did, Abe found himself in a room lit by a single lamp. It hung on a hook above the middle of a great big round table fashioned from a white oak tree with a breast circumference of twenty and one-half feet. Four men stood around it talking and smoking. They wore suits. Trent and Rutherford stood in the corner next to a seated black man who was paring his fingernails with a pen knife.

When the door was shut, Henry Trent said, "That makes five."

Rutherford walked to Abe and held out his hand and said, "Buy-in."

Abe took the fold of notes from his inside jacket pocket. Rutherford licked his thumb and counted five twenties and said to the black man, "Dealer take your seat and split a fresh deck."

Abe took off his coat and hat and hung them on one of seven cast-iron coat trees lining the wall.

He and the other four card players took their seats around the table.

The dealer wore a black satin bow tie. His suspenders were embroidered in redbirds. His shirtsleeves were rolled and his fingernails were smooth as a shell. Abe had heard how good he was and had played once or twice with his son.

The man shuffled. He had fast mechanics and a soft touch. "I'm Faro Fred," he said. "I'll turn cards till I'm dead."

Abe sized up the other men. Each of them he knew, whether by face or by name.

They had all heard of him.

Rutherford poured whiskey into a line of cut-glass tumblers with a bullseye design. He set one before each man. Then he sat down in a chair beside the cookstove and took out his chewing tobacco.

Trent said, "If you're here, I don't have to explain a whole lot."

One of the men had a short-lived coughing fit. When he finished, Trent went on. "The game is pot-limit short stud." He looked each man in the eye. "Go on and buy your chips." He pointed to the orange glow inside the stove and told Rutherford to tend it, and then he sat down in the opposite corner to watch.

Abe admired the table's girth and finish. He did not know that it was the very same table where his Daddy had signed his name twenty years before. *Do not sit down with Mr. Trent,* Al Baach had told him. *He does not speak in truths.* Abe watched the dealer make his little column of chips and push it forward.

Faro Fred looked him in the eyes, as he did each man to whom he pushed chips soon to be thinned.

Abe straightened his stack and kissed the bottom chip and cracked his knuckles.

He played tight for the first two hours. If his hole card was jack or lower, he threw his two on the pile and spectated. He watched them lick their teeth and grimace and rub at their foreheads and take in their whiskey too quick. He noted the liars and the brass balls. He separated the inclinations of one man from another, and he catalogued who would try to outdraw him when he got what he was after. In the fourth hour, he won a little, twice, on a couple high pairs. Then he lay in wait another two.

His time came when the drunkest man with the deepest stack raised to the limit three straight rounds. Abe followed him where he was going, and when it came time to flip his hole card, with two pairs showing, he turned over that droopy-eyed, flower-clutching queen.

"I'll be damn," Rutherford said. "Queens full of fours."

It had taken Abe only six hours at the table to clean out the best stud poker man in all of McDowell County.

The man's name was Floyd Staples, and he didn't muck his cards straightaway. In fact, he flipped his own hole card, as if he believed his ace-high flush might somehow still prevail if only everyone could see all those spades. He watched Abe restack the chips. Staples' eyes narrowed to nothing. He bit at his mustache and breathed heavy through his nose.

Floyd Staples was unbathed and living in the bottle, and his cardsmanship was slipping. That much was plain to all in the room.

He pointed across the table and said, "This boy is a cheat."

Abe double-checked his stacks. He'd told Goldie he'd cash out if he got to four hundred. He stretched his back and said to the dealer, "I reckon I'll cash out now." He pushed his chips forward, and Faro Fred pulled them with a brass-handled cane.

"Three hundred and seventeen after the rake," Fred said.

Trent opened a leather bank pouch and counted out the money.

Floyd Staples stood up and smacked the table with the flat of his hand. He looked from Abe to Henry Trent. "You going to let Jew cheaters run your tables?"

Abe stood up. He looked at the expanse of table between himself and Staples.

He straightened his shirt cuffs. He smiled and kept his temper.

It was quiet. Two men took out their watches and looked at their laps.

Rutherford stepped from the wall and handed Abe his winnings.

Abe nodded to him and peeled off two ones. He folded them one-handed, and on his way to the door, he slid them to Faro Fred, who had pitched the fastest cards Abe had ever seen.

It was then that Floyd Staples said, "Baach, I will fetch my rifle and shoot you in your goddamned face."

Henry Trent quick-whistled a high signal.

Rutherford drew the hogleg from his holster and held it at his side. He told Abe to step back, and then he opened the office door and directed Floyd Staples into the light.

When the door shut behind them, Trent said, "Let's us all just stretch our legs and visit a minute."

And they did. They stood up and smoked. Abe spoke briefly with a man in octagonal spectacles who was more refined than his present company. He was not accustomed to threats of death and foot-long revolvers.

Rutherford stepped inside the room again. "He'll be alright," he said. "Talbert'll get him a whore." He swallowed tobacco juice and coughed into his hand.

Trent said, "Well he damn sure won't play at this table ever again." He gave Rutherford a look and turned to the other men. "I apologize for the unpleasantness. You gentlemen play as long as you like. I've got solid replacement players ready to rotate. Rutherford will pour your drinks and light your cigars, and if you are in need of company, he can arrange that too." He put his big-knuckled hand on Abe's shoulder, opened the door and said, "After you."

Abe stepped into the office.

Before he followed him through, Trent bent to Faro Fred and whispered a question in his ear. Fred whispered back an answer.

The glass rattled when Trent shut the door behind him.

A two-blade palmetto fan hung from the ceiling on a tilt and did not spin. It was yet untethered to a turbine belt drive. Trent had plans to tether it by summer, when he'd salary a man just to turn the crank. The big bookcase was empty, its glass fronts showcasing nothing. Atop the case sat two cast-iron boxing glove bookends.

Abe sat where Trent pointed, a handsome chair with a green pillow cushion on the seat. It faced Trent's double-top desk. He stood behind it and shook his head and laughed at the magnificent young man before him. Trent looked ten years younger than the sixty he was, but he knew his face had not ever carried Abe's brand of chisel.

He opened a drawer and produced a clear glass bottle with no label. "Evening like this one calls for the best." He set two glasses on a stack of ledgers and unstuck the cork. "You heard of Dorsett's shine?"

Abe nodded that he had.

Trent smiled. There were two silver teeth in front. His brow had gone bulbous and so had his nose and chin. "You drank it?"

Abe nodded that he hadn't. He'd only been to Matewan once. Dorsett's shine didn't much travel outside Mingo County.

Trent handed over a glass with little more than a splash inside. "Here's to you," he said. Then he drank his down and sat himself in a highback chair of leather punctuated by brass buttons. He coughed twice and took a deep breath and smiled.

Abe sniffed at the rim and smelled not a thing. He swallowed it and set the glass on desk's edge. There was no burn, only a tingle below his bellybutton.

Trent lit his pipe. "Your Daddy is a fine man," he said.

Abe nodded that he was. He'd long since learned at the card table not to engage in the playing of conversational games, and he'd long since learned not to trust the man who'd promised his Daddy a kind of wealth that was yet to arrive. Al Baach had developed a theory over the years that he'd been bamboozled from the start. *Mr. Trent never wires red cent to Baltimore*, Al Baach had told his boys. *He never sends back Moon's body.* He knew this, he said, because Moon's own son had told him in a letter. The son was grown now, *a good successful boy*, Al called him. He warned his boys to stay away from Keystone's king, and mostly they listened. But Abe was tired of hearing folks complain. Every shop owner and whorehouse madam in Cinder Bottom coughed up Trent's required monthly consideration with a smile. In exchange, the law left them mostly alone. Some whispered that there might come a time when Henry

Trent was no more. Maybe, they whispered, somebody would shoot him, or maybe he'd get choked on a rabbit bone and cease to breathe. But no matter what they whispered, in public they all sang praises to his hotel and theater and all that he and the Beavers brothers had done for Keystone. When the bank had failed the people in '93, Trent and the Beavers had not. They were the kind of men who kept their money in a safe. And for a while, they gave it out. After '93, they took to collecting it with interest, and nobody ever had the gall *not* to pay when Rutherford came collecting. Trent did not himself venture to the other side of Elkhorn Creek any longer. He'd been heard to say that Cinder Bottom wasn't fit for hogs to root.

The way Abe saw it, Trent could say what he wanted on the Bottom. He'd built it after all. And, the way Abe saw it, Trent knew the path to real money, and the rest of them didn't. Abe was relatively young, but he saw a truth most could not. There wasn't but one God, and he was the big-faced man on the big note. His likeness and his name changed with the years, but he maintained his high-collared posture, dead-eyed and yoked inside a circle, a red seal by his side.

He looked across the desk at the older man, who regarded him with humor.

"Your Daddy was here in the early days," Trent said. "He'll get what's due him." He pointed his finger at Abe. "You tell ole Jew Baach I haven't forgot."

It was a name seldom used by that time, a relic of the days when Al was unique in his presumed religiosity. Now there was B'nai Israel on Pressman Hill, a tall stone synagogue equipped with a wide women's balcony. Attendance was ample, though no Baach had ever stepped inside it. Abe wondered whether Trent even knew of such a place. He wondered whether Trent knew that if he hollered "Hey Jew" on Railroad Avenue, more than two or three would turn their head.

There were those who said Henry Trent's mind was not what it once had been.

He poured another in his glass and raised it up. "To half-Jew Abe," he said, "the Keystone Kid." He stood and went to the corner. He told Abe to turn and face away, and when he'd done so, Trent spun the combination knob of a six-foot, three-thousand-pound safe. He opened the inside doors long enough to put five hundred back in his leather pouch, then he swung shut the safe, sat back down, and took out a sheet of paper and a silver dip pen. "You know I had my money on you," he said. "Rufus did too. Rutherford had his on Staples, but I had a notion." He signed his name to a line at the bottom of the sheet. "And do you know what Fred Reed just whispered in my ear?"

Abe nodded that he didn't.

"He said he'd not seen play like yours at the table since old George Devol."

Abe had read Devol's *Forty Years a Gambler on the*

Mississippi nine times through. He'd kept it under his mattress since he was twelve years old, the same year he'd quit school for good. He said, "I aim to best Devol's total table earnings fore I die."

Trent laughed. "You aim to live to a hundred do you?"

"Forty ought to do."

They looked each other in the face.

Trent pushed the paper across the desk. The pen rode on top and rolled as it went.

Abe looked at the figure Trent had written in the blank. *$100.00.*

"On top of what you take from the table after the rake, I'm prepared to offer you that number as a weekly salary." He took out his pipe and lit it. "As long as you play like you did in there just now, and as long as you lose to the company men when I signal, I'll cut you in on two percent of the house earnings, and I mean the tables and the take from stage shows too." He puffed habitual to stoke the bowl, and his silver teeth flashed. "This hotel will be the shining diamond of the coalfields," he said. "They will come from New York and New Orleans to sit at my tables and sleep in my beds, and I have a notion they will come to try and beat the Keystone Kid."

The weekly salary was high—it guaranteed him more than five thousand dollars in one year's time. But the house cut was low, and he didn't like the word *exclusive* on the paper. He started to say as much, but the words hung up in his throat. He cleared it. He said, "Thank you Mr. Trent."

They discussed his daily table hours and decided he'd think on it until the next morning. Trent produced a fold from his inside pocket and peeled off two and handed them to Abe as he stood from his chair. They were brown-seal big notes.

"For your trouble today," Trent said.

They shook hands and nodded. Abe excused himself and headed to the lavatory just outside the office, where he stood and breathed deep before putting the money in his boots. For three years, Al Baach had fitted the insoles of his growing middle boy with a thick strip of leather, and he'd told him once, "If you win another man's money, you put it under there. Then you keep your eyes open."

He walked through the main card room, past the poor suckers who'd never get ahead, and then through the big lobby, past those busy figuring how they could afford the nightly rate, and despite himself, he could not keep from smiling.

Rufus Beavers stood on the staircase landing. He watched the boy smile and knew he'd lived up to his name at the table. He recognized something in the gait of Abe Baach, something his brother possessed. A sureness. A propulsion that had taken his brother all the way to Florida's tip, from where he sent home money and word of adventure.

Rufus made his way to Trent's office, where he found his associate shaking the hands of well-dressed replacement players on their way through the second door. When they were alone, Rufus told him, "Ease up on the Kid's Daddy. No more collecting."

Trent furrowed his brow.

"Got to keep Jew Baach happy," Rufus said. "Otherwise, the Kid will have cause to cross you."

Trent said, "Having the cause don't mean having the clock weights."

Rufus eyed a cigar box on the desk. Its seal was un-familiar to him. "I wouldn't bet against the boy's nerve," he said. "We'll need a Jew on council who's friendly to liquor anyhow, and that boy's Daddy slings many a whiskey."

"You plannin to court the Jew vote and the colored too?"

Rufus tried to read the words on the box. *Regalias Imperiales*. "You know another way?" he asked. "Go outside and look around. Stand there and lick your finger and hold it up. See if you don't know what way the wind blows." He opened the lid and took out a long dark cigar. He smelled it and put it back.

Abe had stepped outside the Alhambra's main doors and was rubbing at the folded contract in his pocket when he noticed Floyd Staples across the way.

Snow fell. Slow, bloated flakes. Staples leaned against the slats of the general store, eyeballing. "I'll git my money back Baach," he hollered.

Rebecca Staples stepped from the big door at Floyd's

left. She was one of his two women, a lady of the evening who had worked for a time at Fat Ruth's. She held their little boy by the hand and he cried and dragged his feet. "I want hard candy," he wailed. Floyd Staples grabbed him away from the woman and smacked his cheek so hard it echoed.

Abe knew the boy. Donald was his name. Goldie sometimes babysat him on Saturday nights.

He grit his teeth and had a notion to walk over and stab Floyd Staples right then with the dagger he kept in his vest pocket. But he knew better. He'd leave that job to someone else, for surely someone else would have the same notion and the wherewithal to act on it too.

Keep your temper, Goldie had told him, and he aimed to.

The boy, who was only four, went quiet and followed his mother and Daddy, a whore and a drunk, onto a sidestreet where a new apothecary was being built.

Abe walked fast to the bridge, where he stopped long enough to spit at the middle and then kept on, smiling at folks who waved or said hello, nearly jogging when he reached the back of the Bottom. He slowed at the corner of Dunbar and a lane as yet unnamed, a spot folks had begun to call Dunbar and Ruth on account of the wide reputation of Fat Ruth Malindy's fine-looking ladies.

The snow had quit. There was a wide dull glow of orange behind low scanty clouds. The glow sat slow on the ridge, and the square tops of storefronts lay in shroud.

A black boy walked toward Abe with a canvas bag strung bandolier-style across his skinny middle. "Evenin edition!" he called. "*McDowell Times* evenin edition!"

Abe fished three pennies from his pocket and held them out.

"Nickel," the boy said.

Abe regarded his wiry frame. He looked to be about ten years old. "Since when?"

"Since my Daddy proclaimed it so." He wore a serious look.

Abe put back his pennies and handed over a nickel. "What's your name?" he asked.

"Cheshire," the boy said.

"Like the cat."

He only stared.

"From the children's book," Abe said. "But you haven't smiled once."

Chesh Whitt didn't read books for children, but he knew who he was talking to. He'd known from twenty yards off. And he'd rehearsed in a mirror how he'd be when he met the Keystone Kid. He'd be poker-faced with a knack for making money.

"Boy your age ought not be in the Bottom after sundown," Abe told him before he walked on.

The men gathered out front of his Daddy's saloon were white and black and Italian and Hungarian and Polish. Some were coming up from the mines and some were on their way down. All were laughing loud at a joke about the limp-dick Welsh foreman with a habit of calling them *cow ponies*.

A fellow who could not focus his eyes nodded loose at Abe. "I got a good one for you," he said.

"I heard that one already," Abe answered. He went inside.

It was an average crowd for Wednesday shift change. A single card game ran at the back, a Russian grocery owner named Zaltzman the only man of six in a suit. A sheet-steel stove burned hot at the room's middle. It had once been airtight.

Goldie was on the corner stage, and the men stood before her with their hats off, whistling and calling out, "Go again sister!"

She had a crown on her head fashioned from tin and grouse feathers dipped in gold paint. In the center, she'd glued a thick oval scrap of bottle-bottom glass. "Bring em back up to me then," she answered the men, and they reached inside their hats and brought forth the playing cards she'd thrown.

On the stool at her side there was a long glass of beer. She finished it with great economy and picked up a new deck of cards. "Inspect those comebackers you tobacco drippers," she called. "I don't want a card coming back to me bent nor split." She wore an old set of her Daddy's wool long underwear, a gold-painted grain bag over that. The bag was big and stiff, her head through a hole in the seam, so that altogether, in headdress and bag, she shone in the rigged pan spotlight as if she'd ridden in on a moon-beam. Queen Bee they were calling her by then, because in Cinder Bottom, at Dunbar and Ruth, that is who she was. Fat Ruth Malindy made the rules, but Fat Ruth Malindy was ugly as ash. Goldie, on the other hand, was a miracle to behold.

On this night her hair was up, spun beneath the crown. She rubbed at her neck where a flyaway hair had tickled, and the men watched, the slope of her shoulder bewitching them. She saw Abe at the door and winked in his direc-tion before getting back to business. "These here cards don't come free boys," she shouted to the men. She stuck out her toe and pushed the coal bucket to the edge of the little platform. "Drop in what you can spare now." A miner just off his shift shoved through and dropped in his change. A house carpenter put in a dollar note and stuck his face out over the stage. He sniffed at her with his eyes shut.

She let him.

Goldie had long since learned to separate a man from his money. There had always been men and money just as there had always been coal trains and mules, and at Fat Ruth Malindy's, a girl could either go prone and give up her notions of fight or she could learn how to talk to a man and take what he had. Before the age of thirteen, Goldie had twice pulled a skinny whittler blade and touched its point to the groin of a man trying to force himself upon her. By the time she was fourteen, most men knew better than to try. The ladies of Fat Ruth's admired the girl's spirit. Some took it up. And there was laughter in that cathouse, and there was always her Daddy, a good man by any measure. And then there was Abe, loyal as they came, quiet when quiet was called for, and, if need be, tameless as the stalking lion.

He leaned against the wall and watched her scale cards. He smiled.

Al Baach stood behind the bar with a rag over his shoulder. He eyed his middle boy, whose path worried him. Al and Sallie had talked on it for years—how the boy was lucky to have Goldie, how Abe and Goldie together were much like Al and Sallie had been twenty years before. But lately there'd been worry, for Al and Sallie had never been quite so old at quite so young an age.

He gave the rag a tug and put it to his nose and blew. He sniffed hard and kept on watching his middle boy. A lad just in front of him let his head fall to the bar top. He was what they called coke-yard labor. He couldn't have been over fifteen and had come into the saloon already drunk. Al wouldn't serve him but the lad had stayed put in order to see Queen Bee.

Al smacked him in the ear and said, "Get in your bed to sleep." The lad was thoroughly awakened, and he stood and walked to the door. On his way, he knocked against Abe, who righted him and headed for the back stairs.

Al called loud to his middle boy.

Abe ignored him. He hit the swinging storeroom door

and jumped to the third riser at a run. He took out his key as he went and unlocked the bedroom door upstairs.

He locked it behind him. It smelled like it always had in there. His.

When Abe and his brothers were little, the Bottom hadn't yet become what it was. Sallie had allowed the boys to be around the saloon, to slumber nights away in its upstairs rooms as their father sometimes did after the boarding house on the hill was booked up perpetual. Respectable boarders would pay a handsome sum to stay up at Hood House, removed as it was from the magnificent filth they so often sought down below. With railroad surveyors and mineral men occupying every open bed, the two oldest Baach boys had moved their playthings to town, where Wyoming Street soon grew awnings to shade its new general store and laundry and tailor shop and tenement-turned-house of ill fame. When Jake Baach was fourteen, he and Big Bill Toothman finished construction of a smaller, second home on the hill, and Sallie aimed to make use of the extra beds, to keep the boys out of the saloon. She aimed to take them from the Bottom altogether, but by that time Abe was a twelve-year-old with the hands of a full-time riverboat gambler. Pretty Boy Baach was good for business. He'd grown accustomed to chewing tobacco when he pleased and playing cards too. School was simple and books had begun to bring on sleep. His head was for numbers. His place was the saloon. He could squeeze tight his mouth and hit a spittoon's dark heart from nine feet off. He could smell a man's bluff sweat at the table without so much as a snort.

Too, Goldie lived across the way. None could keep the young man from Goldie.

Abe opened the big wardrobe in the corner and hung his jacket there. He kept his vest on, and from its change pocket he withdrew a small, homemade dagger fashioned from a four-inch cut-spike nail. It was light as a toothbrush, its handle a lashed leather shoelace. He set it on a shelf inside the wardrobe. From his fob pocket, he withdrew the nickel-silver railroad watch his Daddy had given him two years prior. It was Al Baach's custom to give his boys a sturdy Waltham pocketwatch on their fifteenth birthday. Engraved on the case back of each was the following: *A man without the time is lost.*

Abe thumbed a smudge on the bezel and tucked it back in the pocket. It was half past six.

He sat down on the bed and untied his shoes. From underneath the inner sole, he produced the two twenty-dollar notes, plus the other bills he'd won, folded lengthwise. He kissed them and then knelt at the open wardrobe, where he reached to the back and undid a hidden latch. Then he shifted the false bottom and lifted it out, his old hidden spot under the slat. He set all the money but one twenty inside with the rest, replaced the slat, rehooked the latch, and sat for a moment on the floor with his back against the wall. He took full breaths and let them out slow.

The game at the Alhambra would bring him what he'd always been after. It was something to ponder.

At the window, cold air issued in at the sill. The shade was half drawn, and below him, folks walked the dirt streets laughing. The restaurant beside Fat Ruth's radiated the stench of hog fat burned black. The cook stood out front in an undershirt despite the cold. He picked his teeth with a thumbnail and watched the ladies coming to work. There were more than usual on account of the grand opening across the creek. There were white ladies and black ladies and foreign ladies too. Fat Ruth's was the first in the Bottom to do such a thing, and that was fine by the cook. He said to each as she passed, "You looking every inch a peacock tonight."

Another man stepped from the restaurant and concurred. "Like a springtime payday out here," he said.

Al rapped his middle boy's door, three quick.

Abe had heard someone coming on the stairs. He picked up the spike nail and put it back in his pocket.

When he opened, there stood his Daddy, sweat drops squeezing forth from the pores in his nose. Behind him was Jake, who smiled and pushed his way in and tried to make himself as tall as his younger brother by standing straight. He stuck his face in Abe's. "Don't forget whose room it was first," he said. "Don't forget who can whup you in a fair fight."

Abe wouldn't forget. After Goldie, it was Jake who knew him best.

Al closed the door behind him. "Do you play at Trent's table?" he asked.

"Who's tending bar?"

"You answer my question Abraham." Al spoke loud and set his jaw. None of the boys would ever forget who could whup all three.

Abe said, "I played at his table and I won."

Al shook his head and looked at his hands. He wanted to use them to choke his middle boy, but it would serve no end. Al had known it the first time he'd ever switched Abe, who was ten at the time and had been seen hopping a slow coal train. While Al swung the switch, the boy had whistled with his eyes shut, and he'd spat on the ground when it was done.

Choking the boy wouldn't steer him clean. Al crossed his arms.

Abe thought his Daddy looked old then, and he thought Jake did too.

Jake had a pint bottle in his back pocket. He had a pencil behind one ear and a skinny cigar behind the other. He was supposed to be fixing the storeroom shelves.

"Who's tending bar?" Abe asked again.

"Big Bill. He come over with me," Jake said. He was dark-handsome like Abe, but his nose was bigger and his chin weaker.

Abe knew by the way his brother said "come over with me" that Jake had been at Fat Ruth's again. He'd been lifting from the saloon's money box for two years, just enough to dip his wick once a week. Abe said, "Bill's not well."

"He's better now." Jake put his thumb to a corner edge of peeling wallpaper. "Worry about your own health Abe," he said. "Be dead soon enough you get in with Trent." He walked to the closed wardrobe and knocked on it. "Never was well made, was it?"

"Goldie won't like seeing her Daddy at the barback," Abe said. "He's ill."

"Bill will be okay." Al uncrossed his arms and breathed hard through his nose. He said, "Abraham, Henry Trent has nothing for you. You think he gives you everything, but he gives you nothing in the end." He opened and closed his hands. "As he gives, he takes."

There was a noise outside the door and the three of them turned their heads.

It was Sallie. She'd swung it open without knocking and looked at the men. She toted an unfamiliar baby girl on her hipbone. Behind her was Sam, the only Baach boy forever in need of sunlight. He was skinny as ever and fourteen years old.

"Stand up straight Samuel," Al told him.

The boy did so and followed his mother inside.

"Shut the door," Al told him.

Sallie said to leave it open. She looked at Abe when she spoke. "We're not staying."

The years had not been easy on Sallie, but they'd forti-fied her resolve. After Samuel's birth in '83, there was a still-born. A year after that, there was another, and for a time, Sallie only lay on her back in bed. She'd taken one basting spoon of chicken broth per night for two months. One day she came out of it and never looked back. The Baach boys did what she told them, and Goldie and Big Bill helped at Hood House when it was needed, but mostly Sallie ran the place, and she did so with considerable attention to cleanliness and well-kept books. In '95, she took in the unwanted baby of a Tennessee girl working at Fat Ruth Malindy's and named her Leila. With Goldie spelling her from time to time, Sallie attended that child's every need, sleeping next to her crib up at the second house on the hill. At Christmastime in '96, a wealthy friend of her father's and his thin barren wife adopted Leila, and Sallie had nearly taken to her bed again. Instead she cried for a night and half a day. Then she stopped. "Sometimes, the eyes can't keep from crying," she'd told her boys. "They're pushing out the poison."

Now Sallie's hair was mostly gray. She'd kept it long. She shook her head slow and said to Abe, "You look guilty."

The unfamiliar baby tossed her little covered head and made a noise.

Sam tapped his foot on a floorboard by the bed. He suspected his brother of hiding money underneath.

They had all known that another motherless child was coming to Hood House to live because Sallie had proclaimed it and Goldie had backed her up. The child was born December 30th in a bed at Fat Ruth's. Her mother had left before sunrise on New Year's Day.

Abe regarded the baby and thought on how to answer his mother's accusation of guilt. "I am guilty of making the kind of money that will build you another house, and another one after that. Anybody that wants to live on the hill can do it in—"

"I thought that maple baby carriage was in here," Sallie said.

"Storeroom," Al answered. "But steel brake is broken." He looked at his watch and walked out the open door.

Jake pulled the half-spent cigar from behind his ear and lit it. He said, "Somebody's got that carriage loaded with pickled egg jars."

Sallie hadn't looked away from Abe. She swung the baby to opposite hipbone. "Samuel!" Sallie called.

"Yes ma'am?" He'd sat down on Abe's bed and was fixing to recline.

"Go unload the carriage and roll it to the street."

"Yes ma'am."

Jake opened the dresser drawer and looked at the newspaper lining. He slid his fingers underneath.

Abe turned, stepped to the dresser, and slammed it shut, Jake pulling clear just in time. "Don't forget whose room it is now," Abe told his brother.

The door closed, and they turned, and their mother was gone.

"You got the gold pieces?" Abe asked.

Jake produced a small burlap sack tied with twine.

Abe took it and tossed it on the bed. He retrieved his

jacket from the wardrobe, stuck in one arm, and pulled the sleeve inside out. In the silk lining there was a long, buttoned sheath at the seam. He loaded into it, one by one, the little cedar pieces painted gold. They were hand-cut by Jake, just like the saloon's poker chips. Abe rebuttoned, righted the sleeve and put the jacket back on.

Jake laughed. "Goldie sew that?"

"She is possessed of many talents."

He opened a vest button and put a hand inside. There, in a seam in the lining, were four slick pockets where he customarily kept two of each bill, one to ten. He took out a five and handed it to Jake. "Just watch you don't catch Cupid's plague," he told him.

Jake smiled. "Whatever you say highpockets." He shook his head. He admired the insistent spirit with which his younger brother lived. He only hoped that Abe would stay alive long enough to tamp it down, and that tamping it down might buy him a few more years, and that those few years might carry him to the time in a man's life when he quits carousing, when he's content to read books again, like he'd done as a boy, and Jake and Abe and Sam might get old together, telling stories about how it is to go bald or to watch your shot-pouch sag to your knees.

"You got any of that Mingo shine?" Jake asked.

Abe shook his head no. "I've got to get downstairs." He took a fresh deck from a stack on the dresser.

"You planning to play at Trent's hotel?"

"Not tonight."

"Tomorrow?"

"No." Abe pulled on his shirt cuffs. "But Jake," he said, "I might soon play there every day, and if I do, the money will come back here and up to Hood House both. You can have all the tools and timber you want." He knew his brother was happiest when he built. "Frame another house on the hill, and down here a proper stage, new card room."

Jake shook his head. His cigar was burnt out again. "Trent won't ever give you that," he said.

"Like hell he won't."

After they'd stepped from the bedroom, Abe locked the door again. There was hollering from the storeroom downstairs. They descended.

Sam had dropped a two-gallon jar of pickled eggs. Thick sharp wedges of curled glass sat dead against the cold soak. Brinewater marked the floor in a hundred-point burst. Sam pushed a broom at the eggs, and they rolled, soft and lopsided on the dirty floor, brine-red, some of them split yellow. Sallie had the baby in the emptied maple carriage. She used it like a battering ram to open the swinging door and depart. She didn't look at any of her boys.

Abe told Sam not to worry. As long as there were chickens, there'd be eggs, and as long as there were eggs, people would pickle them with beets, and the world would be a proper place.

He swung through the door, arrived at the stage in three long strides, and leapt upon it to take his rightful place beside his queen. The men at the foot of the stage nodded to him and he bent to shake the hands of twenty or more, patting their shoulders with his free hand. The week prior, a track liner had told another man that his poker luck had swung high since he'd shaken the hand of the Keystone Kid. Word got around.

Goldie said, "Get them hats up swine!" She was fixing to scale and shoot another round of cards. She fanned them in her left hand and took a wide stance. The men before her held their hats high, low, and sideways too. Abe got out of the way. He watched her right arm coil slow above the deck. The men went silent and still. Goldie pinched the first and sprung hard her wrist and elbow. Her fingers, on the follow-through, spread open like honeysuckle. Then came the sound from inside the hat's crown, sharp and dull and full and empty all at once.

Abe closed his eyes and listened to the next and the next and the next after that. It was a sound he could listen to all night.

When she'd finished, she bowed and Abe stepped forward again and said, "And men, when you fish in those pockets for tips, see if you don't come upon another thing too."

And they did come upon another thing. "I'll be durn," one said to the other as they brought forth quarter-sized cuts of wood painted gold. "How in the hell?" one man wondered aloud, and indeed it was a mystery how Abe had gotten the little gold tokens into all of those various workingmen's pockets.

"Each of those gold tokens was hand-cut by my brother Jake, who is practicing to become the finest carpenter these parts have known," Abe told them, "and each of them is good for one beer at the bar." They mumbled approval. "Men, be sure to tip generously, and keep coming back to A. L. Baach & Sons for all your social needs!"

They spewed what earnings they could spare at the coal bucket and moved as a mass to the bar, where Al and Jake and Big Bill worked to pull, pour, and serve every man who saddled and showed his wooden gold. While he worked, Al glared across the barroom at his middle boy.

Goldie poured the coal bucket's contents into a big empty cigar box she'd brought over from Fat Ruth's, where, when business was good, gentlemen callers went through a large box a night.

"What's the take?" Abe asked her.

"Above average." She fastened the box shut and tucked it in her armpit. "I want to hear about your card game," she said. He wore a look she couldn't read. She winked at him. "I want to get out of this get up too."

Abe told her he could help with that and that his take was likewise above average. "Let's get to the storeroom," he said. He looked to the bar, where the more ambitious men were finishing their free beers. "Just watch a minute," Abe told Goldie. "See if my plan works."

And it did. He'd calculated that the men, upon swilling their gold-token good fortune, would be of a mind to have another. He knew that those coming off their shift would've stayed only long enough to see Goldie before they went home, cleaned themselves, and set out to behold the Alhambra. But plans could be changed. Now the men set their dented pewter mugs on the bar top, wiped their mouths, and pulled out their watches. "I reckon I've got time for one more," they said, and they fished once again for coins that would lead them where they wanted to go.

"See that?" Abe said. Then he checked his own watch. "Now let's get to gettin." He pushed Goldie ahead of him and kissed at her neck when they got to the swinging doors. "We got time for me to show you a thing or two."

But in the black damp of the storeroom, it was her who showed him. They'd long since found a corner place, between the wall and the floor safe.

She pushed him against the cold back wall. She set the box of coins on the waist-high safe and put her hand to his trousers and worked the buttons on his fly. He picked her up and set her on the safe. The cigar box dropped and sounded a tambourine call. "Leave it," she said. She tugged at his belt and pulled down his waistband, and when her fingernail cut the pale skin at his hip, he paid no mind. He took off her crown and let it drop. She raised her arms and he skinned the cat and tossed aside the gold feed-sack. Underneath, long-legged underwear was ill-fitted and easily kicked free. He lifted her, one hand under her arm and the other at her thigh. They slowed then and stopped breathing until she had taken ahold and guided him in and pressed herself as close as she could. And it was like that for a moment before they remembered to breathe, and his forearms burned from holding her while she rolled her hips, quickening all the time, toes gripped against the cold panel wall.

They sat together on the gold feed-sack afterwards, and Abe lit a match and showed her the contract. She kissed him. She was pleased at the sight of the long, looping numbers, but she did not say so. She did not say anything, for as quick as they'd brought pleasure, those same numbers struck in her a strong and sudden premonition that life, for a time, would be splendor, and then Abe would be gone.

He burned his thumb and tossed the match. He lit another and showed her a twenty.

She tapped her knuckle on the safe behind her. "What's in this thing?" she asked him.

"Dust."

There was a pickled egg at the floorboard within Goldie's reach. It caught the match's light and shone pink and smooth. She leaned and reached for it. She blew off the dirt and ate it.

When they stepped from the storeroom, the men had cleared out. Goldie took up a dustpan and headed for her Daddy, who was sweeping by the door.

Jake dunked mugs in one tub and rinsed them in the next. Beside the tubs was the stack of little gold pieces he'd cut. He had ideas on putting a hole at their middles or branding their faces with a *B*.

Al stood over his rosewood cash box behind the bar. He sorted dimes from nickels and quarters from halves. He bagged them accordingly. He licked his thumb and rifled the notes and put them in an envelope. The count was high for a Wednesday.

Abe came up behind his Daddy slow and silent. "How'd we do?" he asked.

Al nodded. He closed the cashbox and turned around. "I want to come and choke you when I see the men with the gold, but too busy." He tapped his finger to his forehead. "Now I see your plan."

It was the first time the two had smiled at each other in a year.

"How many normally leave after Goldie throws the cards?" Abe asked him.

"You are a smart boy Abraham."

"How many?"

"Half?"

"At least. They want to get where they're going." In conversation on games of confidence, Abe talked near as fast as he thought. "How many walked out that door tonight?"

"I imagine five—"

"None." Abe reconsidered. "Well, one. But only if we

count the over-served boy who snuck back in after you'd tossed him."

"And then I toss him again."

"There you go." Abe watched his Daddy laugh. He joined him. "Can't count one that doesn't drink and been tossed," he said. "And I'll bet some ordered another after, and another after that, all the while talkin to each other about coming back tomorrow."

Al felt old next to his middle boy. Small, too, for though Abe was not as thick-ribbed as his Daddy, he was two inches taller. He patted Abe's shoulder. "Remember, Abraham," he said, "Even the smart boys can listen once in a while." He tapped his forehead again. "Even the big boys can get hurt."

Al had just turned and picked up the cashbox when the door opened. It knocked hard against the head of Bill Toothman's push broom.

Rutherford stepped inside. Behind him was Taffy Reed, Rutherford's errand boy and son of Faro Fred. Taffy was a year younger than Abe. He was well above average at the card table and had come by his moniker there. For a nickel, the young man would roll up a shirtsleeve, straighten his arm, take the elbow skin between his fingers, and pull it down, a stretch of flesh some five inches in length, highly reminiscent of the elastic properties of chocolate taffy.

"Evenin Baaches," Rutherford said. He gave a foul look to Bill Toothman who was next to him, twisting the broom handle back into the head.

"Evening Rutherford," Al said. He put down the cashbox and took note of Rutherford's sidearm, which seemed to have grown longer somehow. He watched the little man spit tobacco juice on his floor though there was a spittoon to his left.

At the bar, Rutherford climbed on a stool and Taffy Reed stood.

"I'm going to walk Daddy over," Goldie told Abe. She kissed his neck, whispered that she'd be back, and took hold of Big Bill's arm. The sweeping was done. Al had given her an extra two dollars for her Daddy.

Jake dried the mugs and kept his back to their patrons.

"What can I get you Mr. Rutherford?" Abe asked.

"I'm not staying for a drink." He reached in his jacket pocket. "I come to bring you a note from Mr. Trent." He handed over the sealed envelope, *Abraham Baach* on its face.

Abe thanked him.

Rutherford ignored him and looked at Al. "Jew Baach," he said, "your boy played some mighty strong hands today."

"He is a smart boy." Al wiped with his rag at a sticky spot beneath his wedding ring.

"That's what they tell me," Rutherford said. He regarded the strange oil painting tacked up on the wall, a wide crude depiction of a house on a mountain, a homemade job. Below it was a shelf with a half-empty pipe rack and a framed lithograph of Lincoln that stared back at patrons no matter their stool. "You all know Taffy Reed I'd imagine," Rutherford said, motioning to his companion.

Each man nodded at Taffy, who nodded back.

Rutherford looked over his shoulder at the young man. "For all I know, you're in here every payday Taffy," he said. "Baach serves niggers and under eighteen both." He laughed.

"All men are welcome in my saloon," Al Baach told him, "but the patron must be eighteen for beer, twenty-one for spirits."

"I'm only pullin your leg," Rutherford said.

Taffy Reed scratched under his wool cap. He chewed on a toothpick he'd soaked overnight in a jar of homemade whiskey.

"Alhambra's no-nigger policy won't last," Rutherford said. "Mark my words, inside a couple years, Trent will be letting em in like the rest of Keystone does—ain't no other way when they come to be a majority." He regarded his fingernails, which were in need of trimming.

Jake scooted the gold pieces off the counter into his open hand. He put them in his pocket.

"What you got there Jake Baach?" Rutherford asked.

"Nothin."

"Somethin can't be nothin," Rutherford said. He stared down the Lincoln lithograph. "You got any pickled eggs?"

"No," Jake said.

"How about just regular hardboiled."

"Plumb out."

Rutherford looked at the mantel clock under Abe Lincoln. Breakfast wasn't too far off. Every morning of his life, Rutherford ate a half dozen hardboiled eggs. As of late he'd had a penchant for the pickled variety.

"I can put on some coffee," Abe said.

Rutherford just sat. "Seems like your crowd here didn't make it to the hotel's big opening," he said. "Or if they did, they came awful late."

Nobody said a word.

Taffy Reed flipped his toothpick and bit down the fresh end.

"Look here," Rutherford said, turning his attention once more to Al. "Word come down that you ain't on the hook anymore for monthly payments."

Al could scarcely believe his ears.

Rutherford looked at Abe and spat again on the floor. Then he smiled at Al. "But what's say for old time's sake you go on and give me one last handful."

Al said he supposed he could do that.

Abe watched his Daddy turn and open the money bag. He whispered the numbers as he subtracted from his count.

Before they left, Rutherford told Abe, "I reckon I'll be seeing more of you real soon."

In Rutherford's fist was the last of the consideration money he'd collect from any Baach. He muttered as he left. He had work to do. A young coke-yarder had passed out on the tracks and been cut in two. Rutherford would have to drain what was left from him, and affix him again in a singular piece, and pump him full of preservation juice. Or, if he was tired enough, and if he reckoned there was no kin to miss the boy, he'd wheelbarrow his two halves up Buzzard Branch to the old bootleg slope mine. He'd unlock the big square cover and dump the boy down. Either way, he had work to do before he could retire to his room at the Alhambra, where he would skim from the take like he always did and put a single dollar with the rest of his secret things, inside a locked trunk under his bed.

Jake watched Rutherford leave and said, "There is something wrong with that man."

Al shook his head. "He likes to make believe he is powerful like his boss."

"Well ain't he?" Jake produced his tool chest from beneath the bar and poured himself a beer.

"He look like he is to you?" Abe said.

Al thought on acknowledging the cessation of collection. He wondered for a moment if his middle boy might indeed have found the way, if Trent might finally cut them in on the real money. But he was tired. He told them he was heading upstairs to bed. "Please don't hammer tonight," he told his oldest boy.

"Only cuts," Jake said. He was building an arch and batten for the stage.

They watched their Daddy back through the swinging door with the money bags. "Goodnight boys," he said.

They said it back in unison.

Jake finished off his beer, crossed the room, and set to work with a pencil in his teeth.

It was customary for Abe to watch his brother mark and cut. He'd done so for years, ordinarily while he counted his daily take or practiced his card manipulations. He gave Jake the nickname Knot, for Jake would stare at a two-by-four knothole for ten minutes. He would turn lengths of wood in his hand and he'd sniff at butt cuts, and in all those years of moments he rarely spoke a word. Abe found peace in his brother's wood rituals. It was, for each of them, as if they'd found a quiet place, a place both together and alone.

Jake took a measurement with a length of string and wrote it down. He straightened and finished off another beer. He shook his head. "Rutherford doesn't sit right with me," he said. "Don't ever do a thing he asks you to do, and don't ask from him so much as pass the salt and pepper."

Abe looked at the ceiling. The tin wasn't tacked by anyone true-eyed as Jake. "By 1910," Abe said, "I'll have electric lamps in here."

"The hell you will."

Goldie came through the door.

She said her Daddy's back was bad off.

With the pencil in his teeth, Jake said, "Don't let him sleep on his belly. Worsens everything."

"He's on his back now." She'd left him that way with

87

his arms up over his head and his feet against the iron footboard. He said it felt best to have his heels on something.

Goldie gave Abe the eyes. "I'm tired," she said. She wasn't.

They bid Jake goodnight.

Later, they could hear his saw from below—short, clean cuts every one. It was cold in Abe's room, and the two of them huddled under the quilt. After a while, he had to jump from the bed to stoke the little cookstove fire, and she laughed at his shivers when he got back in.

Two or three times, somebody yelled in the street.

They looked again and again at the note Rutherford had delivered. It read: *I have consulted my associates. Let's make it 3%.*

"Who does he mean?" She put her head on his chest.

"I believe he means the Beavers brothers," Abe said. "Or at least Rufus. The other one lives in the Florida everglades."

Rufus Beavers had gotten himself a law degree from Washington and Lee. He had his sights on being circuit judge. He'd sold his interest in the mines and the mill both. He had money to burn, and he was not content as Trent's silent associate. His younger brother Harold grew less refined as he aged, a man who knew no talk but the blackguard variety. He was a fine hunter and had gotten rich bagging Florida egrets for millinery. "Killed over thirty-two hundred little snowies," Harold

Beavers was known to say. "Half of em I squeezed on while they stood in a inch of water puffing up their fuck plumage." He had always been exceptional in the art of concealed approach.

"Sneak-up is what they used to call Harold," Abe said. As a child, he'd been told, like all of Keystone's children, to stay clear of Sneak-up Harold.

He and Goldie pulled the quilt high to their ears. They spoke on the plan. He would refrain from spending his table earnings. She would do the same, plus the take on her skims from Fat Ruth. Before long, there'd be money enough to go around. Big Bill could stay off his feet, and so could Al and Sallie when they took a notion. The saloon would be renovated. A proper wedding would be in short order. And all the while, Goldie had the working girls of Fat Ruth's to teach her about cycles, about when and when not to wear her plumage, about how to cut a lemon in half and wedge it up inside herself before she lay down with Abe. He was happy to respect the cycle and the lemon wedge both. He'd not bring a child into being.

He jumped again from the bed to retrieve a big smooth rock he'd leaned against the cookstove leg. It was hot, and he tossed it on the bed by her feet. He shivered when he got back in beside her.

He expressed his newfound and half-earnest idea of hosting one final game of stud poker at the saloon. A big game for big money before he headed off to his apprenticeship at the Alhambra. "You can serve drinks at the table," he said. "And you'll get a look-see here and there at somebody's cards. We'll have us a system of code words." She would flatter the men at the table with her eyes or her bosom as she bent to give them sustenance. She would eagle-eye what they held with great subtlety.

"Code words have got to seem innocent," Goldie said. "Natural."

They came up with a series of phrases for Goldie to utter, each a cue for Abe to fold or to go all in. At the best of them, they laughed together. "This hangnail's a cocklebur" was one of Goldie's favorites. "That man at the bar is a tallow-faced prairie dog" was another.

They lay in this way, laughing and keeping their feet near the hot rock, and all was right and easy. She watched his eyes close and put her hand to the side of his head and listened to the sound of his sleep-breathing.

Inside Goldie, the premonition remained. She would ignore it as best she could, but it would be there, someplace in her middle. Deep enough to forget most days, but shallow enough so that when things went wrong, she'd have already steeled herself to carry forth in a manner requiring great fortitude.

Such pushed-down knowing will fester quiet in waking stages, but it will come fast after a body that slumbers. And so Goldie's repeating dream commenced that very night, and in it, she found herself sitting way up in the tallest tree there ever was, and though she did not want to look down, she did, and there below her dangling feet was Abe, hung by the neck from a willow-tree limb.

*

Rutherford wore his wool long underwear and two pairs of socks. Lining his fingernails was the root-black dried blood of the man he'd dumped down a three-hundred-foot hole, a young man with nothing in his pockets to name him.

He scraped at the dried lines with a letter opener. He gave up and set the opener down on the bedside table. His newest batch of pickled eggs rested there, a clear-brine jar of six. He took it up and regarded the stirred white specks of membrane where they spun. Cracked pepper ringed the bottom like river silt. A long slice of pimiento pressed against the glass. He'd begun to use the peppers on the advice of Taffy Reed. He'd begun to dropper into his brine a hearty dose of embalmer's fluid, which he believed fortified his resolve. Alcohol and arsenic. Ether and zinc. He'd preserve himself while he lived, even if it killed him.

He got on the floor and pulled the locked trunk from under his bed and opened it. He put the skimmed bills in a old cheroot pail with the rest. It angered him, the cessation of the Baach collection. He touched at the treasures in his cherished trunk. From under the rusted pail he pulled the document he'd secured at fifteen, when his parents told him he was adopted—the torn-out page of a birth register. Just as he had done each night of his life since, he read it.

Rutherford had been raised by a wealthy family in Fairmont, and when he'd gotten old enough to ask why he was so different from them, they told him he was adopted. Soon thereafter, he'd gone to the courthouse and found his origin, and he'd torn it loose and taken it with him so no other would ever find it. In the Marion County Register of Births, someone had written the following for the birth date of Rutherford: *February 30th, 1856*. Such an odd and impossible date was only the beginning of this foul record. His name was recorded *Rutherford Rutherford*. Both *White* and *Colored* were marked. Under *Sex*, both *Male* and *Female* received the pen's slashing touch. And, as the register's keeper must have drowsily attempted mere consistency at that juncture in her hand's sweeping dash across the page, the category called *Born* showed a mark for both *Alive* and *Dead*. *Place of Birth* was left blank. *Israel Rutherford*, a name for which no record could be found, was given under *Father's Name in Full*. *Father's Occupation*: *Laborer*. *Father's Residence*: *Near Lowsville*. Another empty column for *Mother's Name in Full*. Of the forty-three babies born on Rutherford's page, forty-one, under *Deformity or Any Circumstance of Interest* offered the word *Perfect*. One offered *Stillborn*. Rutherford's line read: *Deformity on Ear and Foot*.

A doctor at the hospital in Marion County had taken in the baby Rutherford. He'd found it prophetic that the abandoned boy shared his family's surname. He and his wife raised the boy as best they could, short and strange and funny-looking among all those tall beautiful children bound for college and medical school after the war. At nineteen, Rutherford was angry and bound for southern West Virginia, where he followed a job his Daddy secured him with the railroad. He worked as a station agent, and on a quiet night in 1876, he left a siding switch open to the main track at Welch, as was his custom. But on that night, such a lazy practice resulted in the collision of two loaded coal trains, one moving, one still and unhooked. Rutherford, then twenty years of age, had nearly leapt out of his brogans when the ruckus commenced, and when he ran from the station to the site of the mess, he found the locomotive's engineer unconscious with a wide cut across his mouth. The man was on his side with his arms over his head, one hand gesturing by instinct to grab the brake. Without considerable thought, Rutherford looked around for witnesses, pulled the half-empty pint bottle of homemade wine from his jacket, poured some on the engineer's face and open mouth, and stuck the bottle in his outstretched, grabbing hand. The man's fingers, no doubt happy to have found what they thought was the brake, closed upon the bottle like the jaws of a vise.

Rutherford sucked on a plug of tobacco to cover the wine's smell, and then he waited on the authorities. They didn't like his story.

But a man at Keystone did. Henry Trent had heard of Rutherford, the little station agent with a big gun who moonlighted as a yard bull so he could beat tramps senseless for riding cars. If the tramp gave him a quarter or a necktie or a jackknife, he'd let him go with a singular whack from the butt of his legendary Colt revolver. It was custom-built with a twelve-inch barrel and sperm-whale-ivory grips. Rutherford claimed to have won the thing in a game of three-card monte run by a deaf pirate. The pirate had bought the gun in Hartford Connecticut from Samuel Colt himself, and later, when the deaf pirate happened upon a beached sperm whale in Beaufort, North Carolina, he'd pulled two of its teeth and fitted his ridiculous pistol with ivory.

Trent liked a young man who was short and ugly and capable of violence, who believed himself to be important. He further liked Rutherford's obsession with rich people, and his need to be one, come hell or high water. He offered him a job as his security detail, errand boy, and collector of monies. He had a tanner fashion the longest holster ever seen, open-ended so that the barrel stuck out. He said Rutherford should get trained in the ways of the embalmer, because together they would be making considerable progress in the coalfields, and with progress, Trent told him, come bodies.

Now Rutherford sat on his floor and read, for the 9,495th time, the words and numbers marking his arrival in the world. *Deformity*, he read. *Circumstance of Interest*. Words had always confused him, no matter how many times he sounded them out.

But numbers he understood.

He was forty-one. He'd counted more money than men fool enough to live twice his time. He wasn't through counting, not by a damned sight.

SPRING

1903

IT'S A TOAD-STRANGLER

May 15, 1903

He had not aimed to bed another woman. He had not, in fact, known that he'd done so until the following morning, when he awoke next to her in the altogether.

She had her back to him. They were on his bed at the Alhambra, a third-floor corner room where he slept on two-hour breaks from the big table. The game at the big table had a reputation by then from Cincinnati to Savannah, Georgia. Cardplayers called it the Oak Slab Game. Play had not ceased in six years, for just as Trent had predicted, they came from all over to sit against the Keystone Kid.

But things had lately soured. Abe was twenty-three and had not yet saved enough money to enact his grand plan. He had complained of his staid wages and he had too often behaved sloppily on exorbitant whiskey, and so, on the advice of Rufus Beavers, Henry Trent had turned on the Kid, quietly taking away the very pieces of Abe's liveli-hood he and the Beavers brothers had supplied in the first place. His card show on the Alhambra's stage. His seat at the Oak Slab. The rented room would be next.

The unfamiliar back was nearly pressed against him. The dyed black hair stirred no recognition. He thought of raising himself to look at her face, but he closed his eyes instead, hoping that when he opened them again, she'd be gone.

It did not work. Her small hand sleep-twitched atop the curve of her hip. She wore cheap engraved rings on all four fingers.

It was the sharp quill of a goose feather that had caused him to open his eyes. It poked through the pillow at his throat. He had pinched it tight and pulled it free when there came the sound of the doorknob turning. He sat up, and there Goldie stood. She was stock-still.

There was a quivering hum in her knees. She wore the spool-heeled shoes he'd bought her, and her ankles nearly turned.

Abe could neither speak nor move. There was a push of vomit at his jugular and heat behind his eyes.

Goldie looked only at him, not the woman. She said, "You are a liar," and left.

He did not pursue her.

In the hallway, she couldn't get her breath. She put her forehead against the wall and was faintly aware of the cherubs in the wallpaper art. They rode plum-colored lily pads and drew back their bows. Up ahead, a red-haired boy of nineteen stepped from a room where someone played a harmonica. He wore only a towel, knotted at the waist. He was laughing, but when he saw her, he shut his mouth and stood up straight and secured the loose knot at his navel. "You alright Miss?" he asked.

"I'm fine," Goldie answered. She straightened and breathed deep through her mouth and walked to the stairwell. There, she leaned again on the wall and thought of the time she'd declared to Abe her suspicions about his behavior with other women, and how he'd eased her mind. "I will look at a woman now and again," he'd said, "but I won't look at her twice." And he'd kissed her then, and she'd ceased to wonder much about the nights he stayed at the Alhambra without her, as theirs was a bond built on truth. He'd always been able to look her in the eyes. So it was, that at six o'clock that morning, when the note slid under the door of her room above Fat Ruth's, Goldie had very nearly stayed put. She did not believe what was written, for she and Abe were to marry in July, and after that, they'd cross the country in a Delmonico sleeper, getting off when and where they pleased.

The note was folded precise and penned by the hand of a woman. It read: *Abe is not alone in his Alhambra bed.*

Now she ran from the sight of that bed. Her shoes were off and she took four stairs at a stride.

Abe sat and stared. He'd not felt this kind of sickness in his middle before. He thought he might cease to breathe, and then, from the hallway, came a noise. She hadn't closed the door behind her, and in a slap-second, there came upon him the fleeting hope that he could jump up and hit the hallway, and she'd be there, willing to forgive him somehow if only he could look her in the eyes again. In that slap-second he believed he could nail his colors to the mast and hold life together before it fell apart.

He pulled on his trousers and stuck his head into the hall. Goldie was gone. And so too was his hope, which had never been hope so much as a fast cruel trick played by a drunk man's awaking soul. His was accustomed by then to the ways of his blood, which by night palpitated unearthly glory before spoiling at the cock's crow.

The air in the hallway was stale. He listened for sounds from the stairway.

The red-haired boy was knocking at another door across the hall, calling, in a low tone, "I know you're in there Lucille. I need me a bite of those ham biscuits."

Abe cleared his throat in the doorway.

The boy looked at him over his shoulder. "Hello sir," he said.

Abe wore a hard look at him until the boy's face went red and he looked back to the door. He tapped it light with his knuckles.

Abe slammed shut his own door and his bedmate sat up. Only then did he recognize her face.

Her titties hung pale-nippled. She was slight, and when folks remarked on the quality, she was known to say, "Fit me inside a peanut shell." She'd cut her eyebrows in such a manner as to seem exotic, but it had not worked. Abe had made her acquaintance just four nights earlier at the Oak Slab Game. She was Princess Nina Gyro, the floating gal from Cyprus, though in truth, she was Nina Gill, born and bred in Des Plaines, Illinois. She was the latest lovely assistant and wife to the Great Gus George, stage magician. Gus George was getting old, but he'd played the Keiths once upon a time, and so Trent had hired him both to fill seats and to spite Abe, whose card manipulations, no matter their precision, dissatisfied the Alhambra theatergoers. Henry Trent had also hired Gus George because he'd seen a handbill with Princess Gyro's likeness, and he'd said to himself that he must have that woman. He'd ripped up Abe's stage contract right in front of him, and four nights prior, on the very day of Gus George's arrival, Trent had signaled Abe to let the magician win at the table. But Abe would not fold to a man who took his job. He cleaned Gus out, and afterward Trent spoke to him as if he were a boy, saying, "You do like I tell you to do! Now magic man's liable to powder out of here."

Abe had lost his head then. With other men present, he'd stood and hollered in Trent's face, "Your magic man owes me three hundred!"

Magic man still had not paid.

And here was his wife, naked on the bed.

"You need to get yourself dressed and clear out," Abe told Nina Gyro. He put his hand against the window jamb and leaned hard. He looked up and down Railroad Avenue for Goldie, but a sweat had come on him, and his vision was not sharp.

Nina Gyro licked her lips and patted the mattress and said, "You need to shake off those breeches and bring back one-eyed Jack."

Abe Baach would never put a hand on a woman in anger. No Baach boy ever would because their mother and Daddy made it certain. But inside his foul-sweated skin, Abe knew that he might have to release his hand from the window jamb and let himself fall forward, clear through the glass and down to the road below. This he might have to do in order not to put a hand on the woman in his bed, for he was angry. She had ruined him.

He had never been with any but Goldie.

On the nightstand was a clear pint bottle and one teacup—broke-off handle, no saucer.

Abe walked closer to read what was scrawled in lip rouge oil on the bottle glass. It was difficult to make out at first. *Balm of Gilead*. He remembered then that he'd imbibed from it quite generously the night before. He'd stuck it in his pocket and walked straight to the Alhambra where he'd pounded the locked door to Trent's office. He remembered being thrown out the side stage door by Rutherford and Taffy Reed, and in the alley was Nina Gyro. He'd called her husband a flea-circus man and told her, "that monkey tamer owes me." She'd laughed, hooking her arm in his. They walked together to Faro Fred Reed's club where Abe had his own back room. They passed the bottle and she'd whispered in his ear that she could suck the silver off a dime. After that, he remembered nothing, and this was not customary when drinking Dorsett's moonshine.

He stepped to the bed and she reached for his fly. He slapped her hand and grabbed her by the arm. He did not squeeze.

She giggled.

"You put somethin in my drink?"

She giggled some more.

"Somebody tell you to put somethin in my drink?"

She looked him straight in the eyes and smiled the way she did onstage. When she could hold his stare no longer, she looked around the bed for a cigar. "Well handsome," she said. "You put it in me again like you did awhile ago, and I'll tell you."

He let go of her and walked back to the window. He leaned there again and tried to narrow the number of men who'd pay a woman like that to do what she had done. A few came to mind.

Nina Gyro looked at the long hollow of his spine and the way he hung his head. He was the best-looking boy she'd ever tried to bed, and he'd shown himself to be, in relative terms, a gentleman. She believed that decency still had its tiny place in life. She shook her head at what she was about to do. "Listen to me bonny boy," she said. "I'm going to tell you something, and after I tell you, I'm going to ask you something." She opened the side-table drawer and took out a box of matches. "Then I'll be on my way, and if you want to, you can give me a little something."

There was a ball-knot at his sternum. He thought for the second time of putting himself through the window. "Just please clear out," he said.

She stood from the bed and pulled on her undergarments. "Pumpkin, you didn't put a thing in me," she said. "I droppered the knockout juice at midnight and you was asleep in this bed by two."

He didn't move.

"I stripped you down, then myself, and then I got some winks." A short cigar fell from her balled dress when she picked it off the ground. "Now we're cookin," she said. She lit it and drew deep.

He straightened then and faced her. He needed things made clear. "Are you telling me we did not engage in the act?"

She fixed the twisted bodice of her dress. "Smell your totem," she said.

"How's that?"

"Smell it. Rub your fingers on it and snuff at your fingers." She demonstrated with exaggerated hand gestures and boisterous nasal inhalations.

He did what she'd commanded. The stink was his own.

She could tell by the way of his eyes that he was not yet fully persuaded. "Pumpkin," she told him. "I haven't bathed in a week and a half. I'm what you'd call storm-cellar musty—you'd know if you'd been in there."

And with that, there bloomed again within Abe's blood a notion to fight on. He felt as good just then as he could remember ever feeling, and he was going straight to Goldie. He thought to clean up and then thought better—he'd *not* clean up and he'd get her to smell his totem as proof of his innocence.

Nina Gyro slipped on her shoes.

"Would you come with me to tell Goldie?" His notions, good ones and bad, were coming fast by then.

She laughed. "That's not the deal. I've done a third of what I said I'd do—I told you something." She squeezed a paper tube and put color on her lips and cheeks. Her cigar was nearly spent, but she did not mind its burn between her fingers. "Now I will ask you something, and then you will give me something, and that will be the last of you and me, you hear?"

"I hear."

"What I want to ask is if there is any opium in this shit town, and if there is, would you point me to it."

"There is and I will." And on the back of a handbill for his canceled show, he drew her a map to Cinder Alley and told her to knock at the fourth door on the left—it would be blue—and to say the following when Mr. Wan answered: *There is no doctor like old Doctor Go.*

"Good." She was as happy as she could be without the opium, which she'd not smoked in almost a week. "And if you want to give me a little something for my trouble," she told him, "I would be obliged."

He said he'd take a pass on that last one, and she curtsied to him and was gone.

From the window, he watched her on the avenue. She bent her course to the bridge and the Bottom. To Cinder Alley. He wondered if she'd make it back in time for her stage show that evening.

He got on the floor and used his spike nail to extract four fifty-dollar notes from a baseboard gap. Emergency money. The only other possessions he kept in that place were a change of clothes, a toothbrush, a razor, and a beaten copy of *Forty Years a Gambler on the Mississippi*. He slid the book in his jacket pocket. He rolled the clothes and toiletries, stuck the roll under his arm, and left. He did not take with him the balm of Gilead, for she'd confessed about the knockout juice.

Goldie was not in her room or any other at Fat Ruth's. In the lobby, he spoke with Rebecca Staples. She leaned her hip on the parlor sofa and told him, "I haven't seen Goldie, honestly, in I don't know when."

Rebecca did not look good. Floyd Staples showed up once a month to force himself on her and tell her she was worthless and take her money before he went back to his other woman in Matewan, a woman of unsound mind who'd borne his child in December.

Abe suspected Rebecca Staples of lying to him, but he would not press her. He asked, "How's that little boy of yours?"

"Not so little anymore." She sprayed perfume on a vase of white ostrich feathers.

"How old is he now? Nine?"

She had missed his last two birthdays. "Yes," she said. "Might be ten."

He started toward the door.

"He plays cards all day," she said. She sat down on the sofa, atomizer still aimed at the vase. She squeezed the puffer until the plume sagged.

"I think you've scented that arrangement sufficient," Abe said.

She did not acknowledge, but sprayed once more and quit. She suspected herself newly pregnant, and her mind was awash in quiet panic.

He was almost out the door when a clear thought came to her. "He's in the kitchen right now," she said. Then she raised the volume of her high voice and called, "Little Donnie!" She coughed and cleared her throat. She told Abe, "It would sure please him to see your card play up close. Maybe just a riffle?"

He said he needed to find Goldie. "Another time," he told her. He took George Devol's book from his pocket and set it down on the upright parlor piano. "Tell the boy to read this," he said. "I'll come collect it after a while, show him a trick or two." And then he was out the door.

Little Donnie Staples stepped from the kitchen. "What?" he said.

Rebecca thumped a fist at her ribs to break up the indigestion. She told him never mind.

Across the street, Jake was tending bar. Big Bill Toothman

sat on a stool and rubbed his lower back. Neither had seen Goldie.

Jake told him to try Hood House. "She's likely up there with mother, taking turns at bad-mouthing you." There was plenty of that to go around. Al Baach in particular was angry with Abe. Al had traveled the day before to Welch in order that he might calm his preacher father-in-law, who had heard of the middle boy's penchant for drinking and bucking those that mattered. Before he'd ridden off on his new bay colt, Al had spat on the ground and told Abe, "I would tell you take care of the women and children, but I know better." Al was worried. He'd not paid a cent in consideration money for six years, and he wasn't about to start up again on account of his son. Al had finally been able to put a little away, and Henry Trent had even tapped him to run for council the following year. There was real money to be had in that game.

Abe put his hand on the barstool and leaned. A long house centipede raced from under the kickplate. Saloon sharks they called them. Abe shot out his boot and stomped it dead.

Jake asked if he'd like a drink.

"Just a beer."

He had three, plus the onion-stuffed heel of a breadloaf, before he hiked up the hill. He was halfway home when he stopped and put his hand against a tree trunk. He retched and his knees nearly gave at the thought of losing her. But a single word arose inside him. *Climb*. And so he did.

Goldie was not at Hood House, whose rooms were full-booked. Nor was she at the second house, which they'd taken to calling the orphanage on account of Sallie's ongoing rearing there of the motherless children of whores.

Abe watched his mother through the open door of an upstairs room. She hummed Twinkle Twinkle and worked a highback rocker with her foot. The child she held was Agnes, who had come to her only a month before. Every other unwanted baby had gone the way of adoption, but Sallie was determined that wouldn't happen with this one. Agnes would be a Baach. Agnes would be the girl child she'd never had.

Sallie pretended not to see her middle boy in the hallway. She shut her eyes and hummed until he was gone.

Only when he was out the door and down the hill did Goldie come out of the closet behind the rocker. "I'm going out to the barn for awhile," she whispered.

Sallie only nodded and kept at her humming.

In the nave of the crib barn, Goldie stood and rubbed at the muzzle of her favorite horse. Dot was the mare's name, on account of the white between her eyes. She was a blood bay, one of four horses the Baaches kept. As a girl, any time the notion struck, Goldie would knot a hackamore bridle and throw a leg over and ride. She'd not done so in years, but now she was of a mind to clap spurs to the horse and go.

She looked in the darkwater eye of the horse and saw

there a refracted light beam from the open barn mouth. It curled white along the black roll of the eye, narrow to wide, and it looked to Goldie like the front lamp of a far-off night train, and for a moment, she was inside the eye of the horse called Dot, and she forgot what Abe had done, and she was happy. She scratched at the horse's chin. She said to her, "I bet you still like to get out on a straight stretch."

Samuel Baach walked past the open aisle with a shovel in his hand. When he saw her, he backtracked and said hello.

"Hello Sam," Goldie called. The sun lit his forearms pale. He was the age and size of the red-haired boy she'd seen at the Alhambra. Skinny. She still thought of Sam as a boy. She noted his shovel. "Diggin to China?"

"Shovelin shit," he said.

"Used to make you give me a nickel anytime you cussed."

"That's why I'm flat broke."

She laughed a little.

"Where's Abe?" He set down the shovel and pushed up his sleeves.

She shook her head. "Don't know. Don't care to."

Sam spit out his tobacco. He looked up at the coming clouds. "Goin to get the big rain this evening," he said.

"Don't go into town then."

"It's Friday. My night to pull ale."

She picked at a mud nubbin stuck in Dot's forelock.

Sam regarded her. Even inside a shadow, Goldie was bright.

"I believe I'll ride her before the storm hits," she said.

"You know that mare's pregnant."

She didn't know. It had been awhile since she was up on the hill.

"You can still ride her," Sam said. "She's not too far along."

Goldie patted Dot's big shoulder. It seemed that every matronly thing but her could bear fruit. She'd never wanted to offer a child where so many went unclaimed, but there had once been in her mind the possibility. Then the years passed without so much as a bellyache, and she knew that no lemon wedge or calendar could ever account for that, and so she'd accepted her lot.

She spotted a dirty sugarcube at the foot of the stall door. She fetched it up and offered it to Dot. She said, "I don't have the clothes to ride her anyway."

"Never stopped you before." He'd watched her when he was just a little boy, hitching her skirt and kicking off her shoes. No saddle.

"You feedin her plenty?"

He nodded.

Goldie looked past him at Hood House. "You hungry?"

He was.

*

Inside the third-floor room of the red-haired boy, Floyd Staples sat on the bed. He played his harmonica for the entertainment of a prostitute he'd yet to pay. Its sound was lonesome and full.

113

"Where did you learn to play like that?" she asked him.

He did not answer but scratched his neck and looked to the door, which presently opened. The red-haired boy had traded in his towel for a fine suit. "They're cleaning out his room," he said.

"Pay this woman two dollars and a half," Floyd Staples told him, and the boy produced a billfold and gave her three. She left without a word.

The red-haired boy was from Mingo County. He'd left the mines after only a year to make his living playing cards. He owed Floyd Staples seventy-two dollars.

"When you say they're cleaning," Floyd said, "you mean cleaning up or cleaning out?"

"Looks to me like he's run his course." He stuck out his chest and regarded himself in the dressing mirror. "That skinny nigger was out in the hall and I heard him say to the leprechaun what a shame it was, the Kid shed off like that."

Staples snorted and swallowed. "Ain't nothin you can do with bad blood except to let it," he said. "Oak Slab don't need him anymore. Bigger than he is." He walked to the dressing table where he poured himself a drink. "Not too big for you though, is it boy?" He swallowed his whiskey and poured another and reclined on the bed with the tumbler atop his chest. He considered his banishment from the Oak Slab. He could still see that ace-high flush. "You got your invitation card tucked someplace safe?"

From inside his suit jacket, the red-haired boy produced

a well-crafted forgery. The embossing was professional. Every grain of the table had been mimicked from the original. Talbert would be on the door, checking invitations, and his eyes weren't what they used to be.

The red-haired boy had begun to wish he'd never met the man now lying on his bed, let alone lost to him at the card table. And his stomach had begun to seize anytime he thought of their plan for that night. He'd not spent much time around the likes of Floyd Staples, who, by any human standard, was plain bad. His clothes were in tatters. His beard had last been shaved two weeks on the right side, a month on the left. But he'd promised the kind of money the red-haired boy was after, and it was shortly in sight.

"What time is it?" Staples asked.

The boy checked his timepiece. "Half past four."

"Your Daddy's accountant friend is tardy."

"He'll be here."

"Let's go over it again," Staples said. "I want you to show me your every move after the cue."

*

Abe was high up in the fly lines by nine o'clock. He was drunk, seated on the narrow board of the loading platform, legs dangling. In each hand he gripped a pair of dike pliers. He'd taken them from Jake's big tool chest that evening, thumbing the edges of their jaws for sharpness. He'd not thought twice about stealing them, for his plan to find Goldie had failed, and as he drank, another plan took its place. Now he opened each cutter wide and readied them alongside the blackened wires the audience could not see. He waited for the offstage man to crank the winch. When he did, the crowd could be heard to applaud. Abe watched the wires climb, and when they'd stopped, he gripped each plier tight but did not yet squeeze.

Above him, rain beat the roof with a mighty sound. The storm had begun at sundown and showed no sign of letting up.

The house band was tucked on the floor stage left—the man on upright piano banged slow, joined by an old-timer on guitar and a girl sawing the fiddle. They played the snake-charmer tune in perfect time. Like a trance it filled the place and fought the rain's drone.

Gus George called to the audience, "You see ladies and gentlemen, if I concentrate and position my hands just so, I can hold Princess Gyro on the very air. Indeed, I have made her float."

Abe looked down. The top of George's head was bald. Nina Gyro's gown was white silk. Abe hummed the tune and tried to remember the words. He sang in a whisper, *I will sing you a song, and it won't be very long.*

George went on, "Her trance is deep, ladies and gentlemen. Watch as I prove there is no mere mechanical trickery involved in such a—"

Abe squeezed both grips at once. The pop was loud and metallic, and the crowd gasped as the floating woman came down crooked and hard, blackened wires falling upon her white gown coiled, like rat snakes. Gus George shot a look to the loft, but all was darkness up there. All was shadow in the fly lines.

Abe spat from on high and walked fast across the platform to the small loft window, where he climbed through and ran down the backstage stairs. He elbowed hard the face of the winch man and made the side door in under a minute. He laughed as he went, for he'd shown them all. Magic was not real.

The door to the alleyway nearly clipped Floyd Staples when it swung. He drew his pistol on instinct and aimed it at the man who'd emerged. He could scarcely believe who it was. "I'll be durn," Floyd Staples said. "My luck gets better by the hour."

Abe went still with his hands to his side. The awning above them roared and spit a fast leak. He tried to slow his breathing, and he frowned at the man before him with a gun, his mind unable to place him. His beard was uneven and the hair at the brim of his brown slouch hat was pasted to him by day-old sweat. "Floyd?" Abe said.

"I told you I'd git my money back boy." He shook his head and smiled, his teeth the color of tree bark. "Are you runnin from the poker table? I thought you was out of that game."

Abe could hear a ruckus growing inside. "Could you let me be on my way?"

Even over the rain, Floyd heard the shouts coming from the Alhambra crowd, and he didn't like them. He wondered if the red-haired boy had bungled up the plan somehow and made a scene. "Why don't we both be on our way together?" he said, and he shoved Abe back inside with his pistol.

He kept it pressed to Abe's spine as they made their way past the winch man, who sat on the floor rubbing his head. They emerged from a stage door and maneuvered around the edge of the crowd, now in an uproar over the trickery to which they'd been subjected. They hollered at the downed magician and his lovely assistant, exposed in the heat of the footlights. "You goddamned quacksalver!" shouted a woman in a velvet hat. One man threw a green glass bottle, narrowly missing the bald crown of Gus George, who knelt over Nina Gyro where she lay, clutching her broken coccyx and screaming for a doctor.

Floyd steered Abe to the main card room unnoticed. They moved along the wall and stopped at the door to Trent's office, where Talbert was on watch. He'd just lowered his newspaper, having caught wind of the ruckus, and he said, "Abe, what in hell is going on?" He paid no mind to either the man at Abe's back nor Abe's banishment from the Oak Slab, as was evidenced by what he said and did next. "Guard the door will you Kid? I've got to go see about this noise." He dropped his paper on his stool, mumbled about floodwater, and was gone.

Staples told Abe to open the office door and he did.

There was no one inside.

Staples shoved him forward and closed the door behind.

"I can smell my money," Staples whispered. "I can smell my new life." His bloodshot eyes welled up. "Got me a new baby boy," he said, "and I aim to feed him beefsteak and oysters, buy him popguns and swinghorses and whatever else." His woman in Matewan had been committed to the home for incurables, and he'd heard the boy was with a widow woman up Warm Hollow. He aimed to go and get him.

A plate with a half-eaten mutton chop sat on the desk. Abe looked across the office at the glass-paned door through which he'd stepped every day for the last six years. He wondered who sat in his chair.

Staples kept his eye and pistol trained on Abe as he tiptoed to the card-room door and put his ear to it.

Inside, the men guarded their hands, elbows on the slab. The single kerosene lamp lit their furrowed brows, and the roof over their heads bellowed the rain's steady fall. Henry Trent had made a trip to his office safe and returned with the leather bank pouch containing two thousand dollars. The betting had gone high, and he knew somebody would soon cash out. He stood against the wall and gripped tight the leather.

Rutherford was at his side. He cupped his hand to his ear. "You hear a commotion?" he whispered.

"It's the rain," Trent answered.

Taffy Reed had just dealt fifth street when the red-haired boy's accomplice, a bespectacled coal-company accountant named Boner, said, "It's a toad-strangler ain't it?"

This was the cue.

The red-haired boy stood and drew the pistol he'd smuggled in. He aimed it at Henry Trent's face. "Hand me the pouch," he said.

Rutherford put his hand to the ivory grips of his hogleg.

"Draw it and I'll put one clean through him." The boy moved toward them now.

"Keep your hands where he can see em," Trent advised, and Rutherford did as he was told.

The boy, suddenly bold in speech and movement, held out his free hand.

Before he gave over the pouch, Trent told him, "Son, you will be dead before week's end."

He'd made the mistake of looking Trent in the face when he spoke, and he'd lost his boldness, but he took the pouch nonetheless and backed to the door with the gun still leveled.

Floyd Staples had kept his ear to the door, but now he stepped back and took one of the cast-iron boxing glove bookends from the empty shelf. He raised it up as the doorknob spun, and when the red-haired boy back-stepped into the office and shut the door, he brought it down hard, crushing the skull. The sound turned over Abe's gut.

Staples swiped the pouch and ran. He was out the door and halfway across the main card room by the time Abe could make his feet move.

Talbert returned just as Abe was exiting, and they collided, overturning the stool and spilling to the floor the newspaper and Talbert both. The little man looked up at him. "Kid?" he said.

"I'm sorry Talbert."

It was then that Rutherford managed to shove open the second door. It took all he had to push aside the dead weight of the red-haired boy. The door's bottom rail made a smear of his blood, and Rutherford slipped on it, his long Colt drawn. As he righted himself, he spotted Abe and lined him in the sights.

Abe ran across the card room and into the lobby. He knocked the shoulder of a bellboy at the main door and hit the avenue. He turned south and slid in the mud. The rain had not slacked.

He'd nearly made it to the bridge when he realized he couldn't go home.

The first shot came then. Abe thought he could hear it as it passed over his head.

He ran for the creek. It was almost over its banks. Black as tanner's ooze and moving quick. A buggy wheel spun on the current.

The second shot came. He dove in the water.

It pulled at him hard and carried him fast. He found it difficult to swim toward the opposite bank. His arms burned, and as he bobbed and fought, he could see the railyard up ahead. A slow-moving empty was switching tracks.

He couldn't get across. He would not make the bank in

time to reach the railyard. He was going to die in that water.

This he'd accepted, until he saw the outline of a man running at creek's edge. Light from the railyard lit him just sufficient to see. He was shouting. He carried something long in his hand.

On the order of his wife, Al Baach had gone looking for his middle boy at nine o'clock. She'd made him take her umbrella, and as he'd neared the bridge, he'd heard the gunshot and seen Abe dive in. He followed, and as he ran, he closed the ribs of his umbrella, secured the snap, and prepared to put it to use. Now he'd gotten ahead of Abe, who was fighting hard and almost at the bank.

The ground was nearly black, and Al tripped over the big knee root of a hard-leaning tree. The fall took his wind, but as he lay there in the mud, he grabbed ahold of the very root that had toppled him, and he stretched away from it, extending the umbrella to the water with his opposite hand.

Abe could see it there ahead of him, the metal tip his beacon. He closed both hands around it as he passed, and he kicked his feet and bent his elbows. Al held fast and pulled until he'd gotten his boy at the armpit and hauled him up onto the shore.

Together, they stood and slid and steadied themselves. Then they ran for the railyard. They ducked behind a high stack of brattice wood and watched an empty westbound train switch onto the mainline. It gathered a little speed, and as it passed, Abe saw Floyd Staples sitting in the open door of a boxcar with his legs hanging crossed at the ankle. He waved with one hand and held up his money pouch with the other.

Floyd Staples laughed while he watched the Baaches cower in the dark, soaked to the bone. And when the train had pushed out, he had a look at the big notes in the pouch. Red seals on every one. He smelled them. Then he unlaced his calf-high boot, stuck the pouch tight against his shin, and relaced. He reclined on the rocking floor of the car and pulled a cheap cigar and matches from one pocket and a picture of his woman from another. She wore a fur hat. Her dress was fringed in lace. Floyd had plans. After he got his baby boy, he'd go to Huntington and break her out of the home for incurables. He'd walk right in and pay off the guards. "I am king of all these hills," Floyd Staples said to himself. And for a moment he believed it. Then he thought of the red-haired boy and what he'd done to him, and something happened to Floyd Staples that had never happened before. A fit overtook the man. It came quick and he sobbed, the heaving kind. His head hung. Snot and spit both came heavy, and he nearly vomited when he pictured that boxing glove bookend, the sound it made on thick bone plate. He'd never planned on killing the boy. Something overtook him in that office, and he knew he'd not ever outrun what he'd done.

Against the timber stack, Abe had told his Daddy what

had happened, shouting over the rain. He said that they were out to kill him, that he'd cut the wires, that they probably reckoned he was in cahoots with Staples.

Al was unruffled. "Rutherford will shoot before there is talk," he said. He thought on what to do. "I will go and tell them the truth." Down the line, they could see the brakeman's lantern. It swung as it neared, lighting shapes on the black ground. Al knew the Friday nightshift brakeman—he was Robert, a patron at the saloon. When Abe was safely off, he could slip the man a dollar to keep his mouth shut.

He gauged the lantern's distance, then looked his middle boy in the eyes. "I will tell them it was Staples alone," Al said. "I will put them on his trail going west." He wiped at his brow and took note of the long eastbound train now switching onto the mainline. Its high hoppers were loaded with coal. He put his hand to Abe's neck. "Listen to me Abraham," he said. "You go east." He pointed to the slow-moving train. "You hop that one," he said. "Do not ride on top—the turns will toss you off." For a moment, he was flustered. Then he turned to the stack of brattice wood and pulled from it, as best he could make out, the straightest and flattest cut. He pushed it to Abe's chest. "Lay this on the knuckles," he said. "It will steady your feet. With your hands, you grip the ladder."

Abe looked at the space between the cars.

The brakeman was now at a jog, fifty yards off. "Hey!" he yelled.

"You go to Baltimore—the wharf, at Frederick Street. You ask there for Mr. Ben Moon. You tell him you are my son."

Abe thought of all he'd left undone. He wanted to make a dash for the twelve hundred dollars stashed in his wardrobe. He wanted to tell his father that he couldn't go, that he needed to get to Goldie, that there was something she had to know. It was not his time to leave, he wanted to say, but the ball-knot had returned and risen now to his throat, and he couldn't utter a word.

Al pulled his son up then by the shirtfront. "Ben Moon," he said, and he shoved him toward the mainline.

Abe ran, tucking the board in his armpit. He timed his jump and reached for the hopper's ladder. The train was gaining considerable speed. He pulled himself up.

Al could see him as he got smaller in the distance, slipping between the cars and kneeling to set the board across the knuckles. He hoped his middle boy would get a solid foothold.

"Hey!" the brakeman yelled again. He was twenty paces off with his gun drawn.

"Robert," Al Baach called to him. "It's me. It's Al." He reached for his billfold. The black mud from the creek bank had gotten inside his pockets.

Robert the brakeman slowed up. "Al Baach?" he said, raising his lantern. "What in the hell are you doin out here?"

But Al did not answer. He stood in the downpour and thought of what would come for him now, of what would befall his family. He thought of the Bottom and how Trent had begun to let it be, how he'd allowed the Baach boys to run Wyoming Street and Dunbar too. He thought of the previous spring's Alhambra banquet, where Trent had pointed his steak knife at Al across a crowded table of T-bones and said to the important men, "Gentlemen, right there is your next councilman."

All of that was over now.

He watched the eastbound train push out of the yard and into the bend at town's edge. Its whistle cut the rain and bounced off the ridge. It was the most familiar sound Al knew, but on that night, it hollowed out his very soul.

High above him, on the bald steps of the mountain, Goldie Toothman walked an old skid trail, the loggers' dead slash still tangled in the ruts, piled high as her waist. She carried a big box of kitchen matches in the pocket of her coat. Taffy Reed had sold the matches to her for a nickel, claimed to have soaked them in a solution that rendered their phosphorous heads immune to water's dousing. Goldie had a notion, as she watched the eastbound train curl around a slick-faced highwall, to set the whole tangle afire. She'd left Hood House with no real thought of a plan, only a feeling in her gut that Abe was sure to die.

Now she stopped and stood still and watched the tiny men in the railyard below. They were lit by the glow of the brakemen's lantern between them. They exchanged money for silence.

Goldie did not watch the train as its tail was swallowed

by the woodland hollows ahead. She knew then that Abe rode somewhere inside its rumble, and she wondered if her terrible dream's fruition might come to be on some other ground, if Abe would dangle for his debts on a foreign limb where she could not see him. It would be easier that way.

She looked up and let the rain fall into her eyes.

SPRING & Summer 1910

THE CROWS WERE IN THE EVERGREENS

April 20, 1910. New York

It was not yet four AM when the cardsharp exited the ill-lit Bowery bar. He took long strides to a place he knew inside the wall of a graveyard on Second Street. There he leaned and opened the quartered newspaper in his grip. It was the evening edition. He'd lifted it from the bar's counter before he slid unseen out the door, and when he'd folded it around his earnings, the headline below the crease had declared: *Summer Here Two Months Early*.

The air was June hot.

Now he set the paper on a wall ledge and leaned and counted his latterly money. No light reached the long lawn of vaults, so he sequenced the notes on touch. One hundred and twenty-three dollars. He right-angled dog-ears with his thumb, flatted the stack, and split it in two. He took off his shoes and inside each he made for his money a bed. A man who walked could appreciate the extra cushion.

He lit a cigar and held the spent match until he'd left the graveyard. He walked to First Avenue, stood beneath a gas lamp, and looked about. There was not a soul, and this struck him as peculiar.

He took from his jacket pocket a handbill made by a printmaker he knew. It was folded at the middle, a good stout paper, its dimensions about that of a book. Its artwork depicted a spade which swallowed a club which swallowed a heart which swallowed a diamond. At the center of the diamond there was an eye, with a man inside the pupil. Across the bottom, the handbill read *Watch the Master Card Manipulator! The Incomparable Playing Card Prophet known around the world as Professor Goodblood will astound and delight!* He sat down on his heels and tented the handbill at its crease. He set it as a house upon the street brick. He produced again his matches and struck one and held it underneath until the handbill burnt to a fine black scatter. There was no need for it now.

He'd only gotten the short-run show because the owner of the Stuyvesant Theatre owed him considerable money. It was a gesture of goodwill. Abe had considered the offer and had gone so far as to print a sample handbill, but in the end, the man sold his theatre and moved to Australia, and the new owner had told him, "Listen Goodblood, card tricks are flapdoodle. The people want leg-drop action. They want raincoats and whiskers."

It was of no real import. Professor Goodblood was not real.

Abe Baach was the cardsharp's name, but no one knew it. He was called by many names in those times, names dependent upon location and disguise of mustache or beard or eyeglass. Names dependent upon the mark he roped or the tale he told.

He wore a scar from his ear to his bottom lip.

He had more money than he could spend, and it had not come from paltry vaudeville checks or short-run opening card acts. The freshest of it had come easy on this particular night. His mark at the Bowery bar was a fat crooked rich man who had drunk his weight in gin. Abe had nearly let him walk from the table with dime enough for streetcar fare and a cup of coffee. But the man proved unworthy, ruining a competitive hand of stud poker with too much chatter on such unoriginal topics as the cultural inferiority of immigrants. "The micks and the guineas," he'd said, "are bull-headed ingrates, and the kike panders to the nigger." Abe had nodded and laughed and said how right the man was before he took his last nickel.

Now he walked alone up First Avenue to the apartment where he'd slept most nights for a month. The tenant was a good-looking gal from Kingston, Jamaica, a stage actress and dancer who sometimes passed for white and who pronounced her words in a way that tickled him. On the first night he'd slept over, after enjoying a maneuver Abe had privately named *the low-high side-to-side*, she had said to him the following: "You got good curve in de hose."

He crossed Seventh Street and sidestepped a dried-out pyramid of horse manure.

Up ahead, in the darkened doorway of a flophouse, a man stood. Abe had seen him from the corner and had put a hand to his vest change pocket, where he kept a half dollar and a little two-shot spur-trigger pistol. It was his custom with strangers on dark streets to allow three possible greetings. A passing nod if the gentleman was average. Be he mendicant, the gift of a coin. And should the man be looking to rob a body, he'd meet the empty smile of a muzzle.

Abe had nearly decided on the coin when he made out the man's box calf shoes. They were well-made and seldom worn. They disqualified him from charitable donation.

The streetlamp marked him average. He wore a brown wool suit and no hat. He was middle-aged. His head was bald. "May I have a word?" he said.

Abe stopped, hand still at his pocket. There was insufficient light to study the eyes, only flickering wide circles on the clay-brown brick. Abe said, "What is the word you wish to have?"

"God's word," the man said.

"I heard that one already."

"Have you?" His voice was low and ragged.

"I have." Abe stepped closer to him. The man's face was slack and kind. There was something familiar about him. His left eye was hazel and his right was brown.

"Did you listen?"

"I did."

"What did you hear?"

"Plop," Abe said.

The man was puzzled. He cocked his head and asked, "Holy water?"

"Holy shit."

The man laughed. His hands, which he'd kept crossed at the front, came apart and hung at his sides. "It's the truth," he said. "God is."

Abe took out the half dollar and handed it to the man. "Is what?" he asked.

"Yes."

Now Abe laughed. He told the man he'd not had such fine conversation since he didn't know when.

The man nodded and smiled. "There is nothing without one, two, three," he said. He pointed at the sky. "God is the comet."

"What's that you say about one, two, three?" His ears had pricked at the numerical point.

But the man, who had begun to feel something powerful, only rocked a little at the waist and kept time with his mind. "He has commenced his poison rain and cosmoplast." He smiled. His teeth were yellow. He was preaching now. "They call this comet Halley," he said, "but its name is Elohim."

Abe looked up where he pointed. "Well," he said. "I suppose it is." He nodded to the man. "I've got to be on my way."

The man said he had to be on his way too, and he nodded in return and walked south.

Abe looked where he'd stood. There was a picked mound of birdseed. The old heavy door of the flophouse was painted brown, a slop job, coat cracked by heat and the knuckles of undesirable men. The cracks revealed, here and there, a resolute blue. Above the door, someone had painted the street address on a brick. *123*. "I'll be damn," Abe said, and he looked up at the black iron staircase clutching four stories of brick and dark windows. Then he looked past the roofline at the low dark murk of clouds pushing toward the river, and he imagined the commencement of poison rain and cosmo-plast. He could make out side-by-side drops as they neared, the first landing on the bridge of his nose and the next tapping his shoulder at the stitch. He imagined rain thick as syrup and the color of creek mud, and if it had been real, he knew somehow it would smell of grapefruit and rotten eggs.

He walked on to the apartment of his temporary woman.

She was awake. She ate sweet potato pie from the pan and told him she'd been waiting, that a man had come by with a telegram. Her toes were bloody from practicing her dance.

Abe said to her, "What man?"

She handed over the telegram.

```
RECEIVED at 195 Broadway    213 AM.
Baltimore Md Apr 20 — 10


A. L. Baach wires from Keystone "If
son Abe alive tell him come home.
Jake dying."
   Stay  quiet  here  Come  to  docks
Talk to Bushels.
                    Moon.
```

He went to the closet and unhung all his clothes in one swipe.

She'd never seen him move in such a manner. "Wait," she said.

"I'm sorry. I've got to go home."

She watched him pack his suitcase and pull rolls of money from spots she'd never known—a loose square of molding at the mantelpiece, a gouge at the dressing table's kneehole.

"Who is Jake?"

He didn't answer.

"You going to Baltimore right now?"

"Yes," he answered, and in fact he was. He'd have to stop in Baltimore on the way home to put things in order. But she believed his home to be Baltimore.

"Joe," she said. "Wait."

She believed his name to be Joe.

She walked to the window. It faced west, and on the

inside sill she kept a mint plant. She watered it twice a day and watched it from noon to half past, the only time afternoon sun fit between tenement roofs. "Wait," she said again. She thumbed the little plant and picked a bright leaf, and chewed it to sweeten her breath, as she always did before they lay together on the Murphy bed.

When she turned, he was closing the door behind him.

It was his custom to leave while they slept, departing a woman's abode in the night, his feet trained for silence. He'd left women in Atlantic City this way, and more in Savannah, Georgia. He'd left two behind in Richmond, and two more in Newport News. They'd known him not as Abe Baach, but instead as Joe Visross or Honey Bob Hill. Boony Runyon or Woodrow Peek. Sometimes they knew him for a month before he was gone, other times two or three. It all depended on the mark he was working, on how long it took him to take his touch. By the time they woke up, Abe was back in Baltimore, counting out twenties with Mr. Moon.

He'd never felt much in leaving them, never had given a second look to the beds in which they slept. They had enjoyed their time with him, he thought, and they'd get over him soon enough. It had been this way for most of his working years. He'd started out telling himself he'd go back to Keystone when he'd saved twenty thousand. Then he told himself forty. After a while, he didn't tell himself a thing, and now, here he was.

It was nearly sunup by the time Abe boarded the westbound train out of Jersey City. He'd run from the ferry and climbed into the first car he could, its seats half full of swing shifters, most of them already asleep. He sat and watched a dusty tunnel worker doze, the man's unshaven neck slack against his seatback.

Abe took out one of two full flasks he'd gathered at the apartment of his temporary woman. He drank from it and watched the sun's orange glow split the horizon and squint the eyes of those still awake on the train. He took out a deck of cards and shuffled. Angel Backs, a discontinued line of cheap stock with little varnish, cherubs and wings and halos for adornment.

He thought of his old room above the saloon, the cards he'd laid on the windowsill.

He took out the telegram and looked at it again. *Jake dying.* He tried to sleep.

Nine miles past Philadelphia, the train bucked at a slow turn and Abe caught a whiff of death rising off Delaware Bay. Morning sun lit up a window smudge left by a sleeping man with too much hair dressing.

He drank the last of his coffee. Across the aisle, a woman had the *Philadelphia Inquirer* spread before her. One headline read, *Miracle cure for syphilis discovered.* Abe knocked on the wood of his armrest. It was his own small miracle that his spigot had never leaked so much as a single hot drip. He read another headline. *Islanders at Curacao spot Comet streaking overhead.*

He checked his pocketwatch. He hadn't slept more than a twenty-minute stretch in fifty-four hours. The minute hand appeared to bend and the white face went black for a moment. Abe blinked and shook his head. He turned the watch over. *A man without the time is lost.* He stuck it back in the pocket.

The woman with the newspaper possessed the ankles of an angel. An inch of skin shown between skirt hem and the top of her patent oxfords. Abe beheld that inch. He watched it bobble. He delighted in its map of pores and stubble, and he cleared his throat and said, "Miss?"

She lowered her reading material. Her expression was neither welcoming nor cross.

"I couldn't help but read your headlines," Abe said. He pointed to her lap. "I have it on good authority that the comet reported there will rain poison on the lot of us."

"Yes," the woman answered. "My sister has been stock-piling comet pills from the apothecary."

"Smart gal."

"No such thing as too cautionary."

He nodded.

A man seated ahead of him stifled a cough. A child ran the aisle with an apple-head doll in her fist.

"Where are you travelin to?" Abe asked.

"Lynchburg."

He leaned forward. "I couldn't help but notice the other news, from Germany. The syphilis cure?"

"Yes?" She'd never liked the sound of the word *syphilis*.

"That's my old cousin," Abe said. The train car swayed. The knuckles moaned.

"I beg your pardon?"

"The German fella. One that brewed up the magic serum. He's my old cousin. He give me an advance dose half a year ago, cured me up right. My pipes are clean as polished brass." He winked at her.

She looked around to see if anyone had overheard. It was the strangest conversation she could remember, and he was the handsomest man she'd ever encountered. "Well," she said. "How delightful."

Abe smiled. He liked the way she said *delightful*—quick, as if built from a single syllable. He watched her take in his smile. He watched her own emerge. He told her he was pulling her leg and she chuckled. He told her he was not the type to contract syphilis and then he asked if she fancied playing cards. She did.

Abe reached his hand across the aisle. "My name is Joe," he said. "Joe Visross."

He began calling her Dee. When she asked him why, he said that to him, she was Miss Dee Lightful, and that she always would be. She chuckled some more. He moved to the seat facing hers and utilized the table between them to spread the deck. "Oh my," Dee said. She'd not seen the work of such hands before. They moved as if mechanized, oiled for unbroken ease. He blind shuffled, smooth-talking all the while. She picked cards and he shuffled again, palming without the slightest trace of impropriety. He plucked the cards she'd chosen every time. She was impressed.

Fifty miles from Baltimore, they'd already shared and

finished the contents of his second flask. Abe flagged the porter and handed him a fin to allow them passage across the loud rollicking vestibule to a vacant compartment car. Once inside, he set down his luggage and pulled the window shade on the locking door. Dee lay down on the low bunk and hiked her skirt. Her eyes were wanton from whiskey. Abe was quick and careful to take his customary position astride her, groin to loin, weight on his elbows.

When he shut his eyes to kiss her, he saw, plain as daybreak, the face of Goldie Toothman.

He raised up and hit his head on the iron luggage berth. The blow nearly put out his lights, and when he touched his hand to the back of his skull, a knot rose slow. He'd lost his vision but was able to shove off the bed and stand.

Dee regarded him there, shuffling against the train's rollick. "Are you going to be sick?" she asked.

He put his hand out against the wall. His sight returned dull at the edges and he looked through the window glass at the Susquehanna bridge trusses whipping by. He'd once seen a man hung by the neck from such a truss.

"I think I'm going to be sick," Dee said. She'd begun to realize what she'd almost done with a stranger on a train.

"I'm sorry," Abe managed. He picked up his bags and was out the door without a sound, a steady throb at the back of his skull. His breath was still hung up in his throat at the sight of Goldie.

Memories can be nullified, and when she'd started to fade some years back, he was glad. It had made everything easier out in the world.

Now he stood inside the roar of the vestibule, taking deep breaths in order to compose himself.

Jake dying. They were words he could not outrun. He watched the accordion walls contract around him like the gills of a fish. He looked at the pressed-steel floor of the gangway beneath his shoes. It was nearly reflective, spit-shined. At the corner, it was factory-stamped *Pullman No. 123.* "I'll be damn," he said.

*

Four hundred miles away, locked inside a fitful nap, Goldie Toothman heard another kind of roar, the kind that often accompanies daytime slumber, and she sat upright, ears ringing. She was in an upstairs room at Hood House. She had waked out of breath.

She stood from the sweat-addled bed and cursed the unseasonable heat.

Across the room, Jake Baach lay dying on the other twin mattress.

She checked his pulse at the neck, where the skin had gone purple-yellow. The wrapped dressing there was a foul brown, the wound beneath it a scabbed bullet graze. The one in his belly had gone clear through. Another was lodged in his scapula. Goldie lowered her ear to his face and listened. He still breathed.

She went to the dressing table mirror and regarded her reflection there. It displeased her. The crows were in the evergreens again, making their awful racket. She walked to the window. Somebody had closed it while she slept. There were those at Hood House who believed Jake might sweat out whatever was in him, whilst others believed in the cure of spring air.

All of them knew by then that such things did not matter. Doctor Warble had done what he could. He said it was most likely a blood infection, and that hope was a notion to think about quitting.

Goldie looked into the yard.

She opened the lower sash, pulled from the floor stack a sturdy book, and stuck it in the channel. The window was open wide enough to put her head through. The birds kept at their cawing, and she said to them, in a near-whisper, "Shut your cock-chafin beak holes." When they did not obey her command, she returned to the white iron bed, knelt, and reached underneath. She took the hammerless shotgun from its mount against the slats, checked that both barrels held shells, and took a crouch position at the open window, barrels resting on the sill. She lined up her shot, shut her open eye, and imagined herself squeezing the trigger, and that the room-rattling noise of it awoke Jake Baach from his wretched death nap to behold black feathers and pine needles bursting from the branches.

She opened her eyes. The crows had gone quiet.

She was about to stand from her crouch when one of them cawed again.

"I'll murder the murder of you," she told the crows.

Spending the night at Hood House had put her in a foul mood once again. She'd offered to administer to Jake as he worsened, and she was glad to ease Sallie Baach's load, but the trees and animals did not suit Goldie any longer. She longed for town. She could see it from the window, pulsing already just down the clear-cut face of the mountain.

How odd, she thought, to have such contrary worlds cheek by jowl.

She looked at the table clock by the bed. Nearly noon. She could be on Railroad Avenue by half past.

The washbowl was half full of clean water. Someone had hung a hand towel on the edge.

She lay the shotgun on the dressing table and took a hairbrush from the jewel drawer. When she had her hair up and her face and neck washed, she regarded herself in the mirror again. Her displeasure was mostly set aside. She watched Jake's reflection in the mirror's corner, so still under the sheet. The back of his hand was like a swollen plum, fingers black.

Someone was coming up the stairs.

It was little Agnes. She stopped and stood in the open doorway.

Goldie turned on the stool to face her. "Hello sweetie," she said. How tall she'd gotten for seven years old. Her short pants long outgrown, lean legs with big kneecaps. A tooth had gone missing up top. Goldie wondered if Sallie had buried it in the yard. She'd missed so many such things staying away all the time.

"Is that my book in the window?" Agnes asked.

"Aren't all of em in these stacks yours?"

"Have I read you the story of Krustikuss and Growlegrum?"

Goldie stood and picked up the shotgun. "If you're up for sitting with him till Grandma Sallie comes, I might let you read it to him."

"I'm up for it," Agnes said.

They crossed in the doorway and Goldie kissed the top of the girl's head. She hesitated, asked if the baby was asleep.

Agnes nodded that he was. She watched Goldie descend the stairs, and then she stepped inside the room. She took note of the used water and towel she'd laid out for Goldie. She did not look over at the man she called Uncle Jake, but instead sat in the chair by the window and opened her book and read, "So one was tall and one stout but both were of the same size in wickedness, and as to Krustikuss he liked to eat babies while Growlegrum was fond of young ladies."

Downstairs, a thin line of oven smoke adhered to the kitchen ceiling, dancing there, slow and fickle to the whims of wind through open windows. Al and Sallie sat at the long table drinking coffee. Between them were two plates covered by dishtowels.

They regarded her as she descended the landing.

"Supper won't stay hot much longer," Sallie said.

"I've got to get to town." Goldie set the shotgun in its hooks over the pie safe and headed for the door.

Al picked up a section of the paper and crossed his legs. He rubbed his knee where the ache was deep.

"I just got Ben settled in the cot." Sallie pointed at the little one where he slept in an iron rocker by the sideboard. "We can set and visit a minute fore I go back up to Jake."

Goldie wanted to tell her that they'd visited plenty the night before at that very table. Al had told them then what he'd done. He'd said, "I sent a telegram to Baltimore, to Mr. Ben Moon. And if Abe is alive, Mr. Moon will send him home."

Goldie had nearly laughed. In seven years, Al Baach had never said a word on Abe. Seven years she'd watched the Baaches shrink while Henry Trent took what he wanted from them, and not once did anybody say they knew Abe's whereabouts, or that they might send a telegram his way.

Goldie stopped, her hand on the doorknob, her back to them. "Did you go to the telegraph office this morning?"

"Yes," Al said.

"Was there something there for you?"

"No."

Goldie turned the knob, stepped outside, and shut the door behind her.

A mouse ran the length of the kitchen floor. "Where's the cat?" Sallie asked. Al didn't answer.

She stood and went to the door, watched through the squat square panes. The young woman walked down the dirt path to where the cinder clouds billowed and the train whistles blew. Through the thick water glass, she seemed to fall apart and reassemble with each step, her red and yellow dress twisting like a column of fire.

Sallie just stared.

"Her food?" Al asked.

"Eat it."

"And the boarder's?" The other covered plate was for the only present boarder at Hood House, a scholar of some kind up from Virginia who said he was writing a travel book. It was customary in those times to have vacancies. Henry Trent had long since convinced the railroad and coal company men to spend their boarding money elsewhere.

"Eat his too," Sallie answered. She'd not have doubled her dumpling recipe if she'd known folks were going to be rude. She could hear her husband getting fatter behind her.

She watched through the glass until Goldie was gone.

Sallie had worried on her since Fat Ruth disappeared and Goldie quietly took over the business, a madam who was younger than half her girls and better looking than all of them. Sallie had worried on her more since the passing of Big Bill. Goldie had neither shed a tear nor missed a money delivery to either saloon or boarding house, and it was her deliveries alone that had kept the Baaches afloat.

Trent had been collecting from the Baaches when and how he saw fit, ever since Abe left town. He had more recently wired Sallie's Daddy in Welch, offering a fine price for the land on which Hood House sat. She'd gone to Welch and told her Daddy that to sell would be a sin, but he'd looked at the floor while she talked, and then he'd asked her, "Is it a sin worse than intermarriage to a Jew? Is it a sin worse than rearing the mixed-blood bastards of whores?"

Sallie walked to the iron rocker and looked at the baby boy. He was a year and a half. He was the first half-black baby to come to Hood House, and there were those who found in such offspring nothing more than blather for the front porch.

A train whistle split the quiet. Sallie turned and watched the old man eat.

*

In town, Goldie walked with purpose down Railroad Avenue. The sun had moved free of the mountain and set up overhead.

Two men who looked to be railroad brass stepped into an alleyway, their stiff hat brims pulled low, heads tucked. She knew what they were looking for.

In a patch of dirt next to the Union Political and Social Club, a black dog was rope-tied to a chunk of brick chimney.

It was a sizable ruin, big as a rich man's grave marker. The chimney had toppled in a fire the year before and was left, in pieces, where it fell.

The dog's tongue moved forward and back as if on a timer. It whined with each pant. There was not a water bowl or a puddle of rainwater to be found. Nor was there an inch of shade, as every tree in downtown Keystone had long since met its end—some by fire, some by flood, and some by tooth of saw.

Goldie freed the rough length of rope from the bricks' sharp red edge and pulled the skinny dog across the dirt. When she stepped inside the heavy door of the barroom, nobody paid much mind. There was a card game in the corner where men mumbled low and angry. A girl no more than fourteen sat on the lap of a bearded man whose eyes were nearly shut and whose hands hung dead at his sides.

"Which one of you does this animal belong to?" Goldie shouted. All gave attention, save the half-conscious drunk with the too-young whore on his knee.

Chief Rutherford sat on a stool at the end of the long bar. He'd taken off his gun belt and hung it on the stool next to him. He ate his customary noon plate of pickled eggs prepared by Taffy Reed. "That's my Sambo," he said.

He stumbled when he stepped off his stool. He wiped his hands on his shirt and walked slow toward where she stood by the door.

When he was close enough, Goldie said, "He had neither water nor shade out there in the yard."

Rutherford snorted away the drip on his lip and smiled. "Well, I reckon he don't mind, long as a peach like you wanders by to save him." He looked her up and down and shook his head in slow disbelief that a woman so beautiful could still be stuck in the bowel of McDowell. "Matter fact," he went on, "I believe when I put him out there on that rock I was settin bait for the likes a you." Like every man in Keystone, Rutherford wanted more than anything the privilege of bedding Queen Bee, no matter the cost.

She smiled back at him.

Taffy Reed was tending bar, a habitual vocation in service of his Daddy's customers, the most frequent of whom was Taffy's other boss, Rutherford.

Reed had not seen Goldie in weeks, but they'd nodded when she came in the door. The sight of her always made his throat clench. Nobody but the two of them knew that he was the only Keystone man to sleep with her since Abe had run off. It went on for a month in 1905, ending as abrupt as it began. She'd bedded other men, but only a handful, only tall-money types in from New York, and only if they laid down the big-face red-seal notes.

Taffy Reed knew Goldie well enough to recognize the look she was giving. He watched.

Goldie leaned down, put her lips at Rutherford's malformed ear, and whispered, "If I see that dog tied again without water or shade, I'll knot his lead around your tackle-sack and throw a pork chop in the road." She reached out, still smiling, and took him by the hand. Around his wrist, she looped the little circle of rope and gave it a forceful tug. It hissed as it cinched, snapping snug to his wrist and appreciably illustrating her point.

Reed brought out a cast-iron pan half full of old water and set it on the floor. The dog quit whining and lapped away. Above him, Rutherford watched with glazed eyes.

Goldie walked to the girl on the drunk man's lap. "Come with me sugar," she said, taking the girl by the elbow.

Rutherford snorted again and came out of his stupor. He kicked the frying pan across the floor. It smacked the bar's brass kickrail, loud as a dinner bell. The men playing cards turned their heads. "She don't work for you!" Rutherford said.

Goldie ignored him and led the girl to the door.

He called after them, "You can't just claim any whore you want." He was tired of Goldie Toothman's ways. He said, "I ain't above shooting a woman in the back," and drew a bicycle gun from his waist. "Most especially when she steals what belongs to me."

Goldie turned to face him. "You a slave trader are you?" She let go the girl and walked right at him. "I haven't seen her around here before. You bring her across state lines?" She sniffed twice at the air between them. "Smells to me like you been to Virginia." She looked down at the little gun between them, took a step closer to it. "How about shooting a pregnant woman in the belly? You above that?" She took the wrist she'd cinched with rope, the same one

152

clutching the revolver, and pulled it to her stomach. The short barrel pressed deep, just above her navel. The dog shivered at their feet, his whine reconvening.

"Hold on now," Reed said. He was bent over the frying pan with a rag, oily water under his shoes. He held his hands up as if to plead for calm.

A man stood from the card table. His mustache curled into his mouth. "Rutherford," he said, "Are you holding a gun to a pregnant woman?"

Rutherford recognized his position and said that no, he wasn't doing any such thing. He pulled free of Goldie's hold and dragged the dog to his original spot at the bar, retucking his gun as he went.

Goldie turned without a word and hooked the girl again by the elbow on the way out the door.

Just past the Machine Works they moved quick along the creek. Neither had spoken. A man used a barber's pole to steady himself as he attempted to put one foot in front of the other. "My place is right over on Wyoming a ways," Goldie told the girl.

They crossed the bridge and came into the Bottom. Goldie checked over her shoulder every twenty paces. They passed the Chinese laundry and arrived at Fat Ruth's, its white recoat of paint grayed inside a day, its sign proclaiming *Fat Ruth Malindys. Cheap Rooms.*

There were those who'd advised Goldie to change the name, to make use of her own moniker, but she knew better.

They tucked inside the doorway. Goldie took the girl by

the shoulders. "Rutherford bring you here from Virginia?" she asked her.

"Yes."

"When?"

"Yesterday evenin."

"This is not the place for you," Goldie told her.

Rutherford had brought in too-young girls before, twice a fourteen-year-old, usually on the occasion of Harold Beavers' visits from Florida. Harold liked them young.

Goldie said, "I want you to go and set in that chaise lounge inside and think about how nice it's going to be to go home and see your family." She opened the screen door. "I'm going to keep watch for a spell, make sure he doesn't track you."

Before she went inside, the girl said, "You don't look pregnant."

"That's because I'm not."

Two women came out of the laundry carrying bundles. They were laughing over a joke they'd heard inside.

There was no indication that Rutherford had given chase.

Goldie looked upon the sign of the beat-up saloon across the street. *Al Baach & Sons.* She looked to the empty second-story window where he'd sat and watched her as a boy. The sun was low and hot. She put her hand to her brow and turned and looked up at her own window. She imagined herself there, pretending not to see the boy across the way.

She'd nearly forgotten what he looked like full-grown,

but she knew that she'd soon find out. In her bones, she knew he wasn't dead.

She went inside and nodded to a fine-suited lawyer from Welch who was exiting a first-floor room. He came every Wednesday at noon. Taylor was his name. He always wanted the same woman, a middle-aged gal called Wink from up at Kimball. Wink was far and away the stoutest of any at Fat Ruth's, and she'd charmed the lawyer on his very first visit, recognizing the brand of want in his eye and proclaiming herself the one for him, the only one around who was, as she put it, "meat-boned and black as a tinker's pot."

The lawyer tipped his hat to Goldie, and, as was his custom, held out a strange old two-dollar note as he passed. "Your gratuity, Ms. Toothman," he said, and she took it and told him much obliged. He sniffed a vase of purple laurels on his way to the door and proclaimed what he always proclaimed upon departure: "Sweetest cathouse I've ever seen."

The Virginia girl looked at the floor.

Goldie stuck the money in her cleavage and stepped behind the front desk for a pencil and a slip of paper. "We'll need to send your people a telegram," she told the girl. "Tell em you're on the way." She licked the lead tip. "You got money enough for train fare?"

The girl shook her head no and looked like she might cry.

"There isn't anything to cry over now," Goldie told her. "I've got your fare and enough for something to eat too."

The girl wiped at her eyes and tried to smile.

Goldie said, "Fried eggs taste better on a train."

*

In Baltimore, Abe nearly ran from the station. He checked his watch and thought on all he had to do before he lit out again. He dropped his suitcase at his safe house on Camel Alley, locked it back up, and hit the street to collect from those who owed big. He pulled the brim of his hat low and walked up Poppleton Street to Harmony, where he knocked on the door of a crooked police officer who owed him two bills. The man was home. He paid up. He wore a woman's red silk robe and slippers made of moosehide, and for the length of their short conversation in the doorway, he scratched at his stones. He told Abe, "Your man Buck got fished out of the Patapsco Sunday morning. He was scalped, had six slugs in his belly."

Abe didn't give a damn about a short-con goldbricker like Buck. He said, "I'm on the eight o'clock to Cincinnati." It was a smart lie.

"Tonight?"

"Tonight." If the man had ideas on double-crossing him, his chums could go sniff the wrong platform at the wrong hour.

He eyeballed Abe, then stuck his head out and surveyed the street. From the bedroom behind him, a woman shouted that she wanted her godforsaken peanut brittle. He paid her no mind. "Where are you headed now?"

"My woman's place on Calhoun." Another lie.

He didn't go west, but east, stopping at Barnum's Hotel to pick up three hundred from a laid-off B&O bookkeeper who scared easy. The bellman gave Abe a look on his way out.

He stuck to side streets and made his way to the wharf.

The warehouse brick wore heavy paint meant to withstand seawater carried by the wind. *Radiant Moon Playing Card Company* it read. At the long dock on Frederick Street he looked for the man they called Bushels. He tapped his fingers against the brass piling cap. A wad of chicken wire and driftwood bobbed against the slick pilings beneath him. He looked past the smog and out across the harbor to Locust Point, the place where his father had arrived from Germany thirty-three years before. Birds dived for fish and a high-stacked vessel waited for position to dock.

Bushels stepped from the warehouse and surveyed. When he spotted Abe, he waved him over.

Bushels was what they called Bushel-Heap Lou McKill, Scotsman and former champion wrestler. Now he protected Ben Moon, or whoever Ben Moon told him to protect, and for on-the-side money, he bent nails and ripped card decks in half. He was six and a half feet tall and weighed three hundred and fifty pounds. He was quiet and known to possess an uncommon sense of decency. His sleeves were rolled to the elbow. He wore a compass rose on one forearm and a swallow on the other.

They shook hands. "He's in his office," Bushels told him.

"Before you go up, he wants me to make sure nobody knows you're back."

"Nobody knows."

"There's been some trouble."

"Nobody knows."

"You check for a tail after the train station?"

"I checked."

"Then he wants you to come straight up."

Abe slipped Bushels a fin. "I need twenty-five decks," he told him. "Devil Backs, the ones with the false name and New York address. Ten wrapped, fifteen free. I need the wrappers flat-packed, stamps separate."

Bushels nodded. "I'll bring em to the office."

Abe followed him through the open warehouse doors.

Inside, Bushels made for the packing department and Abe climbed the stairs three at a time.

When he knocked at the big office door, Moon said to enter.

The office was wide and dark. It smelled of hot grease and newsprint. Moon was having his lunch. He stood from behind his desk and waved Abe inside.

He was an average-sized man with a well-groomed beard. The embroidered handkerchief tucked at his shirt collar was streaked in grease. On the desk was a massive book weighted open by a skillet of fried rockfish. He walked to Abe and shook his hand. He took him by the shoulder and there he squeezed and patted heavy. "Sit down for just a minute," he said. "You want some fish?"

"I might have a bite."

They sat and ate with their hands. "I know you need to get on a train as fast as you can," Moon said.

"I'll make the early morning." Abe wiped his fingers on a stack of newspapers and pulled from his inside pockets the bankrolls he'd stashed at his temporary woman's place. "Here's the take from New York," he said. "Fifty-five hundred and change."

It was a good take from a cut-short trip. Moon held his hands up to indicate he didn't want the money. With what he expected to soon rake in, the fifty-five hundred could walk.

Ben Moon was a wildly rich and adventuresome man whose business practices had grown increasingly bold. He was not bound by law or convention. No woman could settle him. Recently, he'd decided to fundamentally alter the path of his life's work.

He spoke with his mouth full of fish. "You keep that and take it home with you. Matter fact," he said, and he stood and walked to the room's corner. There, behind a three-foot portrait, was his wall safe. The portrait was black and white and depicted a man in a flat cap with his hands in his pockets. *King of Aspromonte* it read across the top. He swung it open and worked the combination and returned to his desk with two thousand dollars. "Here," he said. "God knows how long you'll be gone."

Abe thanked him.

From a stack of targets with eight-inch bullseyes, Moon

took up a sheet. "You want to shoot a little?" Moon believed a man must keep keen his shooting ways. He'd installed a single-stall range running the length of the building. Its only entrance was at the end of his office.

"Not today," Abe said.

A tow's foghorn sounded from out on the water.

Moon was unsure of how to tell the young man his news, so he simply told him. "I'm getting out of the card business," he said. "I'm selling this place." He looked at the walls, the ceiling over his head. "It's going to be an assembly plant for automobiles. Can you imagine it? The Chambers Motor Car Company." He shook his head. He said, "I have some investment opportunities in New Jersey and southern California."

"Investment opportunities?"

"Cards are on the downslope." Moon sat back down and continued to eat. "Anti-saloon leagues will be the death of us all," he said. He stared blank at a stack of books about birds.

Abe couldn't think of a thing to say.

"I've partnered with a fella of means who's built one of the finest rigid airships in the world. You should see it Abe," Moon said. He thought for a moment on pulling out the blueprints, showing the young man the oversize rudder and the long sleek gondola basket. He knew Abe would appreciate such work, and the same could not be said for the other men he employed. But time was short. He said, "Took him five years, but it's near done, and it's sitting in Atlantic City now."

"Man's name a secret?" Abe asked.

"No," Moon said. He regarded the cracks in the cold skillet grease. His new partner didn't want their names linked. Ben Moon didn't care for such a policy. "His name is Walter Melvin. You heard of him?"

Abe shook his head no.

"You ought to have. Man's photographed the North Pole. Sydney, Australia, from a hot-air balloon too, with a camera he built himself. Made his money in newspapers, now he's moved on to moving pictures."

"That's somethin," Abe said. "Moving pictures." He nodded, looking all the while at the floor.

"Got to follow the money."

It was small talk by then.

Moon knew the young man had real matters to attend to. "You don't want to be here for a while anyway," he told him. "Swollen Man's got his collectors back in town. They scalped a fella and tossed him in the water."

Swollen Man was better known as Dropsy Phil O'Banyon, a big-time, ill-tempered Chicago bookmaker-turned-gangster who frequented Baltimore and always had bad luck at the tables there. In February, he'd lost nine hundred to Abe at a high-stakes game in Butchers Hill. He didn't shake hands before he left.

"Phil's sore at me," Moon said. "I wouldn't come down on price to sell him my outfit." He laughed. "Crazy son of a bitch wants to get into card manufacture."

Abe unfolded the telegram and put it on the desk. "I need you to help me understand this," he said.

"I'm so sorry about that." Moon wiped his hands again and yanked the hanky from his collar. He produced from a drawer the original telegram. It gave no indication as to how or why. Again, it was only *Jake dying*. Moon poked his finger at it. "Family," he said. "There is nothing without family." He'd lost his mother to cancer the year before. She was the only family he had. When he was a boy, she'd kiss him goodnight and tell him, "You are my radiant moon."

Abe said, "I didn't know you and Daddy had any contact." For six years, Abe had wired money to his father, once in winter and once in summer, but there had never been any telegrams.

Moon said, "Well, once in a while over the years he's checked on you."

"I wish I'd known. There are people there I could have . . ." And he blinked and saw again the face of Goldie. He put his fingers to the pump knot on the back of his head and winced.

Moon watched him close. "They are all just fine until this telegram, far as I know." He had always wanted to tell the young man what little he knew of life in Keystone by way of Al Baach's letters, which came every five or six months. "Your father was grazed in the knee by a ricocheting bullet two years back," Moon said, "but he gets around. Your mother is well, as is your younger brother. Goldie too is well as far as I know, though her father died last year." In all of his letters, Al Baach had written to Ben Moon, in one form or another, the following: *Abraham must not know of what goes on here with us. If he knows, he will come here, and that is still not safe.*

Then came the telegram. *Jake dying.*

Moon said, "I know that your father has managed to keep the saloon open, but business has been slow." He cleared his throat. "I believe he's taken up shoe repair again."

Abe stared at the words on the telegram and tried to imagine his family, less one. "How can business be slow with Keystone the way it is?" he said. "I've met more than a few men who travel there twice a year. I heard a fella in Boston once talking about Cinder Bottom girls."

Moon didn't know enough to answer. He knew some of it lay in the blackballing of the Baaches after Abe cut the wires and left town. He didn't want to rile him. "Listen to me Abe," he said. "I'm going to tell you something about your father and then you're going to get on a train."

Abe listened.

Moon told of a time when he was eleven years old, a time when the first of many letters arrived from Keystone. This first letter, like all that were to follow, was addressed to both Ben Moon and his mother. In it, Al Baach wrote of what had happened that day in September 1877, and how sorry he was about Vic Moon's demise. He inquired as to whether they'd received Vic's body and the substantial monies he'd had on him. Al had suspicions already on the veracity of Trent's promise to send the money, and he apologized for having not taken care of such business himself. A correspondence commenced then between young Ben Moon and Al Baach, and in each letter the boy received, there was a renewed promise to find Vic Moon's body. There was also enclosed money. When the boy was thirteen, all one hundred and twenty-three dollars had been repaid.

"I bet he never spoke to you or anyone else about this," Moon said.

Abe shook his head no. He wondered why Ben Moon hadn't told him before. He wondered at the figure: one hundred and twenty-three dollars. It was chasing him.

There was a low roar inside his head.

"Your father is a good man," Moon said. He opened a box of long cigars and took one. "He is one of the few left." He trimmed his cigar with a letter opener and lit it and told Abe it was time to go home and make things right with his family.

Abe nodded.

"I do know a little bit about Mr. Henry Trent and Mr. R. Rutherford," Moon said. "And the Beavers brothers." He scoffed, but beneath the scoff was the truth. Ben Moon feared no man, excepting those absurd West Virginia men about whom he'd only read in letters, those men living in a place he'd never been, the place his Daddy had died. "You need to ready yourself, maybe bring a man or two along." He cleared his throat. "Trent is mayor now, and Rutherford is chief of police."

A dizziness came upon Abe then. He thought he might fall from his chair.

"You feeling poorly?" Moon asked.

"I'm just fine."

"You certain?"

"I'm certain."

He wished he had time to help the younger man, but too many needed help in this world, and he had always been a man without the time. "You all set for pistols?" he said.

"I'm all set."

"I got a new five-shot .38. Little three-inch barrel." Moon opened the big bottom drawer and took out a revolver. "Easy to conceal," he said. "You still pack a second don't you?"

"I do."

"Might be time to pack a third." He held it out. He said, "It's good for close quarters."

Abe took it. The gun wore not a smudge. Nickel finish, blued hammer. He tucked it at the base of his spine and cinched his belt a hole tighter. "Thank you," he said.

"How about rifles?"

"Not on this trip."

"You want to take along Bushels?"

"No."

"He is a man of many talents."

"No. It's easiest on my own." He tried to imagine himself back in Keystone. He considered a moment on how he might play it, on what he might find. "Second thought," he said, "tell Tony Thumbs to watch for a telegram."

Moon smiled at the sound of the old man's name and wrote it down. "You haven't used Tony in a long while," he said.

Tony Thumbs was an eighty-two-year-old theater operator whose company Abe enjoyed. He had once been a large-scale buyer of Radiant Moon cards. Before that, he'd been a top card manipulator himself until a blacksmith, angry over losing at Tony's monte table, chopped off his left thumb with a hammered-steel cleaver. Now he made small-batch powder remedies for insomnia and brewed syrup cures for indigestion. He ran a theater called Old Drury and kept a stable of actors and short-con specialists and oddball sideshow types.

"You hire on Tony Thumbs," Moon said, "you get two bodies for the price of one."

"How do you mean?"

"I mean Baz."

Baz was a capuchin monkey who rarely left Tony's shoulder.

"That monkey is still alive?"

"I figure each of em is waiting on the other to die first."

They laughed at the thought of it.

They discussed their methods of communication. Ben Moon would wire Abe at the Keystone office on Wednesday mornings. He'd address the telegrams to Joe Visross, and he'd use a false name himself. They'd stick with the codes they'd developed. More than likely, the telegrams would shortly originate from New Jersey, where Moon had business to attend.

"Abe," he said, "I will give you what you need to straighten affairs down there. My father's life ended in Keystone, and many years ago, before all this other got in the way, I resolved—"

Bushels knocked on the office door and came on in. He had the forgery cards Abe requested—two boxes wrapped tight in oilcloth and strung with twine. Abe thanked him.

He shook Ben Moon's hand, and again the older man grabbed him at the shoulder and patted him.

Abe walked down the back stairs and out to the loading docks. He took a last look at the water as he left, and he recalled the peace he'd found at the harbor all those years before, walking where his father had walked as a young man. Then he looked at the tall pilings where he'd nearly lost his life at twenty-three. It was on his second Friday night in Baltimore, just past the Frederick Street docks, that he'd run across a squat man named Dash who was known to parry and slash like his joints were oiled, a trained cutter in a fight. Abe hadn't known Dash's reputation at the time. He'd only known that he was a dip, a no-good pickpocket whose buddy tried to stall Abe by the loading docks. The stall was clumsy when he bumped Abe, who recognized the strategy and kept walking. There was nothing in his pocket to pick. His money was in his shoes. But Dash was frustrated to come up empty-handed, and he hollered at Abe, "Watch where you step you fuckin tomato can." Abe was drunk, and he'd turned and taken a swing. Dash pulled the blade and got him across the jaw on the second slash. Blood came in a sheet, quick, and Dash reared back to go again. That's when Ben Moon shot Dash in the spine with a .45 revolver from where he stood against the back wall of his warehouse. He was more than forty feet off when he fired.

At that time, Moon had been president of the Radiant Moon Consolidated Card Company for two years. Everyone in the harbor knew not to cross him.

He stopped Abe's blood with the fine starched shirt off his back. He used his necktie to cinch it tight, and when the police came, they nodded respectfully at him and said, "Mr. Moon, good evening." He nodded back and stood there shirtless, lighting a cigar with his big bloodied hands.

The policemen knew he walked the harbor at night, watched the docks where his crates full of cards were loaded and shipped off to Norfolk and Savannah. They knew he wasn't the kind to shoot a man in the back for no good reason.

That same night, Ben Moon took young Abe to the home of his personal tailor, who awoke and fed Abe amber whiskey before stitching the cut closed with his finest six-cord thread, and two weeks later, when his face had healed sufficient, Abe was sent back to the tailor, this time with a note from Moon to make the young man four fine suits. Moon had come to understand the rarity of Abe's intelligence and hand mechanics by then, and it wasn't long before he sent him out on the mainlines to every East Coast town worth a damn, and in those towns Abe played the role of card salesman for the Radiant Moon

Playing Card Company, a square paper by all appearances. He wore his fine suits and carried a leather grip full of sealed and unsealed card decks, but Abe Baach was no square paper. He was a confidence man with five fake names. In April of 1910, where he was headed, he'd not be able to use any of them.

THE PULPIT WOULD HAVE WHEELS

April 21, 1910

The journey from Baltimore to Keystone had been a long and fractured locomotion. When the long train crossed the state line into West Virginia, Abe tapped his foot seven times upon the rumbling carriage floor, one for each year he'd been gone. Despite the lengthy absence, he knew every high trestle, every roaring downgrade. He recognized in the echoed sound of the steam whistle a loneliness only heard where hills grow close as camel humps, the narrows between them waiting on floodwater.

The engineer blew his whistle again at the last crossing before town. The engine slowed at the switch, its brakes rattling hard. Inside the passenger car, Abe watched the people sway together in perfect time, a traveler's muted dance. Their fingers and toes were gripped and steadied by habit, and they looked through windows bleared by coal dust. The hillsides rolled by slow on either side, steep-banked and the purest green. It was early afternoon. The sun held its angle and warmed the earth.

Abe sat alone in a wide-backed coach chair. His big leather grip was flat on the seat beside him, a duffel on top. He studied what passed outside his window. A tipple clutching the hill. A line of beehive coke ovens with two men to a hole, one for the wheelbarrow and the other for the shovel. The train lurched. He could see up ahead now the bridge at Elkhorn Creek, the square brick buildings on Railroad Avenue, more of them than when he'd left. Between the buildings were packed-dirt alleys staked and strung across with clothesline—white sheets agitating in the wind, silent, like flags.

The train slowed at the new N&W passenger station. It was of the board-and-batten variety, its tin roof sharp-angled and striped by the shadow of two chimneys. KEYSTONE was painted in red across the building's side. Out front, two buckboard wagons were stacked double with whiskey kegs. A boy stood and waited for someone, his trousers hitched high above his waist, a man's black bowler hat in his hand. Beside him, a policeman leaned against a post and checked his watch. The train came to a full stop. It hissed. Abe tucked his chin, picked up his suitcase and duffel, and jumped from the coach to the platform before the brakeman could set out the stool. It was half past noon.

He walked past the policeman with his head low and his hat pulled down. He nodded hello to a good-looking woman in a plaid skirt, and he snorted at the wind to catch sin's direction. It blew from where it always had, the windows of the saloons and houses of ill fame across Elkhorn Creek. It blew steady from Cinder Bottom.

The Alhambra Hotel was due south, just past the bend. He did not so much as turn his head in its direction.

Nearing the bridge, Abe regarded the water below. It rolled quiet over jutted stones, its color black and its level as low as Abe had ever seen it in spring. Still, evidence of flood times abounded on the banks. A wardrobe with the doors torn off. A bed frame split in two. Like bones in the mud, they held until the next one came. The bridge's boards were fresh cut, and they'd be fresh cut again before long.

At the middle, he spat.

He breathed in the smell of sawdust and dirty water and coke-oven ash. He looked across the bridge to the Bottom, the place that had born and raised him. The streets were yet to be cobbled, a testament to dirt's resilience. Men and women stood upon them and talked, their features unknown from where Abe stood. There were more of them than he'd ever seen, and payday was still a day off.

He put down his suitcase and duffel long enough to adjust his new pistol, secure at the small of his back. Then he walked across the bridge and onto the main thoroughfare, where a man had fallen down drunk next to a horse-drawn wagon. He was snoring, and three little boys stopped to watch him, passing a poke of hard candy and laughing. One of them kicked the drunk in the armpit, but the man did not stir. The owner of the horse and buggy emerged from the doors of the wholesale grocers. He shooed the boys, stuck his fingers in his mouth, and whistled for a policeman. Four of them leaned against the slats of a saloon up ahead. They looked, then went back to talking.

Abe walked down the middle of Bridge Street. It was good to be back in a place cinched by hills. On all sides, they rose up and watched over man's thin attempt at living.

He noted the new clocktower, the fancy striped awnings that stuck out everywhere, some of them lined in fringe. Telegraph wires hung between rough-hewn poles full of knotholes. Men stood on second-floor balconies, and here and there spilled perfectly good beer on pedestrians below. One of them whistled to any woman he supposed a whore, and if she looked in his direction, he'd proclaim his love in a song of questionable discernibility and origin. He hollered the chorus: "And my knob's as hard as hick-ry and it's stiff as a churn."

When Abe had left Keystone, there were three whorehouses. Now, there were twenty.

Everywhere was the smell of whiskey and beer, the way it lingers and heats in the sun. He looked no one in the eye. He stepped into an unnamed side street and the crowd thinned some. A girl leaned against the iron post of a fence and called, "Hey sugarcube," but it was unclear if he was the man in question. He walked on until he came to the corner of Wyoming Street. He could see it now, his Daddy's place. The sign across the front of the building was in disrepair. *Saloon* it read, and underneath, *A.L. Baach & Sons*. It was as if he were looking at the place for the first time.

He only glanced at Fat Ruth's, where an unfamiliar woman in pink stood by the window, before he approached his old home.

There was no fancy awning, only a stoop, and next to it, a wheat-flour barrel acting as a table. It was an old cask with half-rotted staves. Three men sat around it talking, each blacked in coal dust save a clean-wiped spot at the eyes and mouth. Abe nodded in their direction and walked inside.

It may as well have been midnight in there. The window shades were drawn tight—sharp, thin lines of sunlight carried inside a few feet then died. The air was heavy and rank. Vinegar water streaked the floor, and its smell pulled at memories the way smells sometimes will. Two black men sat at the bar. Coke-yarders, both of them, coming off third shift. They turned to look at him, then kept at their conversation on the monetary risks of raising roosters to fight. Next to them, a mop handle leaned against the bar top, its bucket base of dirty vinegar water still settling.

A heavy tarpaulin covered what had been the little stage. Beneath it was the stopped progress of Jake's skilled carpentry, a cobwebbed affair of grandiose intent. A plan never realized.

From the storage room in back, there came the sound of breaking glass and mumbled cursing. A moment passed, the swinging door kicked free, and a young man stepped through it carrying a five-gallon kerosene can in one hand and a jug of whiskey in the other. He was tall and thin and he wore an uneven beard. "You two better sip it slow," he said to the men at the bar. "I broke one gettin it off the high shelf." Then he saw Abe standing there.

"Hello Samuel," Abe said.

Sam Baach had grown hard and wiry and his teeth wore the stain of all that he put to his lips and swallowed. His nose had been broken. He had a voice like an old man.

He set the kerosene can and bottle on the bar top. His mouth went dry. There was a tingle at the backs of his knees. "Abe?" he said.

The men at the bar frowned and traded a look. They had heard the name.

He took off his hat and left his luggage where it lay. His strides toward Sam were long and he spread his arms wide on the way. It was an embrace known only to brothers. Abe cracked a couple of vertebrae when he squeezed. "Boy, you are a pawpaw knocker aren't you?"

"No taller than when you last saw me," Sam said. They stepped back from each another and cocked their heads and beheld. Sam was the first to look away.

The men at the bar looked at one other again and nodded. It was, in fact, who they thought it was, and though they'd lived in Keystone only two years, they had heard tell of the man, and they'd suspected, as most did, that Abraham Baach would not ever come home.

He took a seat at the bar and turned on his stool to face the two men. "Afternoon," he said.

They nodded. The tall man was missing an eye. The short one wore his weight funny and had a chest like a woman's.

Sam chewed his lip and attempted to regulate his breathing.

Abe smiled as he took a small cigar from his pocket and held it up between thumb and fingers. He put the end of it in his ear and pushed, and when it was all the way in, he stuck his finger inside the canal and pushed some more. Then he coughed and pulled the cigar from his lips.

The short man sneezed and shook his head. He'd seen some things, but he'd not ever seen a man stick a cigar in his ear and pull it out his mouth.

"So you the Abe Baach they speak on?" the tall man asked.

Abe smiled. He regarded the pinched hole where the man's eye had once resided, a belly button now, empty at the center. He said, "If they speak on a man with testes spiked like sweet gum seeds, then yes, I reckon I am one and the same."

The tall man laughed. The other was not possessed of an imaginative humor.

Abe closed his fist upon the little cigar. There was a faint sound of paper tearing. "You gentlemen look to be making the notable move from ale to whiskey," Abe said. "I wonder if you'd mind relocating to another establishment so my brother and I might visit awhile." He opened his fist, and in it were two Morgan silver dollars. He slapped the coins on the bar top and pushed them forward.

"Wouldn't mind at'all," the tall man answered, and he examined his coin before pocketing it.

"I wonder too," Abe said, "if you'd mind sparing folks mention of my arrival. It would be premature to speak on it just yet."

Both men nodded. "Lips are sealed," the tall man said. He'd rightly noted a vague danger should they break their word.

"I'm obliged to you," Abe said.

They slid from their stools and walked out the door so that for a moment, sunlight lit the place, and Abe listened close to the croak of the rusty spring and the slap of the wooden screen door when it shut. It was a sound he could listen to all day.

Sam had a shiver about him. He pulled at his beard and watched his older brother. 'Jake alive?" Abe asked.

"As of this morning, yes, but not by much."

"What happened to him?"

"Shot. One in the chest, one in the belly, a graze at the neck." He pointed to the spots on himself as he spoke of them. "One of em still in there. Doctor Warble said blood poisoning."

The door sounded again and Abe hid himself by putting his hand to his face as if dozing.

Sam squinted to be sure of the patron's identity. "How do Chesh," he said. Then he gestured to hold up. "Come back in ten minutes."

Before the young man nodded and left, he sized up the fellow hiding his face at the bar.

"Who was it?" Abe said.

"Nobody."

Nobody was Cheshire Whitt, son of councilman J. T. Whitt, owner of the *McDowell Times* and founder of the Negro Presbyterian Church. Cheshire was the only Whitt to associate regularly with folks in the Bottom, and his father did not like it, for he believed the black man would only make his mark by honest means.

Abe said, "Who shot Jake?"

"Italian fella, name of Dallara. Carpenter. Two of em was thick as glue." Sam cleared his throat. "Happened up on Buzzard Branch Saturday last. Early evenin, three shots. Jake run out of the woods hollerin and carryin on, blood all over. One of the girls from Fat Ruth's seen him, but he was on the ground time we got to him. Never been awake since. He won't just die like most."

"The carpenter?"

"Captured up at Matewan. They're keeping him up there in the jail. Rutherford's one that caught him, tracked him to a hideout up some hollow. Rifle was up on Buzzard Branch, three rounds spent."

"Where is Jake now?"

"Up at the house."

"I reckon I'll head up there." Abe stared at the wall for a moment, then shook his head.

Sam's nerves were getting the better of him. It was as if a ghost had walked in the door. He set out two glasses, poured for Abe and then himself, and they held them up and drank them down. He wanted to ask about the scar, but he couldn't think of how. He regarded the fine clothes of his older brother. He said, "Jake was setting right there on your stool back in January when he got religion."

"How's that?"

"He had a vision, and afterwards, he'd tell anybody that listened all about it." He shook his head and pointed to Abe's stool. "Happened right there," he said. "He didn't take a drink since."

"How do you mean?"

And Sam told how he meant.

On January 23rd, Jake Baach had the vision that changed his path. It was a Sunday. He'd been drinking whiskey all morning. There was no discerning why the one particular slug was different than those before it, but it was. It went down the wrong pipe, and Jake was choked. He drew no air. His eyes popped. And in the darkness that overtook the inside of his head, a purplish cloud awakened. It pulsed and grew and from it erupted roots and limbs and spewed clods of dirt dried and wetted both, and everywhere there hung the shed skin of reptiles. And the shed skins agitated and moved as if they still held life and they sought each other's touch and they twisted and went end to end on the black dirt ground and made of themselves a scroll of words which Jake could not distinguish, but still he knew with certainty from whence the words came, and if he drew another breath, he would be indebted to the God he'd never believed in.

And he did finally draw another breath, and when he came to on the floor with Sam patting his back, he said, "I've had a vision," and he told Sam of it in great detail, and directly he went to see Mayor Trent, who was himself slugging whiskey on the Sabbath at his own establishment.

Jake had addressed him as Mr. Mayor, which was peculiar, first because he'd only ever addressed the man as Mr. Trent, and second because his voice had changed. It was a full octave deeper. He'd asked if they could be alone.

With a wave of his hand, Trent excused his accountant and his favorite whore, but it was clear that Rutherford and Faro Fred Reed, each asleep in a straightback chair, were staying put.

Jake respectfully declared that as an officer of the law he was bound to disallow drinking on a Sunday.

Trent laughed.

Jake continued. He said that it was not meant to be funny, and he proclaimed that in addition to enforcing the state's Sunday liquor laws, he could no longer permit the forced collection of monies from local businesses, an act routinely employed by his fellow officers.

Trent had quit laughing then. He'd worked the stiff muscle in his twice-broken jaw and said, "Now see here Baach."

That had been the beginning of their falling-out.

Abe could scarcely comprehend it all. He said to his younger brother, "Jake was a officer of the law?" He wondered if Ben Moon had known such a thing.

"Around here," Sam answered, "they'll pin a pistol on anybody." There came the muffled trace of a far-off dynamite blast. The floor trembled beneath their shoes. "Abe," Sam said, "I believe when he got choked, his brain went addled. Air was cut off too long or some such. After that, he was off his head permanent. He was framing a church up on the hill. I saw the sign he cut. *Free Thinkers* of something or other—religion words I couldn't even recognize. He was preaching prohibition and didn't give a damn what anybody thought."

"Did he cross Trent?"

"He didn't so much cross anybody. Frightened em maybe." Sam was careful about his words then. He looked again at that long wide scar. "He sure didn't bite his tongue around his highness the mayor though," he said. "You remember how Jake always knew when to keep his mouth shut, taught us the same?"

"I remember."

"Well, those days was over. I heard from Rebecca Staples back in March that when Jake turned in his badge, he told Trent his intention to run for council at the interim, and come the general in '12, he aimed to be mayor of Keystone.

Rebecca said Jake got right up close on Trent, right in his ear, and said, 'I may not win, but there ain't no politics in heaven, and there ain't nothin but in hell.'"

Abe spun his empty short glass slow on the bar top. "You think Trent had him killed and pinned it on the Italian?"

"The thought had crossed my mind." Sam breathed deep. "But it doesn't figure. Jake may have gone a little peculiar, but you know how everybody liked him. He told a good straight story, he was fair. Trent was right fond of him for a few years there. Rutherford and Fred Reed too. Rest of us they'd just as soon piss on, but here they had Jake do a little carpentry at the Alhambra—he built a coat-hook partition wall by the bar, solved the problem of men coat-smuggling things to the Oak Slab—and next thing you know he's on the police force and taking what he wants to take from whoever he pleases. Trent let him roam free and paid him handsomely to do it." He shook his head. "Things was fine up to that day he got choked." Outside, the bell clanged for shift change at the coke yard. "After that, things was bad as ever."

Abe quit spinning his glass and pointed to it.

Sam poured. He watched a long-legged centipede scurry across the floor.

Abe saw it too. "Saloon shark," he said. "Step on it." These were words uttered at one time by each of those who lived and worked in the family saloon. It was ritualistic sport passed down and enjoyed by all.

Sam gave chase and stomped four times, but the little gray bug was fast against the floor trim and took refuge behind a stack of newspapers in the corner.

"You ain't practiced any killin in seven years?" Abe said.

Sam wiped at the sweat in his mustache with the kerosene rag.

Abe watched his brother's hands to see just how they shook. "Well," he said. Then nothing for a time. "Goldie's well?"

Sam thought on it, then answered. "Yes, though she's acquired a mean streak. Cusses not a little." He made a face to indicate the degree. "She runs Fat Ruth's."

"Ruth?"

"Disappeared. Most likely dead." He looked at the wall clock, stopped again and displaying nothing of use. He told Abe, "Mother reckons Jake is holding on until you get there and say goodbye."

Abe nodded and stood from his stool. "I'm going to put my things upstairs before I go." All those years gone and he'd kept the key.

He stepped inside his old room and locked the door behind him. It stunk of mildew in there. The window shades were drawn. There were wood crates stacked beside the window, and each wore a uniform watermark on its side. clay-colored stains as proof they'd once resided flood-level in the storeroom. It seemed most everything had come up from below. A straight-knee snow sleigh leaned against the far wall, rusty runners bent from hitting rock. Once, a month after Abe had turned eight, a blizzard left Keystone covered, and he'd lain on Jake's back astride the sleigh and shot down the mountain, house to town, narrowly missing the bone-hard trunks of thick-coming trees.

The big wardrobe was shoved in a different corner than before. He opened it and bent to the false bottom. He reached behind and tripped the latch and slid the slat and lifted. It had not been touched. He pulled out the money and smelled it. He counted the twelve hundred in notes he'd not been able to rescue the night he had to run. They were neither mildewed nor crinkled.

He put the money back, added most of the seventy-five hundred he'd brought from Baltimore, and slid closed the slat.

His suitcase was open on the bed, and he took from it his suits and shirts, and he hung them. At the bottom of the suitcase were the two boxes Bushels had wrapped in oilcloth. He set them on top of the wardrobe.

He took stock of himself as he always did when the nature of coming circumstances was unpredictable. He double-checked his vest pockets, both the conventional and the hidden variety. He had ample monies and his spur-trigger pistol and his watch and his nail dagger. Because the present circumstances were exceptionally unpredictable, he'd hidden in the barrel cuffs of his shirtsleeves smaller nails to be used, if need be, for picking locks or stabbing a man in the testicles should a desperate situation present itself.

His patting of himself was ritualistic and meant to stir confidence, but this time, it did not work. The weight of what he'd find up at the house pressed on his lungs and moved up his throat, and for a moment he wondered if his lack of sleep might catch him this time.

He walked to the window. He lifted the shade and looked in the street, and there, striding toward the saloon, was Goldie Toothman.

That's when it caught him and put out his lights, and on his way to the floor, his head banged the very sill where he'd riffled those cards and watched her all those years.

His fall produced two heavy clunks, and from below Sam Baach looked at the ceiling. He knew the sound of a man hitting the floor, and he uttered to himself, "What in blue blazes?" just as Goldie came through the door.

The screen creaked and slapped behind her. She'd drunk a pot of coffee. She asked, "Any word from Baltimore?"

Sam pointed to the ceiling. "He's in his room," he said. "I believe he's just collapsed on the floor."

When there was no answer to their pounding, Sam fetched the key ring from the empty money box.

When the door was opened, Goldie went quick to Abe. She knelt at his side and held his head against her thighs. There was a pump knot taking shape under the hair above his ear. There was another long-since formed at the back of his skull. "Good Lord he's beat up," she said. She ran her finger along the scar at his jaw. She listened to him sleep-breathe.

Sam stood over her. It occurred to him then that he was some sort of devil barkeep, that the drinks he poured were bound to curse his brothers. "He only had three or four swallows," he said.

"Looks tired." Still, she thought, he was more handsome than when he'd left.

When he came to and saw her looking down at him, he said, "Well I'll be a tallow-faced prairie dog."

Goldie laughed to keep the crying at bay.

Sam looked at the two of them together on the floor. He said he'd go down to the icebox and fetch a frozen cut of meat for the swelling.

Abe could scarcely believe she was there above him. She was more beautiful than when he'd left. He sat up and asked her, "Can I hug you?"

She said he could, and it was quiet then, and they did not come apart until Sam was back.

They stood and Abe took the stringy cut of meat and regarded it. "Last I heard," he said, "shoe leather doesn't take swelling down."

Sam took it back. "I'll put some salt on there," he said, "lay it on a hot coal shovel over the embers—it's good as any you'll eat."

"It's a real Delmonico is it?" Abe said.

Goldie asked if he'd been up to the house. When he indicated that's where he was headed, she said she'd come along.

"I've said my goodbye already," Sam told them. He said he'd be there at five for dinner.

They'd need to take the long route to avoid Railroad Avenue. Abe did not want it known he was home.

In the woods, they moved fast and single file, Goldie in the lead. He watched her as he climbed. It didn't matter where he looked—the heel of her boot or the nape of her neck or the place beneath her waist—she stirred in him a thing he'd not felt in seven years. He found that his trousers tented unless he looked at the horse path, but he could not look away from her for long, and this pattern of pecker protraction and contraction continued all the way up the hill, and despite his repeated crotchal adjustments, it was the most discomforting hike of his life. He stopped at a beech tree to adjust and took note of a fish someone had carved in the bark.

Goldie hollered at him over her shoulder. "Climb!"

The sound of it made him smile.

At the grass bald below the second house, Abe had gotten his trousers under control, and he'd begun to consider all that had to be considered. He asked if they could stop for a minute. "I only heard about your father's passing yesterday," he said. "I'm so sorry."

When he started to go on, she stopped him. "Why don't we talk this evening," she said.

In the front yard of Hood House, from just behind the fading rate sign, Sallie had watched them come on the horse path, her eye pressed against the blued steel scope of a rifle. She kept watch in this manner three times a day, training on whatever moved in the woods. She had done so ever since Al was shot in the kneecap, ever since Trent had proven himself utterly mad and unpredictable as the wind.

On this day, like most, it was Goldie whom she sighted. But behind her, striding in a manner that Sallie recalled from even his first steps, was her Abraham. She watched him stop at the grass bald and talk to Goldie. She watched him lean against a skinny poplar tree and clean his boot tread with a bark chip. She closed her eyes, took a deep breath, and looked through the long scope once more to be sure. Then she set the rifle against the sign and walked into the yard to wait for him.

She held her hairpins in her teeth while she tightened the gray bun up top. She wiped at her leaking eyes and sniffed. With her shoe tip, she loosed a small rock from the dirt. She bent and picked it up, and thought on heaving it at Abe when he came into distance.

Goldie told Abe she'd meet him inside and went around to the back.

He surveyed the house as he came, the way it was stuck into the hill as if dropped there from above. One of the corner boards was loose, and there was a bird's nest in a second-story sill. Through the glass up there, Abe made out the shape of a seated man.

When he got close enough, he stopped and raised a hand

to his mother. She kept hers on her hips for a moment, then waved him to come on. He did, stopping only when he was close enough to touch her.

She worked her lips together and stared at him with eyes whose color knew no name. "Well," she said. "I don't know whether to hit you or hold you to me."

"I'm only thankful you didn't shoot me with that long gun there." He nodded at the sign.

She smiled despite herself. "Your brother mounted a telescope on that rifle of his. If I'd wanted to, I might have shot you clear through before you hit the property line."

"You'd have been justified."

"Let me feel you," she said, and they hugged one another close and hard and Sallie let out a long, throated breath with her eyes shut tight, and Abe knew how bad he'd hurt her, and she knew, by the way he held on to her, that he was sorry to have done it. When they let go, she said she reckoned he was hungry. He nodded that he was, for he couldn't speak.

Her skirt was the same limp gray rag she'd worn all her life, and he watched her pull it up between thumb and finger as she ascended the porch stairs, her movements true as her attire. He followed her inside. The smell was one he recollected—salt pork and beans, and behind that, ammonia. Sallie went to the kitchen and Abe stood alone in the hallway regarding the old sideboard stacked in paper and junk and a pitcher of dead flowers. A greasy-coated calico cat lay on its side underneath, licking a front paw, its eye on Abe. He bent and held out a finger. The cat stood, stretched, and went for a spindle leg on the sideboard. It worked the wood with its claws, tearing off splinters. All six legs bore the marks. "You like whittlin?" Abe asked the cat, and then every little muscle in its body electrified before it tore off down the hall, for it had seen Sallie emerge from the kitchen with a glass of water in hand.

"I soaked her on Tuesday," Sallie said. She walked back to the kitchen. It did not seem real that her middle boy had appeared, that she could speak to him on everyday things, that she could reach out and touch him.

Abe was about to inquire on the whereabouts of his Daddy when there was a smacking sound from above, and little Ben appeared at the stairhead. He wore only a loose-pinned diaper. Abe took note of his complexion and his furrowed brow. The boy had a look about him of a shrunken old-timer. "Hello little man," he called.

Ben was not yet fully stable on his feet. He glared at Abe. He grunted at him. And then he took another step. "Whoa now," Abe said, and he positioned a foot on the riser and readied himself to charge up the flight if he had to.

But he didn't. Agnes ran forth from the upstairs hall and got the baby under the arms. She swung him up and held him tight against her, asked him just what he thought he was doing.

Ben stuck his finger in her eye.

She squinted tight to ease the blow. "Eye," she told him. "Say *eye*."

"Hello," Abe called again.

"Hello." She looked at him sideways. "Who are you?"

He thought on how to answer. "I'm Abe," he said.

"Uncle Abe?" she asked.

It knocked him back a little, hearing her call him by such a name. "That's right," he said.

Baby Ben worked to get loose of her and she ignored his struggling, accustomed to the wrangle. She raised her voice over his grunts. "I can read books meant for old people," she said.

"Is that right?"

Sallie hollered from the kitchen. "Aggie! You take my biscuit roller?"

"Yes ma'am," the girl hollered back. She'd been killing ants with it on the back stoop all morning, a dozen or more at a roll.

Sallie walked from the kitchen and stood next to Abe. She used her teeth to scrape dough off her thumb. "You be careful with him on those stairs," she told the girl. She leaned close to Abe and said, "You remember Agnes?"

He nodded that he did.

"She believes herself capable of anything."

"How old is she?"

"I'm seven," she answered, careful to keep her eye on the step below as she came, Ben clutched in one arm, stair rail in the other.

"And that's Benjamin," Sallie said. "He came to us last year. Turned one in December." She took the boy from Agnes, who stood on the bottom stair breathing heavy and shaking out her arm. Sallie held Benjamin up for Abe to see. "He's a catbird," she said. "Smart as a switch."

"He's a shade darker isn't he?" Abe said.

"Yes he is," his mother answered.

"Ain't I smart as a switch?" Agnes asked.

"Smarter," Sallie told her. "More like a horsewhip."

The girl smiled and pushed her tongue through the new gap in her teeth. She looked at Abe. "You want me to read to you?"

"Well," Abe said. "You could read a little—"

"What's your favorite book?"

"Well, I—"

"Mine's *Fuz-Buz the Fly*. You want me to read it to you?" She didn't wait for an answer. Halfway up the staircase, she stopped her full-speed ascent and turned back to him. She said, "You want me to take you to see Uncle Jake?"

He nodded that he did.

Agnes said, "He's dying."

Sallie went to the kitchen with the baby.

Abe started up the stairs. The girl waited on him and held out her hand and he took it.

The air inside the room was foul. An infectious scent from someplace inside bone. Jake lay on his side, swollen as a tick at the wrists, a pillow between his black fingers.

The skin at his neck was mottled a purple constellation. A blanket was gathered around his knees.

Agnes said she'd be across the hall if he needed her.

Abe went to the bedside.

He looked at his brother. The eyes were motionless under the lids.

For a time, when Abe was five and his mother could not get out of bed, he was beset by a brand of nightmares no child should possess. Al had hired a woman in town to take care of the boys while he tended to Sallie, and for a month, all three boys lived in the rooms above the saloon. Abe would awake in the night scarcely able to breathe from what he'd seen behind his eyelids. It made him feel better to walk down the hall and stand at little Sam's crib and listen for the sound of his breath. He did so nightly for three weeks. Once, Jake too had awakened and followed his younger brother. He watched Abe watch the baby. "What are you doing?" Jake had whispered, and it startled Abe, electrified his pores. He didn't answer. Jake walked to him and took him by the hand and led him past the sleeping woman and back down the hall to his bed. He tucked the scrap of square quilt around Abe's shoulders. He told him, "Some folks say prayers when they go to sleep."

"Do you?" Abe asked him.

"No." There were still a couple patrons in the saloon below their floorboards. One of them shouted to another that he wanted a dozen fried eggs. "Go back to sleep," Jake had told his younger brother. Then he got in bed and put his pillow over his head.

Abe had shut his eyes then and tried to think of a prayer. He didn't know any.

Now here was Jake, asleep with his eyes still as could be, painted in the onset of death's shallow hue. Abe thought momentarily of putting a pillow over his head and holding it down.

He cried. And then he did not.

He put his hand to the side of Jake's face and told him goodbye.

Goldie came in the room. "I'll sit with him awhile," she said.

They brushed against each other by the doorway, and he nearly pulled her to him.

Out in the hall, he pressed his ear to the closed door of the front bedroom. A man on the other side cleared his throat. Abe thought he could hear a pen scratching paper.

In the kitchen, Sallie cut her rolled-out biscuit dough with a musket-cap tin. When they'd all been cut, she watched the yard outside the window where a single-file line of chickens high-stepped a faint path. She'd told Al to kill one for supper, and she suspected he'd forgotten. For three days, he'd kept to the second house as much as ten hours at a time. His shop was in the living room there.

Agnes sat at the table and read to herself, her posture stooped, her lips forming whispered syllables to conjure in her mind the cannibalism of infants and proper women.

Abe had come down the stairs. He stood in the kitchen doorway. He watched Agnes read, and he watched his mother stare out the window. Baby Ben held her by the knee, his feet on top of hers. "Who is that up in the big bedroom?" he asked.

Sallie held her gaze out the window. "He's our boarder at present," she said.

"Just one?"

"Things have changed." She shooed Ben, opened the oven door with the hem of her skirt, and slid in the biscuits. "It'll be awhile on the chicken. Go on over to the second house and see your Daddy," she said. "He'll be in there working."

Al Baach hummed Yankee Doodle while he worked. He had a boot upside down on his iron stand. He was putting in new ball calks.

Abe watched him through the living room window, stooped over the workbench. His backside rested on a tall barstool. He wore a black canvas kippah on the crown of his head and his hair was unruly and streaked in gray.

Abe tapped on the window. When his father turned and saw him there, he dropped his pincers to the floor and put his hand to his mouth.

Inside, Al Baach held his middle boy and cried.

It was something Abe had never seen him do before.

Then, just as quick as he'd started, he wiped his eyes and picked up his pincers. He groaned when he bent. He sat back against his stool and twisted another calk into the boot sole.

The smell of leather cement was heavy. Al's back was wide and his posture old. A cane leaned against the leg of the workbench.

"I heard about your knee," Abe said.

"You go and see Jake?"

"Yes."

"You say goodbye to him?"

"Yes." It was quiet save the groan of the floor under Al's stool and the cold twisting of his little spikes into place. Abe stepped closer to watch him work. "Cork boots?" he said. "You takin up logging on a bad knee?"

Al looked over his shoulder wide-eyed. "These boots?" he said. "These boots I am making for Mr. Henry Trent so he can better step on us and kill us with a thousand tiny wounds." He scratched his head with the pincers and turned back to his work.

"I've never seen you wear a skull cap before."

"Yes, my smoking cap," Al said. "The wife of my Lithuanian friend make it for me. You like it?"

Abe didn't say one way or the other before Al continued.

"I still don't go to synagogue, but my head stays warm in the cold." And he turned again to his son, and with the pincers he lifted the kippah and bowed his head. "You see?" he asked. "You see how it is to get old?"

Abe could see the scalp through long strings of hair.

Al dropped the cap back on his head. He took the boot

off the iron stand and looked into the black open throat. He set down the pincers and said, "Your mother talks to me at night when she thinks I am sleeping." He picked up an awl and pushed at something inside. "In the morning I tell her I agree with everything she said. And I do. Women are smarter than men, Abraham. We should have had you boys in synagogue, in a church, doesn't matter. Friday, Saturday, Sunday, doesn't matter."

"You always said they didn't want you there."

"I always said what I always said." He coughed and spat in a wastebasket. He asked, "You still are keeping your money in your shoes?"

"Some of it."

He dropped the awl in the boot and threw it on the workbench. "My hands hurt," he said. Then he picked up the bottle of leather cement. There was a picture of a white sperm whale on the label. He uncorked it, put his nose over the opening, and snorted twice. He sat back and smiled and held out the bottle to Abe, who passed on the offer. Al asked him, "Do they tell you I have rats in the attic these days?"

Abe shook his head no.

"Well," Al said, "Mr. Henry Trent has more rats than me."

It was quiet.

From the corner of his eye, Abe saw them coming across the yard. Goldie carried Ben, and Agnes followed.

He went out to the porch and stepped off the crooked stones, and he met them in the high grass.

197

Goldie had been with Jake when he'd ceased to breathe. "It was peaceful," she said.

Al stepped onto the porch and looked at them. He leaned on his cane. "Is someone with him now?" he asked.

"Yes," Goldie said.

"What time did he die?" Al asked. He'd put the table clock in the room and told them all to keep it wound.

"Half past three," Goldie said.

Al nodded. He thought it a good hour. A strong number. He said to Goldie, "Please go and tell my wife that I will be there in five minutes to wash him."

Little Agnes put her face to Goldie's skirt front. Her shoulders shook from the sobs.

Al leaned his cane against the porch post and wiped his hands on his apron front. "Abraham," he said, "follow me."

He'd built a pine box coffin the day before.

It was sitting across two sawhorses under a shed roof that jutted from the house's rear. Al untied his apron and tossed it on the coffin. He said, "I use your brother's tools to make it." He pointed to the sawhorses. "Your brother make these trestles," he said. He pointed above their heads. "And this roof." He pointed to the woods' edge, where long two-by-fours sprouted plumb at the sky. "And the foundation of a cathedral."

Abe regarded the empty chapel husk. Hung head-high from an upright was a sun-bleached signboard. In wide black paint-strokes it proclaimed: *Church of the Free Thinkers of the Merciful Enthroned.*

"His friend helps him with the foundation," Al said. "Strange man from Italy, no English. Thinks and builds like Jake, now they say he shoots him." He put his hand on the coffin top and rubbed for smoothness. He said, "Couple weeks ago, Jake makes a trade for a new ripsaw, and the other man throws in these pine boards. No charge." He shook his head. "He was going to make a pulpit. He draws a plan and show me." Al made circles in the air with his finger. "The pulpit would have wheels, to take on the streets."

Abe only listened, and the words sounded on the air as if uttered by some other man's father, a stranger who spoke of the tools and creations of some other man's dead brother.

"Your brother make this cane for me," Al said, and he held it forth. It was lacquered hickory with a high silver band. Just above the band was a tiny silver button. "Mechanical." He pressed the button and a catch inside the shaft released with a tiny sound. The cane was no longer one but two, no longer a cane but a sword and scabbard. Al unsheathed it. The blade was fashioned from a broken-hilted bayonet. "Everybody says your brother was a lunatic after he choke that day. They say it because he stand in the streets and tell them there will come a drought, a hurry-cane, a blazing fire, a comet, a more terrible influenza." He punctuated his words with the up-pointed sword and scab-bard. "He says over and over again—*It will come swift*. He says it will spare no women nor children nor beast. It will end them same as it does the sinning man."

Abe worked his jaw and thought of the man in the flop-house doorway.

Al made his cane a cane again. He leaned on it and turned to the coffin. "No one can understand the brain," he said. "But your brother makes beautiful things." He bent and blew a little mound of sawdust from the coffin top. "I don't get the handles on it in time," he said. He'd meant to put eight holes in and knot some rope.

Abe said, "You think Trent had him shot?"

Al didn't answer. There was an eastward wind in the treetops, and a branch scratched across the shed roof above them. He sighed. Then he said, "I can know the weather by my bad knee."

Abe looked up at the rafters. There was an abandoned bird's nest at the corner joist.

Al regarded the scar on his middle boy's face. He looked him in the eyes. He said, "Your mother wants you to take everything from the man who shoots your brother. Everything." He worked his lips and kept down all that wanted to come out. He said, "She wants to move then to seashore."

Neither spoke.

Al turned and patted the coffin. "Empty, it isn't heavy," he said. "You and I carry it to the room. Samuel will be here in an hour."

Al and Sallie had decided they would bury Jake in the Hood family plot up the hollow. They had not asked her father's permission, for they agreed it wouldn't matter.

There was no preacher and there was no rabbi. Only the family, and they put Jake in the ground as quickly as Sam and Abe could heft him into the wagon and steer the mare to the circled iron gates, spear-tipped and listing on the overgrown slope.

Abe and Sam wore no gloves to shovel. Blisters filled and opened, peeled back and burned.

Agnes went off alone in the hillside field, and when they'd refilled and patted flat the earth, she set down three handfuls of blue phlox. One for Jake, yet unmarked by a headstone, and one each for the Baach babies who had not lived. *Infant Son* and *Infant Daughter*, the little tablets read.

Sallie pulled up all the weeds.

Back at Hood House they ate together and spoke in happy tones for the benefit of the children, who were not subject, on this night, to a particular bedtime. Sam drank too much as was usual, and Goldie watched Abe delight Agnes by pulling coins from her ear and nose and shirt collar.

Al said he was going for a walk. They watched him from the porch. Twilight's hue lit orange the tops of canted trees on the opposite ridge.

Abe and Goldie walked with the children through a skinny plateau of high goosegrass. The seed heads in the dying light glowed like links of gold.

Between the houses, six crows sat on the jutted branch of an evergreen. They cawed and rolled their throats. "I loathe those birds," Goldie said.

Abe looked up at them. He told Agnes to come over by the tree. He called too to Ben, who was smashing an army-worm in his fist.

At the base of the big tree, Abe pointed to the crows. "Just watch those blackbirds," he told them. "I'll bet you each a nickel I can make them fall from their perch."

"All at once?" Aggie asked.

"All at once," Abe answered.

"You ain't going to shoot em?"

"I ain't going to touch em."

The crows cawed. Ben cawed back.

"Good boy," Abe told him. And he made his own call, a high *look here*, and the crows aimed their beaks at the ground.

He stared hard at them, and they stared back, their heads twitching at first, then going still. Abe walked a slow circle around the low branches of the tree, and where he went, the birds' eyes followed, their small heads swiveling. He circled again. Around and around the tree he went, each time increasing his speed just enough. The crows kept watching. Swiveling. On the sixth time around, the first crow fell. On the seventh, the rest came down. They hit branches as they came, their bodies thudding at the feet of the children.

Agnes stepped back, her mouth open.

Ben kicked at one with his bare foot.

"Are they dead?" Aggie asked.

"Asleep," Abe said. "And if you wait a little while, you can watch em wake up."

They waited. Abe had to pick Ben up to keep him from kicking at one poor crow.

From his perch, the boy grunted at the birds.

Agnes frowned and looked as if she might again begin to sob.

A minute passed, then another, and when one began to stir, Agnes sounded a gleeful note. Two flapped a wing and she clapped and hopped in place.

Then the crows rose from the smashed goosegrass, awaking from their hypnosis on wobbly legs.

"Climb!" Abe commanded, and they did.

Goldie smiled at the sound of their wings on the air, the birds otherwise silent as they flew up past the heads of the children.

Back inside, Goldie lowered the lampwick and got next to Agnes in her bed. She let the girl read to her. Abe watched them before he went to the kitchen, where his mother stood staring out the same window. He rubbed her shoulders.

The boarder descended the staircase. He thought for a moment of leaving without acknowledging the pair, but he changed his path and stepped in their direction.

He was a frail man whose spectacle lenses were thick as lampshade glass. Beneath them, his eyes were small and quick to twitch. They were the kind of pale blue that was not to be trusted. His mustache was thin as gut string, his posture weak. Abe did not like the man from the moment he stepped into the kitchen.

"I am quite a bit more than sorry for your painful loss," the boarder said to them. The sharp enunciations of his *t*'s and *s*'s were not pleasing to the ear of regular folk. "Young Mr. Baach had turned to the Lord and will find his place in the kingdom." He smiled. "I must journey now for my nightly walk." He donned his block crown hat and stepped to the door.

When he was gone, Abe said, "That was a lady's hat he put on his head."

"It wasn't." Sallie turned to the heap of unwashed dishes.

"Put a peacock feather in it why doesn't he?" Abe said. He picked up a stack of plates and dunked them. "What's his name?"

"Ladd," she said. "Oswald Ladd."

"Where's he from?"

"Virginia."

"I don't trust his eyes."

"Hush Abraham."

Goldie came down the stairs and stood in the kitchen doorway. "Agnes enjoys some very strange literature," she said. She stretched her stiffened back. "A man had his nose cut off and buried and sewed back on upside down."

"Did you spy my biscuit roller up there?"

"The man had to stand on his head to blow his nose." Goldie watched the muscles in Abe's neck, the way the lamplight lit his ears transparent.

"Does that boarder's room have an outside lock?" Abe asked his mother.

"I said hush."

"Abe, let's you and me go for a walk," Goldie said.

In the dark aisle of the crib barn Jake had built with her father, Goldie brushed the neck of the mare who'd pulled the wagon to the cemetery and back. She was the only horse on the property then, a chestnut with two white socks and a snip at her nose. Hers was the only stall housing life—five of six cribs kept little more than sawdust and chicken feed. Spun webs thick as cheesecloth linked rafter boards. A square of moon through the loft window lighted the place. Goldie said to Abe, "This mare is Snippy. You knew her mother."

"Dot?"

"That horse could outstrip a downgrade mail train." She could still remember the old urge to throw a leg over.

"What happened to her?"

"Back broke coming down the creek bank." She put her hand to the mare's white spot. "Jake put her down with his Winchester right there in the water." Drool ran from the horse's jutted lip. "This one here isn't half what Dot was."

He neither spoke nor moved to touch her.

Goldie looked in the eye of the horse. She said, "You broke off the end of Nina Gyro's tailbone."

He took a deep breath. There was a whistle in his left nosehole.

"She stayed here in town for a while," Goldie said. "Mostly at the opium den."

He watched her shoulders, her neck. All that brown and gold hair knotted high by an ebonite comb.

"After she fell, it hurt that little woman to so much as sneeze, and that magician husband up and left her. What kind of man leaves his broken-tailboned wife?"

"Not much of one."

"You know I met a man told me the Great Gus George got committed two years back for running the streets of New York raving naked?" She laughed. "Man said it was nine degrees outside. Said old Gus had a mitten on his tallywags." She shook her head. "At any rate, once Nina could walk, she limped into Fat Ruth's asking about work." She shooed a slow fly from Snippy's muzzle and the horse nodded deep. "I was liable to have killed her had she not told me the truth about that night she spent in your bed."

He could think of nothing to say in return.

"Well," Goldie said. "She died of her own accord the next winter."

There was a gust through the aisle. Colder air was coming.

Abe said, "I looked for you that day. I aimed to tell you nothing happened."

The horse had gone still at Goldie's touch. She said, "I imagine you've had your share of women now."

He thought on how to answer. "I've got my rules."

She turned and faced him. "What are they?"

"She's got to smell good, one."

Goldie lifted her arm over her head and sniffed. "Like a pink pasture rose," she said.

He smiled. "Two, she's got to have a little money in the bread box."

She stuck her finger and thumb between her breasts. "Well, I've always got a little in mine," she said, and she produced a tight roll of notes shoestrung in green ribbon.

He laughed. "Is that what you're calling that spot these days?" And he looked at that spot as he had so many times before.

"Any more rules?"

"No whores," he said.

She put back the skinny bankroll. "That ought to have been the first one you said." And she thought about his rules and what trouble he may have found in all those years gone, and she thought too on her own rules and trouble. "Since you are so unaccustomed to the ways of a proper brothel," she told him, "I'll explain something to you. A madam might be what she is, but I'll tell you what she isn't. She is *no* man's five-dollar chippy."

And they said nothing for a time but only breathed and stared, and then they were together and moving to the open stall at barn's end where they fell upon a waist-high hill of sawdust, and they were quiet, and they shed only what needed shedding, and their eyes were wide open all the while.

Afterward she lay with her head on his chest as before, and they began to speak of a new kind of plan, one wholly unconcerned with marriage or their role in the reproduction of the species or Delmonico sleeper cars or seeing the world. It was a plan that aimed to do right by Jake. By all the Baaches and Big Bill Toothman too. It would come to be, in fact, not a plan at all. It would come to be the big con.

Abe had once worked long hours for Henry Trent, but the way he saw it now, even back then he'd merely been putting up the mark, merely been working toward the very moment inside of which he now lived.

Goldie looked up at him. "You're an awful quiet kind of man these days," she said.

He smiled and kissed at the line of scalp he'd made stroking her hair. He said to her, "I need to know everything about everyone."

The air in the barn grew chilly, so they brushed themselves off and moved to a vacant room in the second house, where it was Goldie's turn to talk. They ate cold biscuits smeared in honey. For three hours, she would tell him who was who in town since he'd left. Some of the flush were the same as they'd been and some were new.

On his father's workbench, Abe found a fat stub of pencil and a daily desk calendar that hadn't been used in a month. He tore a fistful of sheets from the high rusted arches. He wrote down what she told him. He wrote down every word.

Trent had maintained his wealth, but his theater had not prospered as he'd planned. After Abe left town, Trent had ignored Nina Gyro and her broken coccyx, and when a preacher found her hung early morning from a low Methodist joist, Trent wouldn't pay to have her buried.

He'd tried to bring in more national acts for the main stage, but news of the cut wires traveled through the circuit and stuck, and no prominent magician would come. For the past two years, he'd been dead set on bringing in Max Mercurio—a magician who'd earned the nickname the Sublime One—and his Beautiful Beatrice. While in New Orleans on business, Trent had seen a handbill with her picture, and on that alone he vowed that Beatrice would come to the Alhambra. At seventy-three, he still thought himself capable of bedding young women, and he'd even tried once to sweet-talk Goldie. She'd walked away telling him to go and find a knothole, but she'd kept her head turned and her eye on him, for above all, she explained to Abe, Henry Trent was ever more volatile. He'd just as soon bear-hug a man as brain him with a rifle butt. None could know his mood from day to day. He'd collected regular from the Baaches since Abe left and blackballed any who darkened their saloon door. He told all company men to board someplace other than Hood House, and he aimed to buy its land from Sallie's father, Old Man Hood.

Rufus Beavers stayed mildly drunk most hours and took bribes to let men walk free. He played regular at the Oak Slab and still held sway with the railroad, overseeing the clearing and carving of bottomland where a new switchout and tipple would sit. His brother Harold brought back on his frequent home visits a considerable sum of greenbacks too, putting his into the purchase of hill land west of town, just beyond Hood House property, where he clear-cut and stair-stepped the ridge. Along with his brother and Henry Trent, he had his sights on building proper Keystone environs for proper citizens. He'd come home mid-March and slept with fourteen different whores before he left, less than a week before Abe's arrival. He took Rufus with him. Extended vacation is what folks called it. A common pleas judge from up at Welch would cover any trial work the judge might miss.

Faro Fred Reed was still president of the Union Political and Social Club. He was loyal to Trent and aimed to be made a councilman in the interim election by splitting the black vote and unseating Reverend Whitt. Fred's boy Taffy aided him in this endeavor, getting in the ear of every black miner in the Bottom, asking them, "You want a colored man favors whiskey or one that wants to take it away? Can't have both." Taffy was a police officer and right-hand man to chief Rutherford.

Rutherford was as paltry and false-hearted as he'd ever been. For six months in 1903, he'd searched in vain for Floyd Staples, and when he gave it up and came home, he made Rebecca Staples his woman, paying for the hospital birth of her child at Welch. It was another boy, born eight months to the day after Floyd's disappearance, and she'd named him Robert Staples. Rutherford hired a nanny for the boy and threw Rebecca an allowance as long as she kept her opium habit hidden and held his little hand in public.

Rebecca's older boy, Little Donnie Staples, had become the finest cardplayer since the Keystone Kid. The Oak Slab game had endured without stoppage, even on the night of the red-headed boy's murder, and now its principal player—the one all others came to try and beat—was Little Donnie Staples. He was seventeen years old.

"The young ones might be gotten to," Goldie told Abe. "Taffy Reed will prove difficult. He shares his Daddy's allegiance to whoever has the most." She worried that Taffy carried feelings for her still, that he'd not take to Abe being back. "But Little Donnie could be useful," she said. "He's got the eye."

All of this she told him that night in intervals between which they affixed at the middle in bouts of flamboyant sexual congress unavailable to the meek-hearted masses. They stayed in bed past noon the next day.

While Goldie moved in and out of sleep beside him, Abe looked down at what he'd written on the brittle squares of calendar paper. *Beautiful Beatrice*. She was a good place to start because she was a cinch. Abe had big-conned many a man like Henry Trent, and most times the play began with a weakness, usually a woman or the sight of ample paper money. Or both. He shut his eyes and saw himself walking straight into Trent's office, laying a stack on the wide desk, saying what he needed to say in order to make the play. Convincers would have to come early and often. Trent was no fool. He'd smell any whiff of shit and he'd see any angle too crooked. Soft spots he'd push. Mistakes he'd kill over.

Abe watched Goldie's eyes behind their lids. He chewed

on the stub of pencil and reread his notes. Beside *Little Donnie Staples* he wrote *Roper*. Next to this: *Inside Men — Tony Thumbs, Jim Fort*. A fast scratch sounded from above and he looked up at the ceiling. A squirrel skittered invisible across joists and beams. Abe followed its sound until it stopped, looked down at his lap again, and put what was left of the pencil against the page. Only a small triangle of white remained at the bottom corner. *Daddy's saloon* — he wrote. *Big store.*

Sam came from town and reported that no one had caught wind of Abe's arrival, so Abe and Goldie ate and drank and talked and slept and planned and set to further coital undertakings for two straight days. His knob went raw. They agreed, without verbalizing it as such, to never speak on any others they may have slept with. She showed him how she'd kept sharp her card-throwing skills, scaling a fresh deck and hitting every target she called out. Windowpane, picture frame, doorknob, cockroach.

He built a midnight fire between the houses and stood by it naked and made a fireball by spewing a blast of corn liquor. They laughed as they had not laughed in ten years.

Together, they read once more what he'd written on the calendar pages, and then he tossed every one into the fire.

No premonitions visited Goldie's slumber. No terrified visions sat her up in bed.

They hunkered together under a blue and white quilt

stitched by Sallie's grandmother. The cold front came slow from the west, but it came nonetheless.

Before they slept, Abe put his hand to her face and his breath condensed white when he spoke her name. "I love you," he told her. "And I'll not ever love another again."

APRIL FOOLS' HAS COME AND GONE

April 25, 1910

He'd walked the long way back to town in the darkest part of morning. He carried no lantern, for Sam had told of lawless night-men who made sport of shooting out fire from great distance. By the burn in his ears, he could tell that it was below thirty-five degrees. He walked from the woods to the creek bank and looked up at the chalk-white moon. It came free of the clouds, full as he'd ever seen. And though he thought his eyes deceived him at first, he held his stare and watched them descend—snowflakes, few and fitful. He reckoned summer had not come two months early after all, reckoned a Bibled man would tell him that snowflakes in April marked the coming apocalypse. He stuck out his tongue to catch one and in his mind was the word *cosmoplast*.

In his little room above the saloon, he took a powder for the ache in his head. He touched his fingers to the twin knots, still tender from the blows. When he touched them, a soft roar sounded way down deep in his ear canals, a deep-tunneled call, like a blast furnace. He touched and listened, touched and listened. He wondered at his own sanity then, wondered if he might follow the course of Jake, of the man in the flophouse doorway.

He shook it off and took stock of himself in order that he might be prepared for all that could come his way. Vest pockets, hidden pockets. Small money, big money. Nail-dagger, spur-trigger, lock-picker, nut-stabber. This time, his ritual worked. He shot his cuffs. No man could best Abe Baach.

At eight A M, he transacted at the telegraph office, sending coded word to Ben Moon and Tony Thumbs both, the latter with an indication of possible future travel.

At a quarter past eight, he stood out front of the Alhambra Hotel. Its face had stood the test of weather. A man was paid good money to once a day scrub down its bricks and wash its windows. It showed.

Railroad Avenue was peopled thick farther on at the station, but it was quiet at his present juncture. He'd half expected armed doormen on the hotel stairs. He stepped around the side of the building to see about the entrance there. Not a soul was guarding it. The awning under which he'd bumped Floyd Staples seven years prior still hung, bleached by sun and striped by dirty rain. A scabied cat scavenged a wad of newspaper spilling fish bones. Abe proceeded, aiming to see about the building's rear. He spoke to the cat as he passed, holding his hand low for a sniff, but the cat showed its teeth. It sounded a hiss and then a low rumble.

No man stood at the building's backside. It was only the double-bricked husk of the longest game of poker in the land.

He returned to the front of the building and opened the big door.

The lobby shined in straight dark lacquer. Abe nodded to the men at the tall front desk. The seated man was hatless and bald. Two others leaned on wide fluted columns, and asleep between their polished shoes was a long-haired dog.

"Afternoon," Abe said, though he knew it to be morning. He walked over and held out his hand. "Abe Baach," he said.

The seated bald man swallowed and sat back and squinted. "You'll have to pardon me." He patted his shirt pocket. "I don't have my spectacles."

Abe looked at him closer. "Mr. Talbert?" he asked.

The man took up his glasses and knocked over a blue-glass toothpick holder in the shape of an egg. "Yes?" he said.

"What happened to your hair?"

The man got his glasses on. "I can't hardly believe what's in front of me," he said. "Norman, pinch my arm." He held it out but neither man moved. Then he felt at the top of his head and said, "Would you believe me that I lost all that hair at once a few months back?" which was neither the entire nor the truthful story.

"Is that right?" Abe said.

"God's word." He raised his right hand. Then he shook

his head. "Abe Baach," he said. "I had hoped someone was foolin me, comin in here proclaiming themselves as such."

Abe said, "April Fools' has come and gone Mr. Talbert."

The dog on the floor sneezed and moaned and reshut its eyes. The other men continued to lean—neither had bothered to so much as stand straight when Abe had offered handshake. They made their eyes as lifeless as they could and took up a spilled toothpick each and chewed.

Abe looked at one and then the other and smiled. It put them off enough—one checked his timepiece and the other walked to the front window and pushed aside a shear.

"These two is new," Talbert said.

That much was clear to Abe when he introduced himself. He'd watched their faces for tells, but his name rung neither of their bells. "They are young yet," he said. He regarded Talbert, who had always worn a kind face.

The dog farted.

Abe and Talbert commenced straightaway at laughing. The other two did not.

Abe frowned at the stench. He asked, "You boys feedin this animal frog legs?"

He clasped his hands in front so they'd know two things. First, that he would stand and wait for what he sought, and second, that he wasn't looking to do anything quick and deceitful. He said, "I'm here to see Mr. Trent."

The man at the window laughed then, for though he was new, he had gathered that Henry Trent was not one to take unannounced visitors at early morning hours.

Abe recognized the laugh as dismissive rather than jovial. It was a suitable sound when made by an older, smarter man. But when emitted by a young fool such as this one, it was lamentable at best. He thought to himself, *Keep your temper*, and he did. He kept his stance too, but turned his neck and shoulders to regard the man at the window, who tried his best to wear a hard look. Abe smiled at him still.

Talbert stood and leaned forward over the desk. He said, "I always thought you was a nice fella, Kid. But last I seen you, you knocked me to the ground and ran out of here in a hail of gunfire."

"And I am sorry for knocking you down Talbert," Abe said.

"I don't know what they're liable to do to you." Talbert thought. He whispered, "Rutherford's in there with him at the Oak Slab."

Abe watched Talbert's eyes. Through the dusty lens of his spectacles, they were genuine. He said, "My brother has died and I have peaceable intentions." He stepped back and announced that he would go ahead and save them the trouble, and with slow and delicate touch of finger and thumb, he withdrew his spur-trigger pistol and handed it grip-first to Talbert, whom he proclaimed trustworthy and wise.

Talbert admired the little gun and put it in a locked drawer. He rubbed at the back of his neck. Inside he was blank, confused as to his allegiances in life. "Well," he said. "I suppose we ought to go tell him you're here." And he stood and told the two young ones to stay where they were.

He led Abe past the grand stage door and into the main card room. Once there, he pointed back to the lobby and said, "Those two are worthless as chicken shit on a pump handle."

The card room was quiet. Four men sat at a middle table hunched and tired. On the left wall, a bartender stood rigid behind the counter, hands crossed behind him.

An electric bulb hung over the bar, and more hung high above the tables, their cords tacked to the black tin ceiling. These were the only electric lamps in Keystone. Trent had said in 1902 that he'd have electric inside a decade, and seven years later, the lines lit up. They pulled straight from the generators of the Northfork Mining Company, where circuit judge Rufus Beavers sat on the board of trustees. Beavers was newly widowed and had lately become a more-than-regular patron of the Alhambra Hotel. He was at the Oak Slab most nights. He kept a third-floor room on permanent. His brother Harold was known to take over the room on his twice-a-year visits home, throwing big money around and nightly taking two or three women upstairs.

The hot orange filaments hummed. Abe watched them dance inside the glass, alive. He'd once told Jake that he'd have electric lamps at A. L. Baach & Sons by 1910. He'd wrongly thought he'd be running the Bottom by then.

On the way to Trent's office door, Talbert tipped his head at the barkeep and whispered, "Nothing between that one's ears but cotton."

A fat man sat on a stool in front of the door to Trent's office. He lowered his halved *McDowell Times* and bit a long stretch of dried beef. "Who's this?" he said to Talbert.

"This is Abe Baach, the Keystone Kid." And with that, Talbert made his customary tap on the door, told Abe to stay put, and went through.

The fat man said he didn't believe that to be the truth, and in the same sentence asked if he'd been frisked, but Talbert had already shut the door.

"I have been thoroughly frisked," Abe said. "I didn't get your name."

"Munchy," the man said. "I'm police." He pulled back his jacket and showed his badge. He aimed his beef at Abe's scar. "What happened to your face?"

Abe told him, "Well Munchy, I was performing cunnilingus on a gal who turned out to have a greased bobtail trap in her pussy."

"You were doing what?" Munchy said, but Abe never got to extrapolate because Talbert came back through the door and held it open and told Abe to go and sit by the desk, that Mr. Trent would be with him presently. They crossed in the same spot where Abe had knocked him off his stool all those years back, and Talbert nodded to him and said, "I wish you luck," and closed the door again.

The office was quiet and Abe kept his eyes on the second door. He sat down in the same chair he'd sat in so many times before.

A fan hung from the ceiling and spun slow on a turbine

belt drive. There was a half inch of dust on each wide blade. The black spade minute hand on the floor clock clicked to six. The desk lamp surged and hummed and the glass-fronted bookcase trembled at a slow passing train.

Henry Trent stepped into his office.

Abe stood.

Trent watched him and kept his hand on the knob as he back-shut the door. He wore no jacket. His white shirt was stained yellow at the armpits. Neck skin hung over his standing collar, and he'd dyed his hair black all the way down to the roothole, so that when he sweat from the forehead, it came out charcoal gray and puddled at the wrinkles running up-and-down and sideways both. He breathed deep through his nose and walked over. When he got within a foot, he stopped, stood with his big hands on his waist, and said nothing.

Abe held out his hand. "Mayor Trent," he said. "I imagine you—"

"Did Talbert's men pat you?"

"Yessir."

Trent started to inquire about the thoroughness, but instead he took a handful of popcorn kernels from his pocket and threw them at the outer door.

Munchy came in and stood at attention.

"Pat him again," Trent said, "and get on up in his armpits. Ankles too."

Abe stood with his arms out and his stance wide again, looking Trent in the face while the fat man located the deck of cards Abe had wanted him to locate. He tossed it on the desk.

"Get in the crack of his ass," Trent said.

When it was done, Munchy nodded that Abe was clean. He went back to his paper.

They sat across the wide desk from each other just as they had thirteen years before.

Trent took up the Devil Back package of cards and turned it over in his hand. He said, "I thought Talbert had lost his mind just now when he came in there and said what he said." His posture in the highback chair was not what it once had been. "He had the tact to whisper it in my ear, but if Rutherford happens to leave his post in there and come through that door, he's liable to tug his shooting iron and put six right through you."

Abe dipped his hand in a hidden pocket and produced an envelope of money. He held it across the desk. "I hope you'll find it satisfactory," he said.

Trent took the envelope and fished out the notes and counted two thousand dollars.

Behind him, the bookcase still sat empty of books, its glass fronts obscured by flat neglect. Atop the case was the cast-iron boxing glove bookend with which Floyd Staples had crushed the skull of the red-headed boy.

Trent was thrown off by the money. He was suddenly dry-throated. He stacked it on top of the envelope. "Why did you come back here?" he asked.

"My brother Jake has died."

"Shameful situation that one. I'm sorry for your loss."

Abe shut his eyes for the briefest of moments, and in doing so, he imagined himself hurtling across the desk with his little nails between the fingers of his fists, punching at the eyes of Henry Trent, proclaiming all the while, *This is what I do when I smell something wrong on a fella!* Instead, he looked at Trent and said, "Doc Warble said blood infection from the slug." He'd wondered if he'd be able to tell, when he finally sat with the man, whether or not Trent was carrying Jake's demise. Now here he was, and Abe couldn't smell a damn thing on him.

Trent said, "Sepsis. Bad luck."

"The worst kind."

"I hope you do not think me somehow complicit in Jake's end."

"If I thought that, would we be conversing like we are?"

Trent sniffed hard and stared back with eyes as dead as the worthless lobby men. He said, "I'd heard Jake had long since got the syphilis too."

"These days," Abe said, "there's a miracle cure for that."

Trent had not heard the news. He readied his hand next to the pistol tucked at the desk's kneehole. "Don't know if you caught wind," he said, "but there's some saying Jake and the Italian was engaged in homosexual relations."

"Is that right?"

"Lovers' quarrel."

Abe swallowed. In his mind he heard her voice. *Keep your temper.* He looked at his hands. He kept his temper. "Mayor

Trent," he said. "I've done considerable growing up while I was away, and I've become a successful man of business." He sat forward on his chair and looked Trent in the eye. "I'd like to apologize to you for my drunken and juvenile ways of old and for the pain I may have caused on the evening of my departure." He cleared his throat. "I believe you know I was not involved with Floyd Staples, but I should have stopped him somehow." He willed a look of remorse to his face.

From beyond the door, somebody at the big table told a good one and the men were made to laugh, loud and in unison.

Trent took his hand away from the concealed piece. He packed the bowl of his pipe and got it going. He regarded the younger man and remembered the way he once manipulated cards. "What line of work are you in?" he asked him.

"I am a salesman for the Big Sun Playing Card Company."

"I've got my card supplier."

"Course. I'm not looking to make a sale."

"What is it that you want?"

Abe told him he wanted a new beginning. He said he aimed to stay awhile and help out his family, and that if it sat right with Trent, he would restore his Daddy's saloon to its former self. "I hope that two thousand will mean something to you," he said. "I hope it might buy Daddy a few months' respite from collection." He said that such a respite would allow him to put the place in working order, and putting the place in working order would allow a decent

224

living for his brother and more equitable footing for his father, who was injured at the knee and of the age to put his feet up once in a while. He said, "And I aim to bring my mother around on selling Hood House to you."

"It's the acreage I'm after."

"Acreage too."

The fan above spun and a piece of dust fell on the heavy desk between them, slow as the snowflakes Abe had seen that morning.

Henry Trent again turned the card deck over in his hands. He took long pulls on his pipe and said, "Goddamn Baaches. You took a five-year king's run at the big table and shat on it, left your Daddy to shovel up and pay the fiddler." He licked his finger and stuck it in the bowl of his pipe. There was a small wet sound. "Your brother finally found the wise way to real money, and what did he do? He shat on it. Went prohibitionist, religified." He shook his head. Baaches were hard to figure. "What happened to your face?" he asked.

"Ran across a man who could wield a blade."

He nodded. He knew the type. "Did you give as good as you got?"

"Only thing he wields now is an invalid's chair."

Trent smiled.

Abe smiled back.

They stood and met at desk's end, and Abe remembered what Goldie had said about the man's volatile state. For a moment he wondered if a gun was to be pulled, but Trent instead raised up his fist and knocked pipe ash on it. He looked hard at Abe's eyes before bending toward the waste-basket and blowing. He said he'd have to run things by the Beavers brothers.

"Of course," Abe said.

But Trent would not run things by the Beavers brothers. He'd manage it all alone while they sunned themselves in Florida, and by the time they returned in June, he'd have locked up a hundred acres more. Prime acres of plateau land where homes could be built and folks with means could live high up from the filth below.

They shook hands.

Trent unlatched the arch doors on his liquor cabinet. He poured two whiskeys from a wide-bottom decanter. He raised his glass and said, "To half-Jew Abe, businessman and crip-pler of the knife-wielding." He opened the door to the main card room and told Munchy to go on break. He stepped through and surveyed. "Too quiet," he said.

Abe followed and they stood in the open and watched the singular table of men, and without taking his eyes off them, Trent said to Abe, "I've always liked your Daddy. I never intended the bad blood and all that's happened." His eyes welled and his voice shook. He was not in full control of his sensibilities.

He cleared his throat and returned to his office, where he poured another and eyed the green-sealed card pack dancing in red devils. He took it up and walked back to Abe. He perched his foot on a rung of the fat man's stool. "Look to be some fine cards," he said.

Abe said that they were indeed. He listed off the towns and cities they supplied, all the way to San Francisco. He said, "And we supply a good many top magicians and sleight-of-hand artists too. Verner and Marlon, Mercurio and Andrews, and we—"

"Max Mercurio uses these cards?" He'd nearly choked mid-swallow.

"Uses them exclusively," Abe said.

Trent thumbed the deck. "Do you know him?"

"We've shared a drink or two." Abe had never met the man.

"Fine stage magician," Trent said. "Doesn't need all the bangs and flashes."

"I couldn't agree with you more."

The barkeep side-eyed them from his station and unclasped his hands. He was ever-ready to grab, if need be, the cut-barrel shotgun. It hung from a pair of broken-down hay hooks affixed to the underside of the bar.

Trent asked, "Do you know Mercurio's gal?"

"Beatrice?"

"That's the one."

"Beatrice is a jewel. Doesn't put on airs."

There was a rising carbonation in Trent's throatway. He didn't know whether it was excitement over Beatrice the Beautiful or indigestion from that morning's fatback and eggs. He said, "I saw the very same in her."

The conversation was playing just as Abe had imagined it, and he did not miss a beat. "I wondered if they'd been down here. I haven't spoken to Max in a while."

"Well, they haven't yet," Trent said. "I met Beatrice only in passing once in New Orleans." He'd met nothing more than her picture on a rectangle of newsprint. Four times since, he'd made written request of rates, but Mercurio had never returned his letters.

Abe suspected Max Mercurio would sooner be run through with a pig spit than come to Keystone. He said, "Well, the Alhambra's first-class. I'm sure I could arrange it."

And it was then that Henry Trent's posture straightened. He looked at Abe with something akin to wonder.

"Max's manager Tony is a friend of mine," Abe said. "He's got them in Melbourne, Australia right now, but I could wire him and see when they might be freed up for a short run. He owes me."

Trent smiled big. His silver crowns were tarnished yellow and black.

There was a sharpness in his stride back to the liquor cabinet, where he poured another for Abe and told him they'd talk more soon. He was feeling nervous on Rutherford. "Take that one for the road," he told Abe. He patted his back and sent him across the main room.

He watched him go and wondered at Abe's angle and his skill in the art of lying. He could not figure what the young man had to gain from such a play. Sallie Baach's father would finally sell, or he wouldn't. Beatrice would come to town with Max Mercurio, or she wouldn't. Either way, he was two thousand richer than he'd been at breakfast.

He wondered how he'd tell Rutherford about the return

of the Keystone Kid, and he wondered, above all, how he'd keep the little man from killing him.

No sooner had he wondered than he ceased. He'd tell Rutherford that patience was a virtue. You only have to wait until the property is signed over, until Beatrice comes to town, he'd say. Or until the property isn't signed over, until Beatrice doesn't come to town. For a time, he'd say, patience. After that, tiny Rutherford, you can do what you will.

*

Abe fetched Snippy the mediocre mare before ten, and he rode her all the way to Mingo County. He used a snake whip and boot spurs both to make her go, and—following Elkhorn to Spice Creek, cutting through a thick-brush pass—he came into Matewan along the Tug River at midnight, a thirteen-hour ride. He cooled down the horse and hobbled and staked her at woods' edge. He watered and fed her. Then he proceeded directly to the small clapboard home of Frank Dallara, where snakeskins hung like wind chimes from the front-porch roof. He stepped careful at the quiet spot on each porch riser, and turned the doorknob slow as any man ever turned one, and went inside and awakened Frank Dallara by tickling him at the nose with a crow feather.

When Dallara opened his eyes, there was the smooth nickel hole of the five-shot .38.

"I wonder if you'd join me for a walk outside," Abe whispered.

Dallara carried a brass hinge lamp and they spoke cordially as they walked to their destination, a squat building backed up to Railroad Alley.

Abe told the man he meant him no harm. He told him he was only trying to find who'd killed his brother. Dallara understood. Abe asked him about the snakeskins.

"My boy Fred likes to catch snakes," he said. "Him and another boy too."

Abe learned from Dallara that his cousin Giuseppe was a strange and quiet man, a bricklayer and carpenter who pulled his flat cap low and kept his eyes on the ground. He'd not been born in the states like Frank Dallara had. Giuseppe had come from Torino to New York, but there was trouble, so he came to Mingo County, like his cousins before him, to mine coal. He'd quit mid-winter. He had no tunneling in his bones, only building. When he walked to Keystone in February for work, he'd met Jake. "And here was a man could build near as good as him from what I know," Frank Dallara said, "and that ain't common. Giuseppe builds better than me, and I learned from my Daddy, who framed and bricked that whole row right there." He pointed to a two-story building across the tracks, lit sufficient by the near-full moon.

"I built that house you just woke me up in," Dallara said.

When Abe asked him why he reckoned Giuseppe was locked up in Matewan instead of Keystone, Frank Dallara said, "Well, you ain't got no judge down there do you?"

In the alley, it was pitch-black and winter cold. Abe

leaned a hollow concrete block on its end against the wall. He got on top to see inside the single barred window of the Matewan Jail. On a table in the main hall, a wide kerosene lamp stayed lit overnight, casting thread-iron shadow on bare floor. Inside cell two, Giuseppe Dallara lay on a dirty stack of grain sacks. Abe fast-whistled four short bursts like a nuthatch bird and the man sat upright.

Giuseppe was hungry. He cocked his head to regard the man at the window square. A stranger, but his face marked him kin to Jake Baach.

Abe nodded to him and stepped down, and in his place was Frank.

Abe spoke to Frank Dallara, who listened and then said through the bars, "*Questo il fratello di* Jake Baach. *Vuole sapere se lo sparato.*"

Giuseppe spoke fast and for quite some time.

When he ceased, Frank looked down at Abe from his perch. He said, "He was huntin squirrels with your brother on Buzzard Branch. He'd set his rifle down against a tree trunk so he could piss off the edge of a jutted ridge rock up there—folks call it Big Brogan—you know it?"

Abe said he did.

Dallara went on. "And when he come back, his rifle's gone. Him and your brother was trying to figure it when three shots come from way far off. Jake was knocked to the ground, but he stood up and screamed and ran down the mountain. Giuseppe followed, but when he got to the bottom, a colored police drew down on him, and he ran out of there.

He came to my house, and I took him to a hideout up Sulfur Creek Hollow. Your chief of police tracked him two days later, said he'd found the rifle dropped up on Buzzard Branch too." He coughed before he clarified. "That rifle *is* Giuseppe's—a good Marlin I sold to him for six dollars and a half—but it wasn't him that fired it."

Giuseppe spoke again from inside the jail.

Frank Dallara listened and waited a moment before he relayed it to Abe. "He says your brother was a good man. He says your brother was like his own blood kin."

Abe nodded his head. He took out his watch. Just after one. The mediocre mare would be plenty rested by the time he walked back.

He pulled a twenty-dollar note from his vest pocket and handed it to Frank Dallara. "For your trouble," he said. He apologized for the rude and abrupt nature of his arrival. Then he told him there might come a time when he was needed in Keystone. "I might clear your cousin's name," he said.

He nodded to Frank Dallara and walked away.

NO BUCKWHEATERS, NO CHICKENS

May 6, 1910

In those days, Little Donnie Staples was employing the bug to win. The bug was a device that hid a card under his chair at the Oak Slab until such time as he needed it to secure his fortune. He'd built it himself from a penny, a steel spike, and a watch spring. It tucked neatly into the gouge he'd made in the seat's underside and could be dislodged with considerable speed if suspicion arose. He'd used it to win ninety-seven dollars with an ace of spades on May 4th. Then, after his four-hour slumber, he'd returned to play, and he'd found in his little bug not the ace of spades customarily reloaded by Talbert, but instead a Devil Back joker from the Big Sun Playing Card Company. It wore heavy varnish and along the bottom it read:

A DROP OF BLOOD IN EVERY RED INK BATCH!

Such an odd development perplexed Little Donnie. The card got his steam up. Still, he won considerable monies without aid from the bug, and later, in his room at the Alhambra—the very same third-floor corner room where Abe had once roosted—Little Donnie studied the card. No black ink was used in its manufacture. It was a three-color print, primarily red. Its yellow company sign was bright as summer squash and was held by a dancing green monkey on a pedestal, while the pedestal was striped in a color that was neither red nor green nor yellow. Little Donnie brought the card close, the lines an inch from his left eye, the one folks referred to as "lazy." It was anything but. It rolled sometimes, but it could see things no one else could. On that night, in the striped pedestal of the devil-monkey, the eye saw:

123123123123123
MAGNIFY
Little Donnie Staples,
Tell Trent I gave you
invite to Baach game.
Come to saloon back door
on Friday 4 am sleep break

The word MAGNIFY was all he could make out. He fetched his pearl-handled magnifying glass and read:

123123123123123
MAGNIFY
Little Donnie Staples,
Tell Trent I gave you
invite to Baach game.
Come to saloon back door
on Friday 4 am sleep break

He could not sleep then for the clamor of possibility in his mind.

Abe Baach was who Little Donnie had always wanted to be.

In the morning, he stood opposite Mr. Trent with his elbow on the long bar. He asked if they could be alone and Trent shooed away the barkeep. Behind them, an old woman pushed floor oil across the boards between tables. She hummed low.

Little Donnie told Trent he'd gotten an invite to a 4 AM poker game at Baach's saloon. Trent sipped at a short glass of soda water and cringed. He was hungover bad and knew another trip to the commode was close at hand.

Their exchange was to the point and feverishly paced. It proceeded as follows:

"You say it's a secret game?"

"I believe so."

"Played on your sleep time?"

"Yes."

"How did the invite come?"

"Abe asked me hisself."

"You go on and do it and report back to me what you find."

And from Trent's throat came a sucking sound and he put one hand to his stomach and the other to the seat of his pants, beneath which his sphincter pinched sudden against the pressure. And in his mind was a long-forgotten boyhood memory of the time he'd half-filled a pig-bladder balloon with mud-puddle water. He'd blown air in it too and toted the tight balloon in the farm wagon for the long journey to church, and on that journey his tied knot had failed, and the bladder burst brown upon his lap and ruined his Sunday trousers. His granny had held up the mule and thrown him to the ground. She'd stepped from the high wagon seat and jumped a ditch to break off a switch from a sourwood tree. She'd yanked down his trousers and twenty-lashed him across the kneebacks. "You are a bad-hearted little boy," she'd told him, and he cried and looked at the ground. The sourwood leaves she'd stripped lay in a rudimentary curl on the dirt, their October color coming in, reddest at the middle rib.

*

Little Donnie went to the back door of A. L. Baach & Sons Saloon on his Friday four AM sleep break. He was greeted warmly there by Sam Baach, who shared his height and slim build. Sam took him upstairs to Abe's room, where, assembled in a semi-circle of unmatched chairs, were the Keystone Kid and Queen Bee, and mother Rebecca. In a ball on Abe's bed slept brother Robert, who was six and a half years old. He was known to kick and talk in his sleep. Little Donnie liked to call him Bob.

There was rainwater pooled on the windowsill. Cigar smoke ribboned above. Rebecca Staples petted the head of her slumbering youngest and smiled at her oldest.

Abe stood and shook Little Donnie's hand. He asked him, "Do you mind if I call you L.D.?" and then he called him L.D. and told him he was truly sorry that he had not showed him a card trick on the afternoon of May 15th in the year 1903. "I was a boy back then who thought he was a man," he said, "and I was six years older than you are today." He tapped at the side of his head and said to think on that awhile. They sat down.

"L.D.," Abe said, "I can appreciate a well-made bug." And he spoke on how he'd once employed the bug just as L.D. had. He said he'd employed mirrors too, sometimes six at once, each no bigger than a june beetle. He'd worked alone and with a partner. He'd blown smoke-ring signals and used the earlobe pull. He'd cold-decked and dealt seconds. He'd crimped, marked, and nicked on the fly. "And L.D.," he said, "I believe you've already seen my line work on that joker. I can go a hundred times smaller than that." He told the boy he'd give him two years' apprenticeship in two months' time. He aimed to stay the summer. He aimed to find out who shot his brother. "And the next time I leave Keystone," he said, "I won't be leaving alone, and there won't be a pocket on any of us that isn't full up with double-eagles."

He said that L.D.'s help in the money endeavors would be much appreciated.

Rebecca Staples then seceded herself from the conversation. Its terminus was known, and its risk was death. She climbed onto the bed next to her boy Bob, who was the kind to roll out and hit the floor and holler out and keep on sleeping.

It was quiet.

237

To be certain he was understood, Abe said to Little Donnie, "The mark is Trent."

"And Rutherford and Beavers too," Goldie said. She watched the boy for tells.

He looked at one and then the other. "It's a spirited undertaking," he said.

"The touch on this is somethin else," Abe said. "Take you two days to count it out. Big-faced red-seal notes, high-stacked."

Goldie nodded her head. "High as your belt buckle," she said.

"A quarter cut to each of us three," Abe said. "The fourth is split by my associates traveling down from Baltimore."

When the boy breathed in, he shook.

Abe looked at Goldie. He took his own slow inhale before he spoke again. "L.D.," he said. "I know by the eyes, straight-away. I know who's iron-hearted, and I know on top of that who's on the wrong side." The boy had eyes opposite his father's. Abe hoped him ripe enough to ally himself accordingly. He held out his hand. "We can show you some things," he said.

Little Donnie nodded. He put out his own and they shook.

Robert Staples kicked his short little legs straight and talked in his sleep. "They do," he mumbled. "Tippy-top."

Sam stepped out of the room for sustenance.

Abe stood and stretched his legs. He put a hand to the wardrobe where his money rested.

Goldie leaned forward in the bowback chair, elbows on

her knees. She asked if Taffy Reed would be amenable to an endeavor such as theirs. Little Donnie said he couldn't be sure, but that he doubted it. Taffy was like his Daddy. He didn't bite the hand. It was what she'd assumed, and it relieved her in fact, for she worried that trouble could stir should Abe and Taffy mix.

Goldie told Little Donnie that such a plan involved, at its conclusion, relocating. She said, "I will never love another place the way I love McDowell County, but there are times when what's required is a journey." She said the Baaches were planning for the possibility of a long one that didn't ever circle back to Keystone.

Little Donnie indicated he wouldn't mind relocating elsewhere.

"Good," Goldie said. And she sat back again, and the spindles moaned at the touch of her ribs and shoulder blades. She called Rebecca over and told mother and son that the following would be required: supreme confidence, discipline, and endurance. She looked Rebecca in the eye and made her profess to stay off the opium and to mislead Rutherford as need be in order that they might all do their best work. "And if we tell you to tell Rutherford you're going away for a while and you're taking little Bob with you, then that's what you do." She looked Little Donnie in the eye and told him he too would have to mislead.

Abe spoke to Rebecca from where he stood. "I've got a man coming to town who makes a powder," he said. "Eases you off the poppy." Tony Thumbs had miracle cures for most any ailment, cures that had righted Abe's own ship more times than he cared to count.

Sam brought up the big blue coffee pot, four straight cups, and a bowl of olives he'd soaked for a month in white whiskey. Taffy Reed had given him the idea. On a winter consideration collection, Taffy had indicated that his toothpicks were booze-pickled. Penny candy too. Licorice, caramels. Tobacco. Garden vegetables. Taffy would brine most anything in whiskey.

Abe sat down again. He sighed and smiled and took up a handful of olives. He tossed them in his open mouth and chewed. He told the story of the coming summer.

"I call it the double-sideways big con," he said, tapping at the side of his head again. "It goes both ways and there will be a good bit of improvising on the side, but our mark will be certain of one thing all the way through." Abe looked at Little Donnie straight and spoke in an even tone. "He'll believe himself the superior confidence man to me, and you'll keep him right on believing."

The boy swallowed and kept his mouth shut.

"You're our roper," Abe told him. "An important job, but an easy one too if you listen when you need to listen and speak when you need to speak."

The boy nodded.

Abe said he wouldn't hold it against L.D. if he decided to double-cross him. "But you need to know, I played Trent already in his office, threw some short stack at him and watched him go soft. Gave him a whiff of the right woman."

"Beatrice?"

Abe nodded.

Sam was too ambitious with a honk of his whiskey-coffee and regurgitated into his mouth with the croak and puff of a toad. He kept his lips shut tight and swallowed it back straightaway. "Pardon me," he said.

Goldie laughed.

Abe went on. "Our inside men arrive shortly from Baltimore." He spat four olive pits rapidly into an open hand. "You're sitting above the big store right now." He pointed to the floor beneath their feet. "We will revive this place. People will know of it for a hundred miles or more, and they will seek out its delights." He pointed at Little Donnie. "But you're not the entertainment, L.D. You are a player of cards." He smiled. "You'll nightly engage in a false game of high-stakes poker with men pretending to be someone they're not."

Sam poured coffee while Abe spoke slow and deliberate on such delicate matters as to convince Trent that Little Donnie was *his* roper, working *his* mark. It was enough to addle the mind.

There was talk of disguises and mirrors and paid actors and forged documents and false jewels.

They all listened to him.

The boy asked smart questions. Abe answered all but one, the boy's last. "How did you manage to put your card in my bug?"

"That isn't how it happened," Abe said. He held out his hand. They shook.

Little Donnie Staples left early that morning a changed young man, and, as he was told to, he reported back to Henry Trent while Abe waited in the Alhambra's fine lobby, small-talking with Talbert.

Trent was by then laid up with bad digestive troubles. A flop sweat was upon his temple. He was still and pale and centered on his wide cane-box mattress. He clutched his bed sheet. He could not figure what the boy was telling him. He said, "Abe is downstairs right now?"

"He is."

"And he told you to ask *me* about all this?"

"He did."

"Why doesn't he ask me himself?"

"I gather he's a little bit afraid of you. Doesn't want to overstep his bounds too quick."

It settled him a little to hear such a thing. He almost smiled. "And if I let you play there? How's he cutting it?"

"I get three. You get forty-seven. He gets fifty."

"Did he say what number he was looking to clear?"

"One hundred grand. Biggest mark will be a fella from Chicago owns some office buildings."

"What kind of game is it?"

"Seven-card stud. The men will all be from Cincinnati and St. Louis and the like. Big money men. No buckwheaters, no chickens."

Trent was having trouble following. The boy was using words that neither pleased his ear nor aided his thinking. He thought of sitting upright but didn't. The clock on his bedside table metered the silence in cold clicks. He asked one of the many questions he had. "Why would they come to a ratshit West Virginia saloon to risk their holdings?"

Had little Donnie been running on ample sleep, he'd have answered quicker. As it was, he felt his throat closing, but he managed to push out the words. "I gather he's been selling cards to these men for six years, and they are all of them hooked bad on the poker table." He told Trent that Abe had recently wired the men and revealed what they'd always suspected—that he'd once been somebody. That he'd once been the Keystone Kid. Back then, like Rutherford and Harold Beavers and so many others, they'd wanted to play him but never had the chance. He'd disappeared. Now he was back. Now they could take him on right smack in the bowel of his own red-light boomtown.

Trent stifled a belch. "Presumably they know of me?"

"I gather they don't."

He grunted. "Why does he need you?"

"I gather he's heard about my play."

"Why does he think I'll let you?" Forty-seven percent on a hundred grand was good money, but Trent had good money enough to wipe at his asscrack if he saw fit.

"The way Abe sees it, we can fleece the Chicago fella twice, once at Baaches, where I'll appear to lose while Abe wins, then again when we steer him to the Oak Slab, confident against my play." He had gotten his stride back.

A crane fly bumped at the lamp's cast circle on the ceiling.

"And he wants a cut of the Oak Slab take?"

"No. Just wants to get his Daddy's saloon up and running again."

Trent thought on it. "I don't know," he said. "Why does he believe we'll do it?"

"He believes we'll do it for the kind of certain money that comes in working the table with him as a partner. These men will think they're lucky enough to play Keystone's best, from way back and nowadays both, and they'll think us enemies rather than cohorts."

"Why doesn't he just beat them without you?"

"I gather he can't play like he used to. He's lost what he had."

Trent knew of at least three men who'd be interested to know such a thing. Rutherford and Harold Beavers and Taffy Reed had wanted a shot at the Keystone Kid for as long as he could remember. He watched the crane fly dance above him. He said, "He gave no indication of another angle?"

"He thinks he's smarter than he is." Now Little Donnie improvised. "I'd say the Jew blood in his veins taints his view on who aligns with who in this world. I could feel it. He wrongly assumes me his friend."

It was quiet.

Trent considered the advantage of having the boy inside Abe's domain. "Go on and do it then," he said. "We'll make something out of it."

"He said he'd be glad to come upstairs and talk to you about it further."

"Tell him in a day or two."

And so it was that Little Donnie Staples would daily come to spend three dark morning hours with Abe and Goldie. They would teach him things such as how to covertly place tiny mirrors at strategic angles inside a man's office. Between lessons, he would nap upright at a fake game of poker populated by salaried stage actors from Tony Thumbs' Baltimore stall. The best of them, a fifty-five-year-old actor named Jim Fort, would play the role of Chicago Phil, millionaire. The diamond stickpins in their silk ties would be made of glass. They would speak one way in character and another alone. This facade they would all maintain in the event that Trent might finally show his face at Baach's place, in the event that he might try and confirm the strange and intriguing tales told to him by the lazy-eyed son of a whore.

CYANOGEN GAS WILL IMPREGNATE THE ATMOSPHERE

May 18, 1910

The people stood in the middle of Wyoming Street and danced on loose legs and sprung knees. They drag-slid their feet, kicking dust into the cool night air. A man in a bow tie sat on a wicker-seated chair and played a guitar. Another stood and played potato bug mandolin. From an open turquoise suitcase, a woman sold single-dose pills for a dollar apiece. The suitcase was rigged with a leather belt around her neck, and she walked up and down the street's center calling, "It's not too late! Comet pills! Get your comet pills!"

It was four in the morning.

Inside, Sam Baach poured generous swallows from a squat-cylinder black-glass bottle. Comet drops, halfdollar a shot. A miner still in his carbide cap paid and regarded the clear liquid. He knew of another man on his shift who'd stayed underground for the earth's impending passage through the tail of Halley's Comet. "What's in it?" he asked.

"Oh, I'm not entirely sure," Sam said. "Quinine, rum, purple wine. And there's secret ingredients too that the doctor doesn't tell of." The doctor was the husband of the woman with the turquoise suitcase. He'd made a display of drinking down five shots of his own product and proclaiming, "No poison gas will ruin these pipes!" and was now asleep, face down on the crowded corner table. The miner looked over at him and said, "Well, here's to living past sunup." He drank it down and ordered another.

Abe was readying one of the performers Tony Thumbs had sent in from Baltimore, a Frenchman whom he hoped would please the crowd. A. L. Baach & Sons had not seen this many warm bodies since before he'd left town in '03. Trent and Rutherford had left him well enough alone, all on the reports of Little Donnie and the promise of a New York telegram proclaiming the impending arrival of Max Mercurio and the Beautiful Beatrice. In the meantime, Abe had brought in some of Tony Thumbs' choicest acts to populate the saloon, and more were on their way.

The stage itself had been finished the day before by Frank Dallara, who was paid handsomely. He made use of an oversize custom workbench in the storeroom, a great big bench made by his cousin and Jake Baach. Its tool well was quadruple deep. It had wide-throated shoulder and tail vises. On that workbench, Frank Dallara had now built, in two weeks, the rails, battens, grids, and drops of a proper performance stage, miniaturized. He'd been paid handsomely, and with a cut of his earnings, he'd paid the jailer at Matewan to feed Giuseppe something other than beans and bacon.

Goldie lit the footlights and stepped behind the curtain. She got on an upturned pail and brushed powder on the opening act's face while he stared at the newspaper. He'd been asking, "What this word means" for twenty solid minutes, pointing at headlines and leadlines both. Goldie looked where he pointed. *Cyanogen gas will impregnate the atmosphere.* "Means poison," she told him. "We're passing through the comet's tail right now."

He frowned.

Abe stood by, watching. He cracked his knuckles and checked his watch.

Goldie made the opening act take another swallow from the brown glass bottle Tony Thumbs had sent along.

"I do not need it," the man said.

"Can't hurt," she told him.

He swallowed and winced and looked again at the newspaper.

"Don't worry," Abe said. "It's no truth in that headline." The cyanogen-gas theory had been largely discounted, but Abe had paid an acquaintance at the *McDowell Times* to run the article three days straight in order that he might stir folks to buy comet pills and comet shots, in order that they would attend the saloon's comet party. The acquaintance was Cheshire Whitt, whom Abe paid handsomely to print handbills reading *You Can Sleep After You Are Dead. Come to A. L. Baach & Sons. Wednesday night into Thursday morning. Dance and drink and be entertained by world-renowned acts on our new stage.*

The acts weren't world-renowned as much as Baltimore-renowned, and the fame came less from stage time and more from habitual drunken exhibitionism.

Now the opening act was powdered and reassured that the world would not end before he took the stage. Goldie peeked her head through the curtain and whistled at Sam, who was having trouble keeping empty mugs filled. Sam in turn nodded to Cheshire Whitt, who opened the door and hollered at the people in the street that the show was starting inside.

It was shoulder to shoulder when Goldie stepped from the curtain. "Ladies and gentlemen," she said, "direct from Paris France, I give you L'homme Péter."

The crowd took this to mean that the man's name was Peter. Had any of them spoken French, there may have been fair warning of what was to come.

He wore a yellow swallowtail dresscoat and a purple flowered cravat. His skin was pale and his tonic-slicked hair a reflective black.

He surveyed the quiet audience before him, turned away from their upturned faces, and bowed toward the curtain. Still bent at the waist, he called out, "Now the automobile, with a backfire," and he lifted the tails of his coat and sent forth with wondrous might a continuous blast of odorless gas. It issued from his anus with the clear tone of a combustion engine, and it ended with an impossible clap that startled those in front. When they recovered from their startle, they began to laugh heartily in a chorus. The chorus rose as the reality of what they'd seen set in, and they only quieted when L'homme Péter looked over his shoulder and said, "Now for the Yankee Doodle." They waited in disbelief. He played it in perfect time and pitch. Some bent double with laughter then. One man left in disgust. For any who questioned the sound's origin, L'homme Péter took a paper sleeve of talcum powder and emptied it over the up-pointed seat of his black breeches. He called, "The Waltz!" and a cloud of fine white particles burst upon the gaslit air, spinning as they fell.

It was as if he'd swallowed an accordion.

They called him out with savage claps and high whistles for an encore, and behind the curtain Goldie fed him another swallow of Tony Thumbs' patented Fart Juice, though L'homme Péter didn't need it. He'd been born with a gift—the fart juice only stirred propulsion. He threw open the curtain, bent again before them, and played the snake-charmer song until their bellies clinched and their eyes watered from laughter.

At five, a yellow-haired Norwegian woman took the stage wearing only three bleached sand dollars held by kite string over her unmentionables. She sat on a barstool with the handle of a thirty-inch handsaw gripped in her knees and pulled a cello's bow across the back of the blade. It sang high weary lullabies until more than one silent man imagined he'd found his bride.

In the storeroom, behind a wall newly framed and bricked by Frank Dallara, a pretend game of seven-card stud proceeded slow and quiet. Three of the five men half-played their hands, but they didn't give a damn about the outcome.

One of them steadily dozed. His shoulder twitched. He breathed through his mouth.

Little Donnie Staples was wayworn, and so it was easy to sleep upright in a hard-seat chair. In ordinary times, he worked his twenty-hour shift at the Oak Slab, slept for four, and was back at the table for another twenty, all the while winning, if he had a mind to. But these weren't ordinary times. There were no four hours on a feather mattress. There was only a chair.

By then he was accustomed to hard-seat-chair-beds and big-city-actor talk and the lessons of a first-rate confidence man and his card-throwing woman. He'd even grown accustomed to the elaborate and constant predicting of another man's whims.

For two weeks he'd been told two things about sleep: you can do it when you're dead, and until then, you can do it in a chair for a half hour, twice nightly, between the hours of five and seven AM. It had proved true, and Little Donnie had begun catching his double-thirty winks in a chair-bed, and he'd maintained control of his faculties sufficient to keep winning at the Oak Slab too.

He awoke from his straight nap to the sound of a comet-gas believer screaming, "I see it! I see it in the air dust!"

He one-eyed his timepiece. He stretched and stood. Trent would be anxious for another report. Each morning, he told Trent and Rutherford how he still slow-roped the big mark, how he would keep alive his trickled losing streak until the mark pulled from his jacket the property deed Abe was sure he'd bring. They knew the Chicago mark as Phil, and they were after the man's eight-story office building on West Superior Street. They knew him to be hooked on Keystone's charms, and presently they would lure Chicago Phil to the Oak Slab, where they'd take more off his hands. They did not suspect the man was only a tale.

The yellow-haired Norwegian finished her set and lifted, ever so briefly, the twin sand dollars covering her nipples. She shot behind the curtain as the men whistled and hooted. Goldie emerged in her place and hollered to the crowd that Saw Girl would be here all week. She declared comet shots to be half price until seven. "You can sleep after you're dead!" she called.

Behind the curtain, she took Saw Girl by the shoulders and said to her, "You only lift those sand dollars once, and you only do it at the end of the show. Then you get off quick."

The girl had a condition that caused her to look through people and to not hear what they said to her. She nodded.

Goldie knew the girl spoke English. "You hear me?" she said.

"Do I not do it just the way you say already?" Even to her own ear, the voice was childish, but she went on anyway. "Do I not?"

The skin beneath her makeup was waxen. It was opium skin.

Goldie made a note to send Saw Girl packing. Back to Baltimore with money in her pocket.

On her way to the storeroom, she spotted Cheshire Whitt tending bar with Sam. She slipped him the write-up for the Sunday and Monday editions. She told him to take his post out front. Her step had spring. She noted the positions of Alva Smith and Rose Cantu, her two most educated ladies. Each was on the lap of a rich man at the mainroom's poker table. Each batted her eyes slow for effect. On the promise of Goldie's good money, Alva and Rose would play it this way for three hours, and then they'd slip out the back, replaced by Goldie's next two smartest ladies, who'd do the same, and so on. There was no coitus whatsoever involved, and thusly it was a much-sought-after shift for the working girls of Fat Ruth Malindy's. And the rich men from Bramwell and beyond could not wipe from their minds the pretty gals with the eyelashes who'd up and disappeared. It was enough to make a man come back to A. L. Baach & Sons Saloon. It was enough to make him tell his friends.

Goldie had found something lost to her a decade before. It was a spirited way of being, and it was better than before. Abe had learned in his years gone to tamp down those reckless habits that had previously sabotaged their liveli-hood. Now there was more thinking than drinking, more talking than fornicating, though all things in moderation were appreciated. It was the sureness of it all that she most favored. The ridiculous certainty that they would come out on top, alive. Only once had she made mention of their endeavor as something fraught with peril. "We might be between the hammer and the anvil on this one," she'd said, and Abe had only kept doing what he was doing. He was practicing his card manipulations before a mirror, watching his own hands. He'd answered: "Well, lion's got to roar."

She met Little Donnie and Abe at the whiskey barrel in back of the storeroom. It was empty. It had a head but no bottom, and under it was the three-foot fireproof safe bolted to the storeroom floor, the same safe she and Abe had long ago retreated to in times of mutual need.

Abe handed Little Donnie an envelope with five thousand dollars inside. He'd retrieved it from under the wardrobe's hidden slat that very morning, leaving little behind for cushion. He said to the boy, "Give it to him straightaway in his office, alone. Use those good ears of yours and that lazy eye too. Use the mirror if need be."

Little Donnie had never held such thickness inside an envelope. "This is five thousand?" he asked.

"Tell him that's fifty percent of our touch. Tell him he needs to cut your three from that."

The boy nodded and put the envelope in his jacket's inside pocket.

Goldie watched him close. She still could not understand why Abe wouldn't accompany the boy on such an errand.

Abe said, "Tell him Chicago Phil left but said he'd be

back in about a month. Tell him the man is hooked and he wants to sit once more against me here before he tries his hand at the Oak Slab. Tell him he's bringing back bigger money and a building deed both." He patted the head of the big hollow barrel. "Tell him there's a safe in back under a barrel," he said, "and that what's in it grows nightly."

Little Donnie committed it all to memory.

Abe had a headache. He touched at the healed spot over his ear where the pump knot had once resided. There came, at his touch, a roaring sound still.

Little Donnie watched him put his fingers to his head and work his jaw open and shut.

"You okay Abe?" he asked.

"Chesh Whitt is out front, armed," Abe said. "He'll tail you and make sure nobody tries to rob you on the way." The young Whitt had proven eager to work whatever job they gave him. He liked the money and he didn't ask questions.

Little Donnie said he needed to drain his bladder before he left. The sight of that much money made him nervous, and when was nervous, he had to go. He stepped into the old pantry where the piss bucket resided.

They waited for him at the back.

Abe patted the boy on the shoulder, unlatched the door bar and lifted it, then turned the big lever key.

Outside, the sun was rising.

When the boy was gone, Goldie crouched at the false-bottom barrel. She pressed herself to its middle and wrapped her arms around and lifted it off the safe. She set it on the floor.

"Strong," Abe said. "Well put together."

She slid her drawers off over her stockings and shoes. She hopped on top of the safe and hiked her dress and spread apart her thighs.

"You been into the comet shots?" Abe asked her.

"I been into remembrance," she said.

*

Rutherford paced the length of Trent's office, eating the fifth of six pickled eggs. He did not care for the sound of Little Donnie's voice. Rutherford's strides were long as he could make them, soft so as not to agitate his bunions. He scratched at his chest as he paced. Bedbugs had roosted in the hair.

Trent leaned back in his big chair and counted the notes in the envelope. He shook his head. "Five thousand," he said. "The easy way. And this fella is coming back for more in a month?" He laughed. "Timing might work out. Rufus and Harold aren't due back until June the twentieth."

Rutherford quit pacing but kept scratching. His mouth was full of egg. "Why in the hell does it matter when the Beavers come home?" he said.

Trent answered. "I told you already. We've got to cushion them with the possibility of a second big touch and the Hood property both. They'll not be happy with the Abe Baach development otherwise."

The Beavers brothers were raising money in the Florida Everglades. They were celebrating Harold's retirement from the slaughter of plume birds, and they'd be home in time to throw summer money at the September primary elections. The midterm meant council seats and new state delegates too.

Rutherford looked at Little Donnie, who looked at his shoes. "You best make this worth it," he said.

Little Donnie looked at Rutherford, then Trent. He said, "There's a safe in back of the storeroom, hidden under a barrel. It's where they put the table winnings, which are growing considerable nightly."

Trent and Rutherford shared a look. "That's good work boy," Trent said. He laid the five thousand on his desk, opened the top drawer, and took out a hand mirror. He raised his lip and regarded his teeth. There was a snag on the tip of his silver incisor. He'd cut his tongue on it twice already. From the same open drawer he took out a long wood rasp that had belonged to Jake Baach. He placed it against the silver snag and filed it smooth. "Rutherford," he said. "Excuse me and the boy for a moment."

The tiny man slammed the door behind him.

Munchy was on his stool with the paper quartered in one hand and a pimiento cheese sandwich in the other. "What's got you so hot?" he said.

Rutherford slapped the sandwich to the floor and wiped his fingers on Munchy's coat sleeve. Four orange stripes dotted in red. "Shut your fuckin mouth fat man," he said.

In the office, Trent stood and said, "For that kind of good work, I'll give you a little more than three percent. Give you an even two hundred." He counted it off the stack.

Then, as was customary, he asked Little Donnie to turn and face away while he opened the safe to deposit the forty-eight hundred. He blocked a direct view with his body.

The boy did as he was told, but he rolled that loose left eye as far to the socket corner as he could. He trained it on the wall-embedded junebug mirror he'd angled precise the night prior, and in that tiny mirror, he studied the spinning knob.

His other eye he shut to better hear the clicks.

A RADIANT AND BLOOD-RED ROOM

May 24, 1910

The night he met chief Rutherford, Tony Thumbs had been in Keystone for only two days, and he would leave inside a week. He'd stepped onto the depot platform Sunday afternoon, his rolling dresser trunk behind him, his white-faced capuchin monkey riding on top. The monkey's name was Baz. He was forty-one years old, exactly half his master's age. Tony Thumbs had bought him for nine dollars in Guyana from a British organ grinder with one tooth. On the platform at Keystone, Baz transacted with a small boy selling the last of his folded *McDowell Times* for three cents. The boy had smiled when the monkey handed him the pennies. Baz had smiled back and held open the paper in front of Tony Thumbs. The headline read: *Now You See It, Now You Don't. The Moon Will Disappear on Tuesday Night.* "Good," Tony Thumbs had told his monkey. "Very good."

Tacked to the first telegraph pole they saw was a hand-bill proclaiming *You Can Still Sleep After You Are Dead. Come to A. L. Baach & Sons Saloon Tuesday Night and Watch the Moon Vanish.*

Now it was nearing midnight of that very Tuesday, and Baz the monkey stood on his pedestal in the street next to his master, who, despite his advanced age and having only one thumb, turned the fastest monte since Canada Bill Jones. He'd grown long the nails of his pinky fingers and used them for getting under the card's surface. He used them too for scooping and snorting the homemade snuff he kept inside a silver necklace box.

His stack of wine crates was set up next to the bow-tied guitar player in the wicker-seated chair, at the same spot on Wyoming Street where the comet pills had sold out six nights prior. A crowd gathered.

Tony Thumbs was stooped in his tall gray hat and matching broadcloth coat. His white mustache was twisted sharp at the tips. Twin kerosene lamps burned high at the edges of his crate. He was all glow and shadow as he called, "Follow the queen! Follow the queen!"

And officer Munchy the doorman did just that, touching his wide middle finger to the blue patterned card-back he knew to be the queen. Tony Thumbs turned it and doubled the fat man's five. The crowd grew.

Munchy smiled at his earnings and stepped to the door of A. L. Baach & Sons Saloon. He aimed to buy a drink for Goldie Toothman. All his life, he'd wanted little more than the touch of Keystone's Queen Bee.

Rutherford stepped into the Bottom without Taffy Reed

in tow. In his fist was a balled-up handbill for the lunar eclipse gathering. He was drunk. He tucked himself between Fat Ruth's and the restaurant, leaning against the siding, looking for Abe Baach.

Through his binoculars, he'd been watching Baach's place from the ridge since the previous week's all-night party. He'd told Trent he wanted badly to make arrests. No, the king had said, just as he had said to the idea of walking in on the secret game of seven-card stud. "Patience is a virtue," Trent had reminded him, "even for the shortest of men."

A woman lost a dollar at the monte table and stepped away to look skyward like everybody else.

A blackness had come upon the full edge of the big clear moon. Like sludge it moved across, wiping away the light so slow it was hard to notice. Men and women stepped onto balconies and leaned forward on the rail, their necks craned.

The guitar player picked an unrecognizable tune and howled like a dog.

When the moon seemed an oval, it began to turn red. Some went inside, afraid that such color hung death on those who watched. Others joined the guitar man and howled. There was much drinking and dancing on dirt and rooftop both.

The hysterical woman from the comet party screamed once again that she could see poison on the dust.

A man burst forth from Fat Ruth's without his trousers fully on. He had looked out the window whilst thrusting away and seen the red-slit eye watching him. Now he ran up Wyoming Street with his waistband gripped in one hand, his shoes in another. He shouted in Greek and fell and cut his knuckles.

Tony Thumbs kept up his patter. "Chase that lady!" he called. "Ten will get you twenty!" Most ignored him in favor of the night sky's show, but not Rutherford. From the dark trench alongside Fat Ruth's where men were known to piss, he stepped to the monte table and laid down a twenty-dollar bill. "Twenty will get me forty?" he asked Tony Thumbs.

"If that's your pleasure sir." And he showed all three cards, slowing up on the queen, before he stacked and squeezed and showed them again.

"I want a new deck," Rutherford told him. He stomped his boots to drop off the mud. He said, "I want Mexican style, flat on the board."

"If that's your pleasure sir," Tony Thumbs said, and he made a sound with his lips like an angry squirrel, and Baz pulled a deck of cards from his checkered woolen vest. He bobbed his head and showed his teeth and handed the pack to his master, who told the little lawman, "Inspect them if you wish."

"I do wish," Rutherford said, and he stared for a time at the missing thumb. He fanned the cards and rubbed their backs and checked for marks or nicks. He pulled the queen of diamonds and the two black jacks. He handed them over and said, "Where you from Methuselah?"

Tony Thumbs showed the card fronts and then worked his hands as if they rode an unseen track. He kept them flat, no squeeze. "I'm not from Mexico," he said, "but I know Mexican style."

Rutherford paid him no mind. He was locked on that queen, his short-statured gaze at perfect level with the crate table's top. When the old man quit his motion, Rutherford grinned at him and pointed to the middle card.

Tony Thumbs turned it. Jack of clubs. "Methuselah lives to turn another card," he said. He took up the twenty-dollar bill and relayed it to Baz, who rolled it tight as a cigarette and stuck it in his lips and puffed. A few in the crowd laughed. Rutherford was not among them.

He turned and ignored the moon some more. He strode to the door of A. L. Baach & Sons and threw it open and spat on the floor. Black women danced with white men. White women danced with black men. Rutherford was of a mind to pull his pistol.

Tony Thumbs extinguished his lamps. He put out his hand and asked his monkey for their winnings. He told him to stay on the door.

Baz perched on a big empty telegraph spool outside the saloon. The long fingers of his feet gripped wood where someone had carved the outline of a naked woman.

Tony Thumbs stepped inside and located Rutherford. He tapped the little shoulder, and when Rutherford turned to face him, the rolled twenty was held in offering. "I didn't intend to take it," Tony Thumbs said. "I was just testing tendency. Some local lawmen will shut down an honest game of monte."

Rutherford furrowed his brow. He said, "What in the Devil Anse are you talking about?"

"My name is Tony Sharpley," Tony Thumbs said. "I manage stage talent, the big variety, and before I send my best acts to an untested town, as I will soon be doing here with Max and Beatrice, I always visit first and gauge the authorities." He pulled a thick card from his breast pocket and handed it over. It read:

TONY SHARPLEY

PRODUCER, VARIETY THEATRE OWNER

57 GREAT JONES STREET, NEW YORK

Rutherford noted again the missing thumb. Stump skin had healed in a white bubble. He looked up at the old man and read his eyes.

A passing miner teetered and knocked into Rutherford with his hip. The lawman drew back and threw a straight right to the testicles, doubling the drunk, before he came round with the left and spilled him to the floor.

"Sweet Mary Magdalene," Tony Thumbs said. "You, sir, are a pugilist of the noblest variety."

Rutherford neither smiled nor came out of his stance.

"Allow me to buy you a drink," Tony Thumbs said.

He did so, after they'd evicted two men from their barstools. Tony Thumbs told Rutherford how delighted he was that

Keystone had a chief of police like him, a man not looking to bust up an honest game of monte, a man who liked to play a little himself. "I cherish a town like Keystone," Tony Thumbs said. "Dearly do I love a town where working men can spend their hard-earned money as they see fit."

Sam was behind the counter. He poured the men their second and gave the nod to Chesh Whitt at the end of the bar.

Chesh walked the long way to the storeroom door and swung through. He gave the earlobe-pull signal to a young actor who'd been put on the door. Folks had started to refer to the secret game of poker therein as the Ashwood Wobbler. Abe had coined the term when he tired of shimming a loose corner leg on the cheap ashwood table.

The young man knocked his knuckles against the door in rhythm with the code he'd been shown. Inside, Goldie ceased her target practice and left twelve cards in the corkboard. The men sat up straight and watched her unbolt the lock. When she cracked it open, they all heard his words.

"Tiny is at the bar."

Goldie took up a velvet satchel from the table. She opened it and brought out a pendant necklace. The cut glass was polished high to look like a big emerald diamond. She pushed it down between her breasts.

Back at the bar, Sam positioned himself so that he was in Rutherford's line of sight.

Goldie approached him with a tray of empty tumblers in her hand. She tucked herself at counter's end, set the tray on the bar, and called, "Samuel, six more." He came over and poured. She leaned across so that she was close to him. She whispered gibberish. Her breasts pressed hard on the bartop.

Rutherford looked to the breasts immediately. They transfixed him. He nodded mechanical-like at the story Tony Thumbs spun.

"The more I think about it," Tony Thumbs said, "the more July fourth seems a splendid day for Max and Beatrice to arrive." He wrote the date on a fresh business card, *fourth day of July*, and next to it he wrote *Mercurio's arrival*. Rutherford half-listened and smiled and took the card, staring all the while at the perfect full skin of Goldie Toothman's cleavage.

She yanked forth the necklace and let it glint ever so quick in the lamplight. Sam took it and put it in his pocket, just as she'd shown him, and she whispered, with her lips forming carefully the words, "Abe said to look at it through your jeweler's lens before you put it in the safe."

Rutherford had so long been around liars and cheats and the tellers of other men's secrets that he was amply skilled in the art of lip-reading. He tried once more to listen to the man he knew as Tony Sharpley. "Yeah," he said, looking at the business card. "July the fourth is splendid." It was a word he'd never before used. *Splendid*. It sounded funny coming from his mouth. He looked up from the card to find Goldie Toothman between himself and Tony, her cleavage now at his shoulder.

"Rutherford," she said. "I've been meaning to apologize

for my behavior at Fred Reed's place a month ago." Now she brushed against him, and she made her eyes heavy too. "I drove you to act the way you did by starting trouble myself. I'm working on my language now."

"That's good," Rutherford managed. "Vulgar tongue don't belong in no woman's mouth."

"You're not so bad Rutherford," she said, and she leaned in and kissed him on the cheek and walked away.

Munchy stood by the stage and watched. He followed her. He figured if she'd plant one on the smallest man in town, she might plant one on the biggest too.

Rutherford just sat on his stool and looked at the business card in his hand. He was too stunned to watch Goldie go.

They were playing it just as she and Abe had envisioned and written on paper and spoken in whisper and with volume both—they were playing it like they'd practiced.

And, as was their custom, all were playing it as if Abe was seated at the Ashwood Wobbler. He wasn't.

He was clear up the hill.

*

Inside his mother's empty boarding house, he sat in a chair at the head of the long kitchen table, conversing in a pleasant manner with Mr. Ladd the God-fearing chaste Virginian, the only boarder to be had.

The young man was explaining, in over-enunciated pronouncements, why it was that the anti-saloon league would sweep away every sinner in every town like Keystone.

"Isn't but one Keystone," Abe said.

"I'll give you that." Ladd pushed up his glasses and took a drink of his buttermilk.

Abe took a drink of his own and listened to his stomach squeal. He couldn't remember when he'd last drunk buttermilk.

Mice scurried in the rooms above them, where Sallie slept with little Ben beside her and Agnes read by candlelight.

Out in the second house, Al Baach put together a peculiar pair of shoes.

Mr. Ladd noted a strange tang to his milk. He coughed. He drank some more.

Through the window, the sun's impossible remains cast against a moon yet eclipsed, and the two men sat inside a radiant and blood-red room.

Abe took note of the thick white droplets hung up in the man's pathetic mustache. He wished Ladd would take a swipe with the back of his hand, but it was not to be. As he'd been trained, the young man took up his napkin, made it a tight triangle, and dabbed the remnants care-fully away. Abe looked past him then at the big floor clock. The minute hand was stubborn. It stuck and pulsed immobile.

The roar was in his head again.

A heavy-framed map of the United States dropped from the wall, its big glass square cracking in two upon landing. For thirty years, it had hung by a nail next to the pie safe.

Oswald Ladd jumped at the sound. He looked to the split-glass map. "Gracious," he said. "How does that occur?"

Abe watched him swallow and dab. "You don't have much of an Adam's apple do you Mr. Ladd?" he said.

Ladd released the empty tumbler. He'd been careful not to slice his lip on the rim's chip. He said, "I beg your pardon?"

"You'll not be pardoned by me sir." Abe did the math in his head. Ladd had begun to drink his buttermilk at ten past one. Now it was twenty-three past one. He guessed the little man would be asleep by half past.

In the kitchen, just after midnight, Abe had dropped in a hardy dose of muskroot, valerian, maypop, and opium, ground fine as ash. A Tony Thumbs custom powder, guaranteed reliable.

He looked again to the big clock. A little carved mahogany swallow perched at its peak. Its wings seemed to move, and Abe shut his eyes and said, "Tell me again how people pass the time where you're from."

Ladd had begun to sweat at the brow. "They don't pass it Mr. Baach. They wring from it the blood of Christ."

"They do, do they?" Abe regarded the other man's white dinner plate. A fly lighted upon the hinge of a chicken bone. "And how does everybody get by without whiskey or beer?"

"I don't comprehend your question's meaning."

Abe sighed. For him, one of life's most tiresome realities was a conversationalist with no sense of honesty. He moved on. "You say you believe a business with a no-negro policy is better?"

"I believe it is what I am accustomed to."

"And you don't want me to teach you any cards?" He produced a deck from nowhere and fanned them next to his plate.

Ladd smiled. His blood was beginning to run hot with that ole good-time muskroot-valerian-maypop-opium-buttermilk punch. "I once played setback," he said.

"You did, did you?"

Ladd nodded. Loose as a goose.

"And tell me one more time why you picked this house to board in."

"I'd heard tell of your brother's vision." His speech had ceased its enunciation. He thought. "Too, this house needed God's touch more than most."

Abe said, "I'll give you that."

Ladd's head sagged. His mouth was open.

Abe left the cards alone and looked at him straight. "I do have a question for you about the birth of Jesus Christ," he said.

Ladd tried to perk. He worked his lips. "Please," he said.

"In particular, I'd like to know something about the three kings."

Ladd nodded, drawn despite his drowsy state toward conversion of the wicked.

"How is it," Abe went on, "that those three kings arrived

there?" He pointed a finger. "How did they come to be right there under your dinner plate?"

And Ladd drooled on his chicken bones and lifted his plate and saw there, underneath, perfectly aligned, the king of spades, the king of clubs, and the king of diamonds. He laughed through his nose before he dropped the plate back and let his head roll the way of his eyes, toward a fireworks borealis in the blackest night his skull had ever known.

Abe watched Ladd lean slow and then capitulate all the way to the floor with a dead man's thud.

The room key was in the first pants pocket he checked.

He stacked the dishes in the sink before he collected the limp little man and climbed the stairs, toting him to his room like a father carries a child, Ladd's neck against one forearm, his kneebacks against the other.

Abe was able to unlock the door without setting him down.

He lay him on the made bed.

He struck a kitchen match on his thumb and lit an old lamp. The glass chimney was smutted gray at the mouth. It illuminated the man's desk, where empty papers had been stacked precise and the capped glass inkwell was half full. The dip pen beside it was gold.

Abe opened a drawer and found another stack of paper, this one marked in Ladd's fine scrawl. He lifted the dog-eared cumulation of words and set to reading.

Ladd was writing a book.

He'd marked through five titles before he came to the one he wanted:

HISTORY OF KEYSTONE WEST VIRGINIA
OR THE
SODOM AND GOMORRAH OF TODAY

Abe laughed. He turned over the first and read the second, a page of notes.

Trent is present Mayor. Also owner of Alhambra and a timber outfit and mine and is financially interested in several enterprises.

Rutherford chief of police. Often beastly drunk, as are most.

Fred Reed, jonah negro. Owner of social club where all mix and drink on Sabbath.

Council is the postmaster, a pharmacist, a Russian Jew, a negro doctor, and a negro newspaper owner.

He turned to the third and then the fourth page, where the writing became fuller and more boisterous, the handwriting still controlled.

How long before a Ku Klux Klan is organized here to rid the place of low-class colored men who have authority over the white man?

Abe thought it a strange notion—the Klan in Keystone. He flipped pages and read passages, their fervor increasing with accumulation.

Those that recognize the workings of the Almighty Father are wondering how soon he will rise in his wrath and destroy the town of Keystone as he did Sodom of old. Some great calamity will befall the place, for wickedness has reigned here so long.

Abe laughed again. He'd known the first time he saw the man that a slate or two was loose.

He studied the loops of Ladd's *l*s and *es*, the snake tails of his *g*s. He set down the stack and looked again to the open drawer, where a Holy Bible of fine brown leather remained. He took it up and noted the bulge at its center. He opened it to find a collection of letters.

Each was from Ladd's father. Each was penned on official paper stock of the Virginia General Assembly. In the most recent, he'd written:

I am sorry to hear of the shooting of the young Baach. It will always be this way for those who speak the truth. We will always be in the sights of the wicked. You must stay now and find a new method with which to reach the sinners of Keystone. You must spread the message of our prohibitionist cause to the vile places of the lesser Virginia. You must be steadfast in gaining advantage for us in the purchase of the property. If I am ever to convince Old Man Hood to sell us his land for less than others are offering, you must aid me in finding how, lest we lose our chance to build the movement there.

"I'll be damn," Abe said.

He thought.

He studied further the handwriting of the younger Ladd.

He set a sheet of lined paper on the desk. He took up the gold pen and dipped it in the ink. He wrote:

Dearest Father,

The brother of young Baach has returned to Keystone. He is the nearest man I've yet encountered to what might resemble a second coming of our Lord Jesus Christ. He will work out the sale of the land with Mr. Hood.

There was a creak from the hall floorboards and then a knock at the door. He lifted the pen mid-stroke on the spine of a capital *S*. He did not move.

Agnes put her mouth to the keyhole. "Uncle Abe?" she whispered.

He let her in.

When she asked why Mr. Ladd was asleep like he was, Abe told her, "Because I dumped a powder in his buttermilk."

"Why?"

"Because I suspected he was up to no good."

"And was he?"

"Yes."

He checked his watch and told her he was a little short on time. He asked if there was something in particular he could help her with.

"Entertainment," she answered.

"How do you mean?"

"Well," she said. The lantern flame waggled. Her face swallowed her eyes. "You been bringing in an awful many entertainers for the adults in the Bottom."

He nodded.

"Well. I wondered if you might bring in some meant for children."

And he knew as soon as she'd said it that he had failed her. "Aggie, that is a fine idea."

"I like puppets."

He put his hand on her shoulder. "Tomorrow morning, I will wire the best puppeteer I know. I'll offer him so much money he'll be bound for Keystone before you finish that book." He pointed to the thin volume of riddles in her clutch.

She looked down at her bookmark, a wood shim that baby Ben had scratched with a red wax crayon. "What if I finish it tomorrow?"

"Read slower."

She smiled. She looked at the stack of papers. "What's that?"

"A book Mr. Ladd is trying to write."

"Is it any good?"

"Not particularly."

"What's it about?"

He thought for a moment. "I don't know," he said. "Condemnation."

Agnes picked her nose a little bit. She said, "Sounds wearisome."

He nodded. "It's a twice-told tale at any rate."

She stood and went to the door. She stopped and put her hand on the knob and yawned. "Any magic in it?" she asked.

"Not a shadow."

Abe watched the door close. He listened to Ladd breathe.

He would finish the forged letter and hold it until the time was right, and in the meantime, he would pay his contact at the postal office to show him any letter Ladd brought in to mail home.

He returned everything to its precise place on the desk and in the drawers. He took off Ladd's shoes and eyeglasses, crossed the man's hands over his rib cage, and returned the key to its pocket.

He'd wait a day or two before he made mention of his slow conversion to Ladd's godly ways. When the time was right, he'd talk subtly of his family's wish to sell their land to a proper sort of man, a man of God.

*

At the long counter of the Chinese laundry, Abe and Tony Thumbs talked in hushed tones. Abe had asked after any puppeteers Tony might know back in Baltimore. Tony shook his head and said "Can't think of a one." Early morning light came diagonal through the transom window. Wyoming Street was quiet.

When Mr. Wan came back with their pressed shirts, they ceased their mumble.

He handed the shirts across the counter and smiled. "You talking about secrets," he said. "But I hear." He had only bottom teeth. He wore all black, as was his custom.

Abe noted the black cap, nearly identical to that of his father. He said, "Wan, you got a Lithuanian Jew for a head tailor?"

"You talking about puppets. I hear. I have a cousin."

Abe was peeling off a dollar for the wash. "He a puppeteer?" He gave over the money.

"The best." Mr. Wan had saved every handbill and news-paper clipping his sister had sent him over the years. He kept them pressed in a pictorial book of the world's rivers. "He cost big money."

"What's his name?" Tony asked.

"Tong." He held up a finger for them to wait and walked again to the back.

"You heard of him?" Abe asked.

Tony said he hadn't.

Mr. Wan returned and spread open the heavy book to a marked page about the Yellow River. A handbill loosed from the vise of the spine. Abe recognized the artwork straight-away—same printmaker who'd fashioned his Professor

Goodblood sample. *Tong the Towering!* it read. *Special Children's Engagement. Saturday Matinee at Stuyvesant.*

"I'll be damn," Abe said.

Tony Thumbs frowned. "He's out of New York?"

"He's in New York for one year," Mr. Wan said. "He's born in Los Angeles." He raised his hand up over his head. "He's very tall, speaks good American." He did not tell them of his cousin's propensity toward tardiness and being out of touch.

Abe looked at the small black-and-white drawing on the handbill. It depicted a hook-nosed clown in a sugarloaf hat. Inside the eye of the clown was a man.

Mr. Wan tapped his fingernail on the drawing. "Best Punch and Judy man in the world," he said. "Best sleight of hand."

"Well," Abe said. "Let's get him on the books."

Mr. Wan stood for a moment with his hands on the counter. He'd imagined too clearly the face of his cousin, and this had brought upon him unwanted memories of his uncle and his father and the smell of set fire and the shrill call of terrible laughter and the hands of his mother covering his eyes and pulling him inside where she made a sound no child should have to hear.

Abe watched the man lose himself to what was in his head. He said, "Wan, I need to know where to wire him."

"Booking fee," said Mr. Wan. "Twenty dollar."

HIDE THE WHISKEY AND BEND THE KNEE

June 22, 1910

Sallie Baach's biscuit gravy had the immaculate texture of something neither liquid nor solid, a savory treacle only possible at the hands of a woman who knew how and when to use her bacon drippings. She carried the biscuits and gravy outside in a chafing dish with a bright nickel finish. She'd spit-polished it the night before with a cut piece of old cotton diaper.

Important men required such reflective chafing dishes, and it was important men who now remarked on the biscuit gravy's texture and unearthly flavor. They sat on wicker throne chairs and chewed slow, remarking on the absurd relative flatness of Hood House land. Harold Beavers shaded his brow with a marble-board ledger book and surveyed the space between houses.

The goosegrass was no more. A week prior, Abe had bought an Acme lawnmower with four cutting blades. He'd paid five dollars for it to Cheshire Whitt, who'd won the mower at the Union Club card table.

Out front of the main house were parked two black Oldsmobile Runabouts. They'd come in on a flatcar from Cincinnati two days before, their arrival orchestrated to mark the Beavers' return on the state's forty-seventh birthday.

Sunlight refracted in the chafing dish, and Sallie squinted as she laid plates on a big lawn table. Al had fashioned it by bolting a de-hinged barn door on two sawhorses. It was covered in a white bedsheet.

Harold Beavers lowered his ledger book and sat down. "Some piece of hill plateau," he said. He unscrewed the cap on his flask and poured its contents in his coffee.

Al Baach sat across from him, Abe to Al's right. Rufus Beavers and Mayor Trent sat at the heads of the table.

Al stretched his bad leg, his boot sole pressed against the sawhorse, and he thought of how very strange it was that two months before, his oldest boy's coffin had sat atop the very same prop.

"Mrs. Baach," Harold Beavers said, "these biscuits is savory."
She thanked him kindly.

Harold was going to run for the House of Delegates. Never mind he hadn't lived in the district, much less the state, for twenty years. He had an address at the Alhambra. He had a new young wife who'd once won a Bathing Beauty Pageant in Rehoboth Beach, Delaware. She was still in Florida, awaiting his summons. He told her he had business to attend to before she graced his boyhood home. He didn't tell her the business, a substantial portion of which was to throw a leg over every new whore in town.

Rufus Beavers thought his brother's fresh wife too young. She was less than half his age. He ate fast and dredged every inch of gravy he could. He watched his brother laugh and blow his nose. Once, Rufus had his own sights on the legislature, but that time was long past.

Harold Beavers' seated posture was bad and he wheezed at the chest. He craned his neck to watch Sallie's backside as she walked to the house where she'd manage the chocolate cake. When she was out of earshot, he said, "Let's us cut short the tittle-tattle and get something done."

Trent had no appetite. He said, "Democrats are surging. Mid-term will more than likely bring about a swing."

Rufus shook his head. "There's movement," he said. "But it's only the panhandles, and they been halfway there for a while anyhow."

Trent was not in agreement. "There's a Raleigh County man throwing money. Braxton too."

"Them two is preaching prohibition," Rufus said, "and any fucking Democrat who goes dry is a loser."

It was the truth. Republican or Democrat, no dry candidate would ever carry the black belt, or any county for that matter, for temperance was not the workingman's way.

Harold chewed with his mouth open. He looked at Al. He asked, "Is there any Jew that will court the prohibitionist candidate?"

"No."

"How many Jews in Keystone now?"

Al thought. "Three hundred?"

Abe looked at his food while he ate. He'd begun to wonder by then if it was Harold Beavers who'd pulled the trigger on Jake, for no other had the man's accuracy from long distance. And, from what Abe could gather, the Beavers had lit out for Florida the day after the shooting on Buzzard Branch. But here the man was, and though Abe listened to him close, he heard no guilt in his voice. Though he looked at him careful, he saw no culpability in his eyes.

Harold took up his knife. He put it in the jar of apple butter and commenced to spread his toast. "How many niggers?" he asked.

"Thousand," Trent said. "Give or take."

Harold laughed wheezy. "This has become some kind of place." He'd heard the Baaches were rearing a half-black child. He aimed to get a look at the boy before day's end. "I remember when there wasn't any road or rail for twenty miles." He waved at the ridges around them with the butter knife. "I climbed from peak to post like a goat." He drank down his coffee and set the mug back hard. "That's back when they used to call me Sneakup," he said. "Sometimes Harry." He laughed at the memory of his old good times. "Or they'd use my full moniker, you see. They'd say, 'Lookout! Here comes Sneakup Harry Beavers.'" He laughed harder and raised up the empty coffee mug and banged it back down as a gavel. "Order!" he shouted. "Circuit Judge

Rufus Beavers in session, kept in the black by way of his little brother, the newly minted delegate-elect from the county of McDowell, Sneakup Harry Beavers!"

Abe laughed genuine. The man had a way with words.

Harold took note of his enthusiasm. His good looks. "Boy, you've always had a smile that could sell used snuff, ain't you?"

Abe shrugged his shoulders.

"How many nicknames you had boy?" he asked.

"Oh," Abe said, "two or three." He wondered how many straight days Harold Beavers had been stewed. He knew the look of those eyes. He'd worn them himself and some-times still did.

Such eyes couldn't see through a ladder.

"Man needs three nicknames at a minimum," Harold said. A crow alighted on the high branch of a pitch pine and cawed. "What nickname was it they called your brother?" He pretended to search for a word. "Mary, was it? Nancy?"

Abe smiled. "Knot," he said.

Al cleared his throat. "Preacher. Some call Jake Preacher." He had his arms crossed over his belly. His black cap was sweat-stained in front.

Harold took out his tobacco and a paper and made a cigarette.

Abe said, "Why don't we speak on your purchase of this land."

"This boy has always been full up on the finest ideas," Rufus Beavers said.

Al stood and walked toward the sound of the children.

"You'll have to excuse Daddy," Abe said. "He's not yet come to peace with the transaction." He put his elbows on the table and leaned forward. He explained to the Beavers brothers the finer points of the transaction's time-line, which he and Henry Trent had been speaking on for weeks, alone in Trent's office, Rutherford having been excused each time. The price had already been negotiated. The closing date was set for Monday, July the fourth, the only day that both Mr. Hood and his lawyer could travel to Kimball for the transfer of deed. The name on the contract would be Rufus Beavers, and on the sixth day of July, a crew of builders would break ground. They'd stand alongside Harold Beavers and have their picture made for the paper, and the headline would proclaim that two things were coming: the Westward Addition and the ascending sixth district delegate-elect.

"It will be a fine affair," Harold said. He was getting itchy for town.

"Indeed." Rufus eyed the second house and imagined it as campaign headquarters. He looked beyond it to the bones of a madman's chapel and imagined its foundation laid across with dynamite and lit by a lengthy wick. *Boom*, he wished to intone aloud, but he refrained. He shut his eyes and saw the Westward Addition in full swing. He saw switch-backed roads, paved, leading to terraced homes, redbrick foursquares with milk-skinned children playing out front. The children made gleeful sounds. None were colored.

None had crossed an ocean to end up in the Westward Addition.

Trent said, "It will all come together nicely," though he wondered at the very sound of the words if it was so.

Al strode back toward the table, his weight on his cane.

Harold Beavers wrote dates in his ledger book and slammed it shut. "Why in the hell ain't we signing papers today?" he asked.

Al sat down stiff. "The lawyer of Mr. Hood finds mistake on surveyor's plat," he said. "You will have ten acres more than was known, to the east." He pointed up the mountain. The men looked where he pointed.

Abe could scarcely keep back a smile. His Daddy had told the lie they'd rehearsed, and he'd done it convincingly. The truth was that the lawyer had already gotten the papers in order, and the sale had already been made. The buyer was never to have been Rufus Beavers. The buyer was in fact a newly retired politician. He was a prohibitionist preacher and friend of Mr. Hood. The owner of the land on which they now sat and dined was a man who'd never set foot there, a man with unquestioning faith in his son's written word. He was Oswald Ladd Sr., smiling signer of power-of-attorney forms, father of the frail boarder Abe had seen off to Virginia the very day before, deed and documents in hand, telling him, "Just give us two weeks to clear off and it's yours." Abe had groomed the junior Ladd for a month, and the man had boarded the train grinning, content in the knowledge that his Daddy was the next owner of Hood House and its acreage, that together they would draw up plans for a prohibitionist temple of godly converters who would settle on the mountain, look down upon Sodom, and configure their cleansing of the three thousand lost.

Up the ridge, a turkey vulture soared. The Beavers brothers watched it, happy at the thought of more land.

Harold imagined the bird exploding mid-flight.

Rufus wondered about the status of the chocolate cake.

The children could be heard in the trees at yard's edge. Baby Ben made a squirrel call and Agnes answered.

Harold Beavers said, "When do we get to sit and turn over some cards?" He'd been playing more as of late, and he was looking to separate somebody from his bank-roll, preferably Abe Baach or the big city marks he'd roped.

"Abe and I have worked all that out," Trent said. He resented having to repeat what he'd already told Harold the night before, but he was accustomed to the man's lack of memory. "Chicago Phil is due back in Keystone either today or tomorrow." He eyed Abe for confirmation and was given such in a nod. "Abe has kept him on the line by way of enticement."

"What the fuck does that mean?" Harold Beavers said.

"Means he's in love with Rose Cantu," Abe told him. "Goldie's best-looking girl. He couldn't stay gone less you castrated him."

They laughed a little.

"It isn't only that," Abe said. "I've been in his ear about who plays the Oak Slab. I told him Little Donnie is the best there is, and he already thinks he can beat the boy."

"Why does he think such a thing?" Harold was getting irritable. Thirsty. He smacked his throat where a mosquito fed.

Trent put his hands at table's edge. "I told you all this last night," he said. "They partnered at Baach's table and the boy pretended to lose while Abe won." Trent had begun to worry that Harold's reckless ways might corrupt their plan. It was best to keep him in the dark on finer points.

"I'm going to rope him for a week back at our table," Abe said, "let him go up a grand or so, and then send him and the others to the Oak Slab on Independence Day."

Trent nodded. "I've got their invites pressed and a row of third-floor rooms on reserve. Tickets to Mercurio's opening night too."

"Phil's a magic enthusiast," Abe said.

Harold shook his head. He said, "And you going to treat that ole magic enthusiast like a king, are you?"

Rufus grew tired of it. "We'll treat him like the goddamned hero of San Juan Hill if we have to Harold," he said. "The man's carrying in property that will bankroll your sorry run and then some."

Harold held up his hands in compliance and said, "Simmer down brother." He pointed at Abe. "It's him who I want to play anyhow."

Abe looked straight at him. "Soon as Phil and the others push off," he said, "you can come on over and sit at the Wobbler."

"The what now?"

"It's the name of Abe's table," Trent said. "Rutherford aims to play too."

The screen door on the main house slapped hard against the jamb and Sallie came on with the cake. Beyond thank-yous, they were quiet as she doled out wedges the size of axe heads.

They ate and grunted to express their pleasure at the dark ambrosial icing.

Harold wondered if it would be improper to ask for a little brandy in his after-supper coffee. She was gone before he could. "What about this championship fight?" he said.

"What about it?" Rufus did not care to speak on Jack Johnson, a man he despised. He'd let his money talk for him. He planned to bet upwards of five hundred dollars on Jim Jeffries.

"Just more money to be made," Trent said.

"I hear Fred Reed is having a big ole party at the Union Club." Harold's teeth were smeared brown. Black crumbs fell from his lips.

"He's running a special telegraph wire for it," Trent said. "Hauling in French wine."

Rufus scoffed. "Thinks foamy wine'll win him a council seat does he?"

Harold finished his cake and wiped his mouth with the back of his hand. "July fourth shapin up to be one busy day. Best be sure your police is ready to put down any sore-loser niggers when Jeffries lays Johnson on the canvas."

"No need for that," Trent said. "They'll have their money on Jeffries."

"Who will?"

"All of em. Most anyway. They ain't fools when it comes to a smart bet. No colored man can beat Jim Jeffries." Trent looked at his associates. They'd been in Florida too long. He said, "Fred Reed plans to put two hundred dollars on white."

The children hollered and laughed in the woods. The hider had been sought and found.

Little Ben waddled quick across the cut weed lawn toward the house. Agnes followed. "Well hide the whiskey and bend the knee boys," Harold Beavers said. "God's children comin this way."

They paid him no mind. Children had no use of men like those at the table. Agnes leapt from grass to back stone step. She glanced in their direction and let the door settle quiet behind her.

Each man aimed his ear then at the sound of an approaching automobile. Its engine roared louder than the Oldsmobiles that had struggled up the same rough path that morning.

"I believe that might be Phil now," Abe said. He stood.

The other men did not, though they turned their heads to see a top-down vehicle of Persian red cresting the hill.

It was piloted by a slick-haired man in a gray lounge suit. Beside him was Tony Thumbs, monkey Baz in his lap. They picked up speed on the flat and tore a straight line at the lawn's big table.

Now the men stood, for they sensed they might be run over otherwise.

Ten yards off, the driver cut his wheel and mashed his brake pedal. The white spokes of his wheels seemed nearly to bend. The gold-gilded headlamps and grill flashed like a smile, and cut grass spat on the tablecloth.

"Good Lord in Heaven," Trent said. He'd tripped on his chair and hit the ground.

The slick-haired man cut the engine and stepped from his seat. He was sixty years old but had the frame of a man much younger. He wore no hat. He smiled and breathed in deep through his nose. "Ah," he said. "That is real air."

Tony Thumbs emerged slow, his old joints sticking. He made a beeline for the evergreens to relieve his troubled bladder. Baz rode on his shoulder bone.

When he'd finished his dramatic inhalations, the driver stepped toward the stunned lot of standing men. He thrust out his big hand. "Phil," he said. "Pleasure." He shook the hand of Rufus first, then Harold, then Al.

Last was Henry Trent, who rubbed at his newly injured hip. He narrowed his eyes. He said, "You're the man we've heard so much on but never yet seen."

"Well, here I am," the man said, "and Master John Goodfellow has already found lodging in the parlor of sweet Rose Cantu." He situated his groin. "And she is still bright as sunshine and as pure as dew."

Harold Beavers only frowned.

It was quiet for only a moment before Phil made a declaration. "I've got a case of rye whiskey in the rumble trunk." He turned and walked brisk to procure it. He was having the time of his life already. Playing Chicago Phil on a West Virginia mountain was a welcome departure for him, a man who'd spent most of his acting life soliloquizing Shakespeare in the decrepit Old Drury. "Who's thirsty?" he shouted.

Abe smiled. Tony Thumbs had been right again. The man introducing himself as Chicago Phil was a veritable ham. Jim Fort was his true name. Telling big-money lies was his momentary game.

Harold Beavers liked rye. He watched the man procure it from the rack. He regarded the vehicle. "That is some automobile," he said.

"Chambers-Detroit," Phil said. "Touring."

"What's your top speed?"

"Thirty-eight miles per hour." His smile widened. He set the case on the table. He pried it open with a bowie knife he wore on his hip.

"You have a last name?" Rufus asked.

Phil gave no reply, but instead uncorked the rye. He drank from the bottle and handed it to Harold. "Yes," he said, "there is ample legroom in the touring. I won that pretty thing at a basement game in Cincinnati. She's worth thirty-five hundred new."

Now Tony Thumbs stepped from the trees and went to each man, his hand extended in greeting. "Not to worry," he said. "Didn't spill a drop on it." Baz bobbed his head and offered his own little hand for the shaking.

Harold did not accept. "Hell zounds," he said. "Carnival come to town." He took a second snort from the bottle and passed it to Abe.

Tony Thumbs looked square at Trent as he shook his hand and said, "Pleasure. I've met your chief of police and admired his gumption."

Trent nodded.

"Wonderful town you've got here. Wide open." Tony was careful not to lay it on too thick. "Couldn't stay away. Those Cinder Bottom girls can stiffen up even the shriveled old-stagers like me." He winked at Harold Beavers, who gave no expression in return. Tony went on. "Max and Beatrice are all lined up. I've just finalized their arrangements on Tuesday. They'll arrive on the fourth, five PM train."

"Good," Trent said.

The rye made its way around with all but Al imbibing. He'd limped off to fetch two more chairs.

"You say you won that vehicle?" Harold was fond of the particular burn of this strange rye whiskey. He poured it in his coffee mug generously.

Phil smiled. "I had kings full of fours," he said. He noted the children as they peeked from behind a window curtain. He cleared his throat. "I gather from Abe that all of you gentlemen are aces at the table." He looked to Rufus. Then Trent. "I gather too that the Oak Slab is the finest and most-established game in a hundred miles or more."

Trent said, "Thirteen years that game has run without stoppage."

Phil whistled his admiration and clasped his hands on the table. "I'd sure like to sit and play when I finish at the Baaches."

"You ever play any cards in south Florida?" Harold asked.

"Well, sure. And on top of it, I won my first clean grand in Bay Biscayne."

"Is that right?"

"Yes sir. That was back when I still kept my monies in a bank, fool as I was." He laughed. He noted the Beavers' nod of approval. "Anyway, back then I'd been depositing my table winnings at this fancy bank on Flagler Street, a hundred or more dollars a day, every day, for a number of months, and one particular Friday, as I was leaving, the bank president asked for a word. He was a small, sickly man, but his office was beautiful. Had a chandelier in there I'd still like to get my hands on."

The men listened.

"So we sit down and he asks me how it is I'm able to deposit like I do—wants to know what line of work I'm in. So I tell him. I'm a professional gambler. He says to me, 'Don't gamblers lose now and then?' I said they didn't if they knew their business. He said 'No man knows his business that well.' I said I'd prove to him that I never lost a bet. I said I'd bet him right then and there two hundred dollars that at noon the next day, I'd come back to his beautiful banker's office, and his balls would be spiked all over, like sweetgum seeds."

Each man laughed then. Abe especially enjoyed the tale, as he'd been the one who told a version of it originally on a late saloon night. Jim Fort had been tickled by the story, asked if he might use it in his role as Chicago Phil. "By all means," Abe had told him.

Phil went on. "So the banker, a real square paper, he can't pass up what he knows is impossible, so he says, 'You're on,' and shakes my hand." Now he had them hooked. He was talking fast enough to keep them on the line and slow enough not to lose them. "Next day, I go back. Accompanying me is the richest son of a bitch in Miami at that time, a man who'd just as soon gamble on cockroach races and back-alley nickel pitches as he would a title fight. We step in the office and close the door and I tell the bank president to drop his trousers. He does so, red-faced, but content in the knowledge that his balls are round as they'd ever been. Still, he's got to prove it, so I step over to where he's standing half-naked under that big gleaming chandelier, and I reach over there between his puny thighs and cup those nuts in my hand, and the banker turns redder still, and across the room, the richest son of a bitch in Miami drops his head to his chest and takes out his billfold."

The Beavers brothers just sat there a moment. Henry Trent too.

"I'd bet that rich son of a bitch twelve hundred dollars that on Saturday at noon, I'd have a bank president's balls in my hand."

They slapped the table and roared, Harold especially. It was one of the finest tales he'd heard.

They emptied the bottle and uncorked another.

At two o'clock, Tony laid on the table a bottle of beer, a cigarette, and a match. He said he'd bet any takers his monkey could open the beer, drink it down, light the match, and smoke the cigarette in less than two minutes. The Beavers brothers inspected the bottle, and indeed it was tight-sealed with the new variety of crown cap. They each laid down ten.

At the sound of Tony's whistle, Baz leapt from his shoulder and bared his yellow teeth at the bottle. The men were startled by the length of his canines. His movements were newly quick. He used his middle incisors like a vise, tore off the cap and spat it in the grass, and sealing his lips around the bottle's neck, he pointed its bottom at the sky. His swallows were fast and consistent. It was empty in forty-nine seconds. He lit the match on his big toenail whilst already drawing on the butt. They'd not ever seen a body puff so swift, and when he'd finished he dropped it in the bottleneck hole.

Hiss.

The Beavers said it was the best ten dollars they'd spent.

Tony held Baz like a baby then, and the monkey went right to sleep. Tony took him to the car and held him there still, humming a made-up tune. He didn't like to see his little friend do the trick they'd dubbed the bottle-and-smoke, but Baz had long since known it by the time he came to Tony, and it had always proven stellar in the making of friends.

The men spoke on the rarity of the ladies of Fat Ruth Malindy's. They spoke on the Reno title fight and the current price of coal per short ton.

At half past four, the two men and a monkey departed, trailing dust. Phil shouted a verse as they rolled on: "Let's drink to our next meeting lads, nor think on what's atwixt!"

The other men leaned and slumped and watched them go. Rufus said, "Those fellas is somethin else."

"Climb in your chariot Rufus," Harold answered. "Let's us see who can lay off the brake longest into town."

Goldie was on her way up the hill as the Beavers came careening down. She hid herself behind a poplar tree and cringed at the sound of their vehicles.

When they'd passed, she went on.

She'd put Rebecca Staples and little Bob on the four o'clock to Princeton. She didn't know why, but she'd nearly cried as the train pulled away.

Now she came into the clearing out of breath. Her feet were tired and even the sound of Ben and Agnes couldn't lift the lilt at her middle. They exploded from the screen door in a burst of high-spirited calls and hinge-croak and wood-slap, and Goldie paused to watch them.

The cut grass seemed somehow wrong.

Sallie Baach was at the big table, stacking dishes. She leaned across it to fetch a butter knife and her back seized up, a charge coursing the muscles to the right of her spine.

Goldie did not move from her anonymous spot at woods' edge. She watched Sallie stiffen and go still. She recognized the posture of pain from all those years her Daddy had struck the same pose, but still, Goldie did not budge. She'd not offer assistance with the dishes or the infirmities of a body gone bad. She'd not engage Sallie in any sort of talk about the shame of leaving Keystone, of giving up Hood House land. They'd started such a conversation in the near-emptied barn two weeks prior, and Goldie had ignored Sallie then, listening instead to the soft bursts of wind from the long nostrils of Snippy the mediocre mare. Goldie could still lose herself in the darkwater eye of a horse, could still see things there. The last thing she'd heard Sallie say was that the world's compass was set straight to hell, and no one, once there, could walk back out.

Now Goldie stood across the cut grass bald from the older woman, who'd straightened and turned to face her. It was quiet, not a crow to be found on any pine branch. They regarded each other before Sallie carried her load of smeared dishware back to the house she'd soon have to vacate.

How old she seemed then to Goldie.

BET YOUR LAST COPPER ON JACK

July 4, 1910

Before the sun rose, Cheshire Whitt had already taken care of the coupe. He'd already laid the *McDowell Times* Independence Day edition at the three doors in town that mattered most. Trent and the Beavers would awaken to the following headline: *Boilermaker Jeffries or Galveston Giant Johnson—Who Will Wear the Crown?* The article that followed was dry and bereft of humorous insight or mention of racial superiority. Chesh's father had insisted on such a tone. "No need to salt what's already boiling," he'd said. It was more than money riding on this fight.

There was a quarter-page advertisement below the fold inviting all to come to the Union Social and Political Club, where a special telegraph line had been installed for round-by-round returns direct from ringside in Reno. Adjacent to this was a smaller advertisement proclaiming the arrival of the Sublime One, Max Mercurio, with his Beautiful Beatrice.

Seats were already sold out for the opening-night show on July 6th.

On his way from the Alhambra to the bridge, Chesh saw, from a distance, the Baach family boarding the early morning train. The platform on either side of them was dark, but the porters had laid out two lanterns by which to load, and they lit the Baaches like footlights. Al carried little Ben. Sallie had an arm around Agnes. Sam stood motionless, nothing in his hands. Chesh regarded his friend. He knew Sam was loath to leave.

Abe had forced his younger brother to go with the rest of them. "It's your duty," he'd told him.

The porters worked fast at the baggage car, lifting suitcases and shoving at iron-bottom trunks.

Before they boarded, the Baaches looked up at the hills they couldn't see.

Agnes cried, a quiet whimper. No puppeteer had ever come to frighten and delight.

Chesh Whitt watched them step from platform to stair. He listened to the final boarding call. His pocketwatch told him it was a minute past five.

In less than twelve hours, his role would commence, and he wondered if Abe and Goldie's plan might actually play out. Regardless, his job was easy. "Start a ruckus, whether Johnson loses or wins," they'd told him. The beckoning of authority by way of drunken foolishness was a vocation with which Chesh was familiar. This time would no doubt prove different.

But Chesh Whitt knew one thing. The white fighter

would never best Johnson, and his own celebratory whoops would come genuine.

*

At quarter past five, the sun still not up, Little Donnie stood in the back of Baach's storeroom. He unlatched the steel arm and lifted it. The heavy door swung slow and quiet. Abe had oiled the hinges.

In the alley was Rutherford. He stepped inside carrying a lantern. Neither spoke as they moved to the barrel. Little Donnie lifted it and Rutherford crouched, swinging his lantern for a better look. Just as the boy had said, the floor safe bolts were no more. He'd undone them an hour before, as he'd told Trent and Rutherford he would.

They locked eyes and nodded, and he set back the barrel.

He pointed to a low shelf behind him. Rutherford held out his lantern.

Little Donnie shoved aside a sack of coffee to reveal a six-foot length of steel chain. The links were a half inch thick. Hitch hook on both ends.

He pointed to the corner, and Rutherford aimed his light at a four-foot warehouse hand-truck with a long steel nose.

When the time came, rolling away the safe would take no time at all.

They peeked from behind the shelves and stepped together to the pantry where the card-players-only piss bucket sat. Inside the tiny room, it smelled of ammonia and mold. Against the wall was an old Western washer with a broken crankshaft. Little Donnie lifted off the top and Rutherford swung his lamp. Tucked in the bottom corner were two .41 caliber double Derringers. Little Donnie opened the breech of each to show they were loaded and Rutherford noted the *S&W* on the rim. Guns tucked back in place, they stepped quiet from the piss pantry.

Back behind the shelves, they locked eyes and nodded once more, and Rutherford walked out the open door.

Little Donnie relatched the heavy arm and turned the key.

He let out the deepest breath he could ever remember taking.

*

The fight wire was spooled and ready on a temporary short pole by noon. Already it was eighty degrees or more, and men stood in the side yard of the Union Social and Political Club, some of them hatless and crowding under a wide tarp. It hung at an angle between the building and the chunk of brick chimney at yard's middle. Beneath it, the telegraph operator sat at her relay board and tested the key spring. She fanned herself with a ledger book.

Taffy Reed surveyed from the open side-doorway. He estimated seventy men, most of them toting big money. Two-thirds were black. *Proper coloreds*, his father called them. The white men present were mostly politicians, there to glad-hand and get votes in the upcoming interim. They'd leave long before round one's bell.

Two more police officers stood with their hands crossed

at opposite corners of the yard. They were new on the force, former coke-yarders who'd come up from North Carolina two years before. Black men whom Taffy did not trust. The tall one was missing an eye. The short one had the chest of a woman. Fred Reed was paying them overtime to watch for trouble. "Any black man hollers too loud when Johnson wins, you shut him up," Fred had said. "Remind him he claim to've bet on white."

A man in overalls approached, pushing an iron-wheeled railroad dolly strapped with two crates of champagne. They were last-minute extras shipped in special from Norfolk.

Fred waved the man up the ramp fashioned from two-by-fours. When he'd told him where to put the crates and paid him his tip, Fred stepped to the open doorway and stood beside his son. Together, they watched as councilman J. T. Whitt stepped into the yard. He wore a tall Knox hat and tan bluchers. He smiled and nodded hello and asked each man he greeted, "Newspaper still to your liking?"

Fred leaned on his boy. "He knows he can't win again, but here he is."

Taffy nodded.

"Man don't even take a drink," Fred said.

They watched J. T. Whitt shake the hand of Harold Beavers.

"Now that man," Fred said, pointing to Harold, "will win in a landslide." He laughed a little. Shook his head. "He knows *how* to win. Knows you got to be crooked as a bucket of fish hooks."

Taffy didn't laugh. He'd heard that one before.

Fred put his arm around his boy. "And we right there in that bucket boy," he said. "We on the side that wins."

Taffy half-listened. He wanted to go play a few hands of seven-card stud before he sat at the Wobbler that afternoon. He knew he was the second-best poker player in Keystone, but he'd never played the likes of Abe Baach, never been allowed at the Oak Slab. The Alhambra main room may have changed its no-negro policy, but the Oak Slab never would. It had long since loosened formalities, ceasing employment of a dealer in 'o1, but no black man would ever be seated. The Ashwood Wobbler would be Taffy's turn at the table.

Harold Beavers too had his mind on poker, but still, he kept right on glad-handing, working his way across the dry yard. He handed out slugs of his Chokoloskee whiskey. He put his arm around half the men present. "Call me Harry," he said. He told several men how sharp he found their suits. To Mose Zaltzman, fat in a black tailcoat, he said, "Russia, that jacket is sharp as a rat's turd in a glass of buttermilk."

He'd had cards printed on quarter-inch stock, the following proclamation on the front:

VOTE FOR
HAROLD BEAVERS FOR
HOUSE OF DELEGATES

YOU WILL FIND MY NAME ON
THE REPUBLICAN TICKET AND YOUR VOTE
WILL BRING NOTHING BUT GOOD

Rufus and Trent sat on ladder chairs by the chimney chunk, the tarp low against their hats. They compared their leather-bound pipe cases. Trent's was velvet-lined. Rufus preferred satin. "Doesn't get stuck with crumbs," he said.

Trent couldn't get his mind off that morning's transaction, a sale at which he'd not been present. "So everything came off without a hitch you say?" His voice was pinched. His stomach was ailing him again.

"There was Old Man Hood's signature," Rufus said, pointing to his lap, "and there was mine." He'd met Goldie and the lawyer that morning at an office in Kimball, halfway to Welch. "The drive was more than pleasant," Rufus said. "Very few bad spots along the way." The road had finally been finished as far as Kimball, and it was the first time he'd tested his Oldsmobile at such distance.

He had not suspected for a moment that the lawyer was Mr. Taylor, the Wednesday regular at Fat Ruth Malindy's, happy to draw up false papers for the madam of the sweetest cathouse he'd ever seen. Old Man Hood's signature on the power of attorney was forged by Abe. Taylor had handled the true sale of the property just two weeks before.

"And you put the deed in the safe?"

"How many times are you going to ask me that question?"

Trent took out his watch. "I best head next door to welcome Phil and them others," he said. All men currently at the Oak Slab had been given notice of their impending eviction. They did not possess the city money of their coming replacements.

Rufus watched Taffy Reed carry a schoolroom blackboard from inside. It was the size of a front door. He set it against the bricks and laid out three lengths of chalk. The betting would be heavy.

Rufus cocked his head and studied the younger Reed's movements. He said, "You think this is all going to come off this evening?"

"How do you mean?" Trent had already stood and taken a step.

"You think Rutherford and my brother can do what they say they can?"

"I do."

"And you think Taffy Reed will sit pretty for it?" He still watched the young man where he stood at the blackboard, drawing columns with exceptional straightness.

"Taffy will never question Rutherford on a goddamn thing."

Rufus wondered if it was true. "And you think your Little Donnie has been both thorough and wholly forthright?"

"I know he has. I raised that pup."

Rufus coughed and snorted. Swallowed. He took off his hat and rubbed his head.

Trent didn't like the last-minute inquisition. "I'll say it again." He lowered his voice. "Rutherford saw it with his own eyes just this morning." He stared down at his old friend, who did not change his attitude. "The boy had unbolted the safe just like he told us."

"You don't think Abe might sniff something tonight?"

"So what if he does? He won't have any protection on hand. Nobody's packing a piece at his table—they frisk same as we do."

Across the way, Harold laughed too loud at his own joke.

Trent kept on. "You'll have eyes on the Oak Slab the whole time, and you'll have Munchy and barkeep and Talbert too."

"Fine lot."

"They know how to fire a gun don't they?"

Rufus said he supposed they did. "And you're still planning to meet this magic man and his gal at the station, despite all that's got to happen?"

"I am."

Rufus put away his pipe and crossed his legs. He looked up at the man with whom he'd built Keystone. "And Goldie?"

"What about her?"

Rufus kept on looking.

"Brought it on herself, didn't she?"

When Rufus didn't answer, Trent walked away.

*

For the first time in two months, the barroom of A. L. Baach & Sons Saloon was empty. Only Abe and Goldie sat at the bar. The stage was empty, its gaslights cold.

"Doesn't seem right," Abe said, "Sam not behind the bar." He recalled the day in April when he'd walked in on his brother like a ghost. "Saloon sharks won't know the difference—he never did stomp one dead." He thumbed a mug-bottom divot in the bar top.

Goldie held his other hand. "You did the right thing sending him off," she said.

He nodded his head. It was full up again with ache, strongest at the base of his neck, and his left ear rang on and off. The night before, as he'd practiced his card manipulations in front of a mirror, he'd shut his eyes against the ringing, and when he'd opened them again, he saw in the mirror his hands, precise and mechanical as they front- and back-palmed and passed and fanned and riffled. He looked down to see his true hands motionless against the dresser top, while in the mirror they kept at their furious routine. He shut his eyes and shook his head and looked again. In the mirror, they moved. In the flesh, at the end of his wrists, they were motionless as death.

Goldie squeezed his fingers. "Samuel belongs with your mother and Daddy," she said.

He nodded again. From his jacket pocket he took out a paper sleeve. He unfolded its little triangles and tipped back his head and poured the powder on the back of his tongue. He swallowed and made a face.

"Go down easier with a little milk," Goldie said.

He only smiled. The bitterness on his tongue nearly gagged him, but he'd found that Tony's headache powders worked fastest when administered in such a dry fashion. The old man had added a new ingredient, a thing called curare he'd procured in Guyana. He said it might numb the pain Abe suffered.

The mantel clock under the Lincoln lithograph read quarter past one.

"We'd better get ready," Abe said.

When they kissed, their eyes were open.

A knock came at the locked saloon door.

Abe cracked it open to find a tall Chinese man in a tan fedora and three-piece suit. "Abe Baach?" the man said, and he was taken aback. He recognized the face inside the saloon.

Abe didn't answer. He moved his hand to the small of his back.

"My name is Ah Tong," the man said. "My cousin is Gene Wan. I've come for the short-run puppet show."

"You're about three weeks too late." Abe looked beyond him, where men bunched in front of the restaurant and whistled at the ladies going by.

"I apologize for my tardiness," Ah Tong said. "I got in a little trouble the night I wired you my acceptance." His chin was squared and his eyes genuine. "Had to pass a little time in the pokey," he said. He'd cut and run during a prisoner transfer on Friday.

The cook across the lane threw his cigar in the dirt and tore off the undershirt he wore. He took a boxer's stance and called out, "Jack Johnson going to whip ole Jeff tonight boys!" and they cheered him hearty and loud.

Abe ignored them and took note of the Chinese man's

silver watch chain. "It's too late," he said. "You don't want to be around here anyhow." He nodded and pushed on the door.

Ah Tong stuck his foot in the channel. "Wait," he said. He took out his billfold. He held forth two ten-dollar notes. "The booking fee you paid," he said.

Abe cocked his head. "Keep it. Cost of travel."

Tong put the money back and nodded. He said he was obliged. He thought a moment before he pulled back his shoe. He was on the lam and predisposed to keep things private, and he'd even thought on hiding out a few months in his cousin's laundry storeroom. But as he stood there, it struck him how he knew the man behind the cracked saloon door, and it seemed too odd to let go. He swallowed before he spoke. "I saw you play cards once in the Bowery, back in April." He'd taken note of the play that night, for even then he'd recognized the player. "You bottom-decked a fat rich man and cleaned him out, and I remember thinking I'd never seen mechanics like yours before. Smooth," he said. "Like Canada Bill Jones."

"Wasn't me," Abe said. "Got the wrong fella." He wondered at the man's angle.

"Professor Goodblood?" Tong said.

But when he pulled back his shoe, Abe shut the door in his face.

Tong turned and watched a woman dance in her underclothes behind the big front window of Fat Ruth Malindy's. He struck a match and lit a cigarette and stepped past the empty spool table. He regarded the black men bunched across the street. The sign above their heads read *Food Good and Cheap*.

The cook put his undershirt back on. "What you lookin for Chinaman?" he said.

Tong didn't answer, but walked on to his cousin's laundry.

Cinder Bottom recalled the streets of his boyhood in Los Angeles. It recalled to him Calle de los Negros and the railyards where he once played hide-and-seek.

*

Jim Fort had not ever perspired before stage lights the way he perspired now at the Oak Slab. *You are Chicago Phil*, he repeated in his mind, eyes shut, cards on the table before him. He wished he'd played more poker on his free time, wished he'd drunk a little more courage that afternoon.

He'd been fine on the way in, introducing the other men to Trent and Rufus Beavers as he'd rehearsed. "This is Mr. Boony Runyon from Cincinnati," he'd said, "and this is Mr. Woodrow Peek and this is Bob Hill," and so on. All was smooth, even the handing over of his locked metal case. "I trust your safe will be secure housing for what's in here?" he'd said, and Trent had assured him that neither raging fire nor blast of dynamite could split his big steel bank.

Now Jim Fort mucked his cards. He wiped his sweat and thought, *This is the sweat of Chicago Phil*.

Across the dark room, Rufus Beavers whispered in the

ear of Henry Trent. "Old man Tony Sharpley just came by the bar." He showed Trent the telegram Tony had given him.

```
RECEIVED at 1 RAILROAD AVE   413 PM.
New York NY Jul 4 — 10

Missed the first train. Will arrive
Keystone on the 7 PM
  B says tell H. Trent sorry. Looks
forward to meet.
                 Max
```

Trent felt young for the shortest of moments, seeing her *B* in line with his name. Were he physically capable, he'd have sprouted a hard-on.

Rufus regarded the card players. He leaned into Trent and said, "That old man's monkey stared at me funny." He took out his hanky and blew his nose. "I don't particularly care for that monkey," he said.

*

Abe felt the calm he'd always felt at a card table. He smiled. He looked at the faces around the Wobbler. Taffy Reed. Harold Beavers. Tiny Rutherford. Those who had always longed to sit and play against him. Those who'd practiced sufficient to clean out most professional men.

Still, by any account, it was an odd four-man game.

Taffy Reed had folded every hand.

Rutherford played a more conservative style than he had as a younger man.

Harold Beavers played loose as a goose.

Abe had asked them already, "How do you find the cards?" They were playing with Big Sun Devil Backs.

Taffy Reed said he liked the varnish. The other two said not a word.

Now Taffy studied his hand and folded again.

Rutherford pulled his chips and drank from the tall rye that Goldie had refilled a half hour prior. He stifled a belch.

Harold Beavers yawned and asked once again, "When's that whore comin back around with more?"

Abe smiled. He said, "A madam is no man's five-dollar chippy."

"Say again?"

"She'll be back presently I'd imagine," Abe said.

Rutherford was winning. His chip stack was plenty high, but still he was uneasy. He knew there was no reason to be—after Abe had frisked them, he'd returned the favor and searched every inch to be had on the body of the Keystone Kid. After that, he'd checked the table and chairs himself, running his hand along their undersides and legs. Nothing was hidden inside the little brick room.

Harold Beavers lit a cigar and Abe shuffled before his own deal.

Rutherford could wait no longer. "I've got to drain it," he said. He stood and walked to the door and unlocked it. "That the piss hole I seen across the way?" he asked.

"That's it," Abe answered. "Bucket's in the back." He thought a moment. "Watch out for the snakes," he said.

Rutherford's neck skin pricked. He swung open the door and stepped through.

"Leave that open," Abe said.

"Why?"

"I've got to keep my eye on you."

"You want to shake it off when I'm done too?" Rutherford said. He shook his head and left open the door and walked to the pantry.

"You'd have to be able to find it first," Harold said.

They laughed.

Goldie came in with a tray of fresh drinks. She set one down in front of Harold. "Extra tall for you," she said.

"Well, I knew you were sweet on me." He tried to put his arm around her but she was too fast on her feet.

She went around the table and stood next to Abe. She set down his drink and regarded her fingertips. "This hangnail's a cocklebur," she said.

Abe put his arm around her waist and stared at Harold Beavers. He smiled and moved his hand to the small of her back. Under the knot of the apron she wore, his five-shot .38 was snug at the base of her spine. He took the gun in his hand and slid his arm down and put it in his lap beneath table's edge.

To the two other men, it had looked to be only a back rub.

Harold leaned back in his chair. "Madam, you say?"

Rutherford returned from the pantry. He stepped inside and looked at Goldie.

"Sugar, you look pale," she said. "Did you want somethin different to drink?"

Rutherford said he was fine. He smiled to her and held open the door.

She called him a gentleman as she stepped back through. He locked it.

Abe had finished his shuffle. He pointed to the deck before him, then leaned back, hands at his lap. "You want to cut that deck?" he asked Rutherford.

Rutherford remained standing. From his side jacket pocket he withdrew both Derringers. He aimed one at Abe's face and handed the other to Harold Beavers, who stood accordingly and aimed his at the heart.

Abe smiled. He looked at Taffy Reed for tells. The young man was wide-eyed. He swallowed and breathed from his mouth. He'd had no idea.

"Why the hell you smilin!" Rutherford screamed.

Abe said, "Man can't smile while he's dyin?"

Rutherford looked at Harold Beavers, who looked him back. They nodded and turned their heads back to Abe and shut one eye each and squeezed.

The shots were loud inside that little brick room.

Taffy put his hands to his ears and shut tight his eyes.

Abe twitched little more than to blink.

Harold and Rutherford looked dumbly at their guns.

Abe drew his own and stood up. He put his back to the wall and his finger inside the guard. He two-handed his weapon's grip, right arm extended straight. He thumbed back the blued hammer and said, "You didn't know they made blank cartridges for a .41, did you?"

Harold Beavers recognized his position. He thought it best to go on and make a move straightaway, so he threw the little gun at Abe's head and was fixing to jump across the table when Abe dodged, aimed, and fired. The sound was thrice as loud as the blanks. He'd hit the man in the dick.

Harold dropped to the floor and curled.

"Lord Jesus," Taffy Reed whispered.

"Those smokeless soft points bark, don't they?" Abe said. "I got four left. I think you've seen my aim."

Rutherford dropped his Derringer on the table and put his hands over his head.

Taffy put his own up high.

Harold moaned and cursed unintelligible.

"Oh, hush now Harry," Abe said. "That snake was syphilitic anyhow." He moved to the door with his weapon still trained. He unlocked it blind.

Goldie stepped inside with an armful of cut rope lengths, burned at the ends. She took the long way around the table and tossed the whole mess in Taffy Reed's lap. She took out her own gun then, Abe's little spur-trigger pistol. "Tie up these other two and after that I'll tie you," she said. Then she winked at Taffy Reed.

Abe said to Rutherford, "After he binds Harry, take off your jacket and stanch that blood." He motioned with his gun at the man's crotch.

When the blood was stanched and the hands and feet of all three bound, Abe and Goldie sat on the Ashwood Wobbler and looked down at the men, their behinds on the dirt floor, their backs against the brick. Taffy Reed tried his hardest not to cry.

Abe trained his eyes on Rutherford, then Harold, then Rutherford again.

Harold moaned low and worked his jaw and rocked.

Rutherford stared at the floor.

Abe said, "For a while, when I was cooking all this up in my head, I thought I'd interrogate you, play you one off the other, and then for another while I thought I'd just kill you both."

Harold Beavers growled then. He looked up at Abe and snorted and spat on his pant leg.

"You ought to save that spit," Goldie said.

He spat again, missing her shinbone.

She shook her head. "Ought to save that spit to grease your shot-up prick. Pig might amble by." She smiled and looked at Rutherford. "I'm sorry Rutherford," she said. "I suppose I haven't worked hard enough on my vulgar woman's tongue."

Abe crossed his ankles where they hung from table's edge.

He went on. "I figure both of you was up on Buzzard Branch that day. Figure ole Sneak-up is the only man capable of swiping that rifle and climbin up the ridge without a sound."

Now Harold hung his head as Rutherford had beside him. For once he'd shut his mouth. He'd not argue death. He'd welcome his last bullet with nothing.

Taffy Reed looked on. He'd begun to understand Goldie's wink. They didn't aim to kill him. It was the other two they were after.

Abe continued his thought. "Only man capable of the marksmanship with a stranger's rifle too, I'd imagine." He considered the thousands on thousands of birds Harold Beavers had shot from the Florida sky in order that rich women might don a more reputable hat. He wondered what that did to a man, such daily taking of life in flight. He looked at the crown of Harold's bent head, the spiraling whorl of the small bald circle, the over abundance of staled hair dressing. "Maybe Rutherford paid you to pull the trigger," he said. He remembered what Jake had once told him about the little man. *Don't ever do a thing he asks you to do, and don't ask from him so much as pass the salt and pepper.* His headache had ceased. He spoke without thinking. "More than likely it was Trent told you to track Jake and cut him down." He uncrossed his ankles and slid from the table and stood. "But I'm not killing any man. My mother spoke nothing on killing. That's not her way." He considered a moment. "Not the way of her boys either." Now Goldie slid from the table and stood at his side. They regarded the bowed heads before them. Abe said, "It's the taking my mother was after."

He sat down on his heels in front of them, forearms against his knees. The gun hung lazy in his hand. "I'm taking everything," he said.

*

Trent stood on the passenger station platform and took out his watch for the second time. It was a quarter to seven.

In his fist was a bouquet of wildflowers, still wet at the cut stem bottoms. He'd earlier sent Taffy Reed to pick them from a dry midden ditch out back of Fred's club. "Put em in a dish a water," he'd told Taffy.

He hadn't noticed until now the dirt and tiny brown glass shards spoiling the bouquet. The glass caught the station lights and sparkled along purple soapwort petals. He blew on the flower and brushed away the filth. He tried to stand straight.

In the distance, somebody shot off a skyrocket.

Tony Thumbs materialized from the station's dark overhang. "Evening," he called to Trent.

The monkey was still on the man's shoulder, and Trent thought immediately that Rufus had been right. The animal was staring him down. It wore a lethargic scowl.

Tony's bow tie was brightly colored. His pants were black satin striped. He held forth an old round flask in offering.

"No thank you," Trent said. He looked again at the monkey. "He looks like he could use it," he said.

"Oh no," Tony said. He chuckled. "Baz only drinks ale."

Trent looked again at his watch.

Tony forced a smile. "I trust you got the message about Mercurio's delay?"

"I wouldn't be standing here if I hadn't."

There was an ache in Tony's hand. It happened when he grew nervous. There were times when he swore he could feel his old thumb twiddling. "I suppose not," he answered. "I only—"

Another skyrocket boomed in the gray cast air over the Union Club.

Baz watched the outward yellow burst and screeched. He moved his head side to side and nibbled nervous at Tony's ear.

Trent squinted and regarded the far-off evening sky around his establishment, too distant to make anything out. "It's not even dark yet," he said. "Who's shootin off fireworks?" He didn't care for the wind's present direction. It happened sometimes, a southerly gust. A carrying-in of the coke-oven cinders from across the creek. It was why he employed a man to scrub his palace. It was why he wanted land high up on a hill.

Baz made a sound like a cat pushing hairballs.

Trent frowned at the monkey and checked again his timepiece.

*

Peering out from under the telegraph tarp, Chesh Whitt wondered who was firing skyrockets before dark. He watched the tail of smoke mix with the cinders blowing off the ridge like summer snow, their hot brick ovens of origin blurring night with day. He fanned himself with the top of a cigar box and tucked back under. "Anything?" he said.

The telegraph operator was growing annoyed at the young man. She ignored him and took the latest wire. "Ninth round is over," she said. "Johnson left hook to liver staggers Jeffries."

Chesh bobbed again from under the tarp. He took up the tin bullhorn. "You hear that men!" he shouted. "Left hook to Jeffries' liver! He's on his way out! Gettin chopped like a big white birch tree!"

One man whooped and fell off his chair. Most ignored Chesh in favor of reconsidering how to best use their bank-rolls. They were oiled up on booze and coiled and cocked at the thought of their black champion finally whipping white man's best. The one-eyed policeman chalked the board and took side bets on round ten.

Fred Reed whispered in the ear of the short policeman, "Watch that Whitt boy."

Chesh's Daddy came over on his way out of the yard. He'd seen enough. He scolded his boy for the second time. "You're embarrassing yourself," he said. "There are a few men here among the trash who have character." He straightened the knot of his necktie. "Write up the fight as soon as it's done. I want the morning edition off the press by four."

Chesh told his Daddy he could give him the headline

right then and there. He moved his hands and fingers on the air as if setting type. "How about this?" he asked. "*Negro proven superior to white man in every regard?*"

"Stay off the whiskey," J. T. Whitt said. He donned his hat. "And keep your mouth shut."

*

Talbert walked to the long lobby's far wall. He moved aside a shear and looked out the side window and watched Rose Cantu pull the Chambers-Detroit into the alley. He stepped back and sighed and returned to the front desk. "You two," he said to the stupid lobby men, "go cross the bridge stand in the Bottom and keep your eyes open. Don't do a fuckin thing but look around unless I tell you, and stay posted until I come call you back in."

They walked out the big front doors without a word.

Talbert watched them through the tall front window before he returned to his desk and double-checked that the grain bags were tucked inside the kneehole.

It was quiet and dark at the side stage door when he swung it open. Abe and Goldie were there just as planned. They stood beneath the awning holding hands. No one spoke. Abe nodded to indicate they'd not been seen, and Goldie shut the door behind. She handed Talbert a black Russian dogskin coat left behind by a patron of Fat Ruth's. It was Christmas Eve when the man's wife had tracked him there, and she'd run him out onto Wyoming Street with a tack hammer raised over her head.

Talbert folded the heavy coat over his arm.

They followed him to the emptied lobby, where they crawled into the kneehole of the big front desk. It was dark. They pulled their knees to their chests and rested their chins. They faced each other and listened.

Talbert stepped into the main card room at two minutes to seven. Three tables of mid-level poker men paid him no mind. He stepped to the long counter, put his boot on the footrail, and waved over the barkeep with two fingers.

The man set down his rag and ambled over slow.

"Girl just come in out of breath," Talbert told him. "She'd run clear from the Bottom, your neighbor I believe. Said your wife had fallen off the short ladder and cracked her head on the range."

"What?" He'd stood straight from where he leaned. He untied his apron with trembling hands.

"Best get home. I'll tend to the drinks."

Nothing else was spoken. Barkeep was around the counter and gone.

Talbert stepped behind the bar and bent low to the hay-hook shotgun. He broke it open quiet, replaced the two shot shells with black powder blanks, and hung it back.

From the kneehole, Abe and Goldie listened to the barkeep's footfalls as he passed and hit the big front doors. Abe squeezed Goldie's hand tight. "Just one more and you're on," he whispered.

Out on the bridge, the stupid lobby men leaned against

the handrails and laughed at the barkeep's desperate gait. "He ain't got the wind for that," one said.

Munchy was on Trent's office door. He'd noticed the barkeep's hasty exit, and now he awaited Talbert, who presently approached.

Before he stepped to Trent's office, Talbert made for the corner partition wall, where he hung the heavy coat on the farthest hook. He remembered when Jake Baach had framed the wall up, and it seemed fitting to him then as he double-checked the right pocket.

When Talbert stepped back out and came to the door, Munchy asked after the barkeep. "What's crawled up his shit shoot?" he said.

"It's what's crawlin out," Talbert told him. "Venison had turned and he ate it anyhow. He'll be out of the lavatory in five minutes or so."

"Well," Munchy said. "We all got to eat a peck of dirt before we die."

Talbert said he reckoned we did. Then he made his customary tap on the door and waited a moment and went through.

Munchy took up his halved paper again.

Around the Oak Slab, it was quiet save the clack of thrown-in chips and the mumbled repeat of "check" and "fold." The men paid Talbert no mind as he shut the door and took a seat against the wall next to Rufus Beavers. It was dark there in the corner, and Talbert leaned to the man's ear and whispered what he'd rehearsed. "There's trouble next door at Fred's. Johnson is whipping Jeffries. Mr. Trent sent word from the station, said to have you step in."

Rufus shut his eyes and shook his head.

Talbert kept on. "Said to take the cut barrel from under the bar, make an example of any coloreds get too proud."

Rufus sighed. He handed the leather bank pouch to Talbert and looked him in the eyes. He kept his voice low. "You stay right here in this room." He pointed to the pouch. "There's a six-shot under the money," he said.

Talbert nodded.

Rufus stood and stepped to the table. Little Donnie had just folded, and the one they'd named Woodrow pulled his chips. Rufus forced a smile and said, "Men, I'm going to see what's holding up the drinks. I won't be long." He gave Little Donnie a look.

Little Donnie nodded that he understood. These city boys needed close watch.

When he'd gone through the office and closed the door behind him, Rufus grabbed the halved paper from Munchy's fat grip and threw it across the floor. "You keep your eyes here," he said, motioning at the room behind him. He inquired on the barkeep's absentia.

"Diarrhea," Munchy said. "Back in five minutes."

Rufus shook his head yet again and marveled at the ineptitude of his associates. "Tell him I took the shotgun," he said.

When Rufus stepped lively through the lobby, Abe recognized the sound of his gait.

The front doors shut, and they crawled from the kneehole.

*

The seven o'clock train arrived eight minutes behind schedule. Trent held his drooped bouquet with both hands and licked his teeth to be sure no food remained. He watched a mother step on the platform stool with a squalling baby bucking in her arms. A young man jumped off behind her with his cardboard grip half-open, a faulty latch swinging loose. "*This* is Keystone?" he said.

Trent had an uneasy feeling, and it wasn't indigestion.

Tony had scooted into the overhang's shadow once again. On account of his nerves, he'd earlier taken too much of a new powder, and now he was foggy. He'd forgotten the details of his role upon train's arrival. He could remember neither his exit cue nor the whereabouts of his luggage.

An older gentleman stepped off the train with an umbrella hooked on his arm. He straightened his suspenders. He squinted and adjusted his spectacles. He had superior night vision when he wore them, and so it was that he spotted Baz, and in turn, Tony. "Tony Thumbs?" he called.

Trent's ear perked on the nickname he'd not heard from any other. He turned to see the suspendered man approaching the darkened depot wall.

"What in the name of scratch are you doing *here*?" the

man said. He stepped within a yard of Tony, who backed away. "Thought you never left Baltimore."

Tony could only swallow. It didn't seem possible that an Old Drury patron would step off a train in southern West Virginia.

A searing heat rose from Trent's middle. It climbed up his chest and into his neck, and though he was unsure of precisely how, he knew then that he had been conned.

The suspendered man kept on. "That monkey still alive?"

Tony backed into the armrest of a long pine bench. His knee gave and he pitched forward, catching himself with a hand. Baz had no recourse but to jump from his shoulder to the platform boards.

"You okay?" the suspendered man asked.

And then Trent was upon them. "Beatrice ain't on this fucking train or any other!" he shouted, startling those close by. "Who are you?" He didn't wait for an answer. Tony had barely straightened back up when Trent let go an overhand right. It landed flush on the old man's mouth and put him down hard.

The war call that came from Baz then was enough to split the eardrum, a scream too high for the human to know. He sprung onto the thigh of Henry Trent and sunk deep his canines there.

The people on the platform were unable to comprehend what they saw.

The suspendered man had taken a knee at Tony's side,

and now he looked up. He saw the animal tear away a strip of Trent's pant leg and a hank of flesh both. Blood flung from the points of the long yellow teeth.

Trent bared down and grabbed the monkey around the neck before he could bite again. He spun on his heels and flung Baz, and the little body shot forth in a line with considerable speed, and the sound of his head against the train's sheet-steel side was loud as an anvil strike.

Henry Trent drew his Colt and made for Railroad Avenue. His stride was broken and slowed from the bite. He hollered, again and again, "It's a setup! Put every man on the office!"

*

She'd walked with loose neck and turned ankles across the Alhambra's main card room, winking at Munchy all the way. Two cardplayers took note but returned to their hands.

She lured him off the door in twelve seconds flat.

Goldie could play drunk with the best, and she'd come out of the floozy gate hard, putting her hand to his crotch and whispering in his ear, "I want a man inside me what's got some beef on his bones." She led him by the hand to the corner wall.

Now he had her pressed there, hidden behind the coat-hook partition, his breath a pinched wheeze. She shut her eyes against its foul stench.

Abe pulled his hat low. He walked across the card room unnoticed by all but one at the tables. The man was losing interest in losing hands and had begun to wonder at the stillness around him and at the woman who'd led off the fat man. He watched Abe go past. He did not know Abe, but found it strange that one so thin could be so swollen at the front. He watched Abe turn the knob and step inside the office of Mayor Trent without knocking.

Inside, Little Donnie had already opened the big safe doors. He stood open-mouthed before the high clean towers of money, and behind him, the other men did the same.

Without a word, Abe untucked his shirtfront and pulled out the six-stack of four-bushel grain bags. They commenced to filling.

Out in the main room, the curious, losing man stood from the poker table. The one who was shuffling said, "You cashing out?" He received no answer.

The man walked toward Trent's office. He heard labored breathing from beyond the partition wall. "Hello?" he called.

Munchy quit his groping. He was motionless, his red face buried in the cleavage of the most beautiful woman in the world.

What Goldie had most feared was happening. She lifted her arm from the sweat-soaked back of his jacket and quietly reached for the pocket of the hanging dogskin coat.

The man stood by the bar and listened. He said, "If anybody wants to know, I believe I just seen a man walk unchecked into Mayor Trent's fortress."

Munchy knew without a doubt then that he'd been had. He straightened and put his hand to his belt holster. He'd pulled his gun and nearly drawn back the hammer when Goldie got her own pistol free of the fur-lined pocket. She fired twice.

The quiet afterward made everything slow. She hated that he looked her in the eyes when he dropped. To see such a thing up close was too much for Goldie.

Abe recognized the double report of his spur-trigger pistol. "Go!" he hollered, and threw open the door. They cinched their filled grain sacks and went, shoulder-toting the loads swift of foot. They left behind nothing but the locked metal case of a man known only as Phil.

Gun drawn, Abe stepped to the partition. Goldie was flat against the wall. She'd moved only to drop her weapon and put her hands to her mouth, and her face was drained of color. On the floor, Munchy tried to gather air, his wide mouth a useless bellows, his jaw hinging hard like a fresh-caught fish. Abe knew by the sound that both his lungs were collapsed. He told Goldie they had to run and they did.

He knocked down the curious losing man on the way.

Not one other stood from his poker table seat as the safe-robbers ran past in a line. As he went, Jim Fort hollered, "Tell em they shouldn't a crossed Chicago Phil!"

Rose Cantu had piloted the Chambers to its place at the head of the line. Behind it were the twin Oldsmobile Runabouts, ready for the open road.

When the safe-robbers emerged from the side stage door, they spread into all three cars. They held the fat grain sacks like children on their laps. "Where's Chesh?" Abe said to Rose, and she only shrugged and mashed the gas.

They hit Railroad Avenue and made left to travel west. Rose took the lead carrying four. Talbert followed in the second, and Abe drove the third. Goldie rode silent and white at his side. He stopped at street's middle and looked back to Fred Reed's.

Chesh Whitt burst from the yard, the short officer trailing him close. He was twenty yards from the car when Henry Trent hobbled into range.

Trent could see now what was happening. He somehow knew what they'd done. He stopped in the road and leveled his Colt.

The officer giving chase dropped to the ground at the crack of Trent's first shot. The man was not hit, but he played dead just the same, and he wondered why he'd quit his coke-yard job.

Trent fired slow and even, and the fourth caught Chesh in the side. He fell and got up to keep coming, the Oldsmobile five yards off.

Abe left his foot on the brake but stood at the tall curved dash. He took a wide stance and turned his hips. He steadied his center as Moon had taught him inside the long shooting stall.

Trent put his sights on the man who'd stood, the man he now saw was Abe Baach.

Abe fired first and Henry Trent dropped to the hard-packed dirt where he'd stood.

Chesh jumped on the gearbox in back and Abe sat down and took the tiller. "Hold on," he said, and Goldie turned to clutch Chesh's wrist, and they drove, a crowd in the street behind them circling their mayor, who lay on his back with a soft-point bullet in his heart. Rufus and Fred Reed took a knee on either side, and Trent looked up at the sky between them where the coke ash gusted gray. His head grew light and tingly. He said something about skyrockets before dark and a monkey and a train. He swallowed. Again and again he swallowed.

Fred Reed took off his pressed white shirt and wadded it over the bubbling hole. "Go get my vehicle!" he hollered to the one-eyed officer standing at his back open-mouthed. Rufus stood and took the man by the sleeve, and together they ran for Fred's coupe. It was parked beyond the yard, the only automobile left to be had.

When Rufus turned the crank, there was nothing.

Chesh Whitt had dismantled the carburetor.

*

Dusk came on the drive to Kimball, the sun muted deep beneath the ridge. A mile out, they'd emptied their grain sacks into hat trunks and leather cases. They ditched the vehicles by a tipple at Kimball's edge and boarded the train bound for Huntington.

At Matewan, Abe stepped off the coach in full dark. Frank Dallara stood by the bulletin light. Giuseppe was not with him as planned.

Abe had wired two hundred dollars that morning on word that the jailer could be bribed.

Now Frank Dallara was stooped and red-eyed. "They found him hung from the window bars at supper," he told Abe. "Said he knotted up strips of that burlap he slept on."

They'd planned to bring him to Baltimore, find him work bricking mansions along Druid Hill Park.

"I'm sorry Frank," Abe said.

The conductor called stragglers to board. "We're six minutes off!" he hollered. "I'm letting her go!"

At the big Huntington station, Goldie spoke to a ticket agent she knew. The man was a monthly regular at Fat Ruth's, and as per her instructions, he'd requested extra hours on Independence Day. She slid a silk-knotted roll of twenties between the bars of his window. "When they come askin," she said, "You tell em Chicago. We were all of us bound for Chicago with transfer at Cincinnati."

She procured their tickets to Baltimore and Atlantic City, and they boarded the Pullman sleeper in a line. When the porter tried to take their luggage, Abe told him to kindly step back. The old man eyed Chesh Whitt, who was bent at the waist and leaking blood through his dressing. "Colored ain't permitted in the sleeper," the man said.

Abe put a finger to his lips and said, "Shhh." He held out a ten.

Chesh grunted as he made for the step stool. He looked back at the porter, who reminded him of his grandaddy.

He said to him, "Don't fret George. One of *us* runs these rails tonight."

At the passenger station in Charleston, they were joined by Sallie, Al, Agnes, and baby Ben, all of whom had spent the evening there, waiting. When Abe inquired on Sam's whereabouts, his Daddy said only, "He is gone. He run."

They'd last seen him at two that afternoon, while they ate cold chicken behind the station. They'd just spread a quilt on the bank of the Kanawha when Agnes saw him above and pointed. "Is that Uncle Samuel?" she'd asked, and there he was, high up on the river trestle, running just as fast as he could.

*

Everywhere were riots on Independence Day streets. Jack Johnson had won easy, and as night became morning, men were stabbed in the dark for being black. The quarrelling on Keystone's dirt lanes was relatively tame. White men mostly mumbled and glared. There were celebratory calls not unlike those of Chesh Whitt, even as Mayor Trent was tended and kept still. He somehow kept breathing, his heart languid but alive.

He was toted by Fred Reed toward the hospital at Welch, his chariot a horse-drawn rig meant for coffins. By the time they hit Bottom Creek at nine, he was dead.

It was Rufus who discovered the others. He'd walked to the Bottom and into Baach's saloon with the cut-barrel shotgun level at his hip. He'd followed the sound of their calls and nearly turned away when he saw Rutherford and Reed hog-tied on the floor by his brother. *Here*, Rufus thought, *here is delegate-elect Beavers, his member gunshot and bled nearly dry.*

He cut them all loose.

Rutherford and Reed chained the de-bolted Baach safe to the hand-truck and rolled it to the alley, where they blew off its door with dynamite. Inside was nothing but a Devil Back Joker. Stuck to its front was the business card of Mr. Tony Sharpley, 57 Great Jones Street, New York.

Rufus Beavers returned to the Alhambra, where he could only stare at the emptied insides of his own thrown-open safe. It was taller than he, and it had not been so bare since the day of its purchase in 1894. All that remained was a foreign metal case. Rufus pried it open to find twenty card decks and one business card. The decks read:

BIG SUN PLAYING CARD COMPANY
NEW YORK CITY, USA.

The business card read:

PHIL O'BANYON
1 EAST SUPERIOR STREET
CHICAGO, ILLINOIS.

*

Tony Thumbs had survived. Knocked unconscious, five front teeth gone, he'd been helped to the train by the suspendered man, who'd thought to seek out and load the luggage too. On the eight o'clock eastbound, the old man rocked with his head against the window glass.

He rode in this fashion through Princeton and on past Lynchburg too, the fear in his bones subsiding as the mountains gave way to flat. He held a frozen Delmonico steak to his mouth and rocked in his red velvet seat. He looked at the empty cushion beside him. Baz had not been so lucky as him.

The monkey was wrapped in the suspendered man's jacket and stuffed in Tony's medicine trunk. His little body was cold and stiffening quick, clacking against brown and red bottles of curare and opium and valerian and maypop.

At Silver Spring, Tony peeked inside the trunk to see his oldest and dearest friend in this world. He pulled back the lapel of the fine worsted jacket and looked at the white face and cold open eyes. He cried, and he did not care who saw.

He drank from a red medicine bottle before he closed up the trunk.

He hoped the others had made it out alive. He hoped they would meet him in Baltimore, and that they'd let him rest awhile. He was eighty-two years old after all.

At Ellicott City, he finally slept. He dreamed of Abe and Goldie, flying on the air above the Old Drury stage before the glow of new electric lights. They had no need for wires. They tossed money upon the air, and it floated there, as if unbound by gravity's rule. And Tony stood at stage's edge and asked if he could have his cut of the touch, and they told him yes. Of course, Goldie said. Of course. And she looked at Abe and commanded, "Climb!" And the Kid and the Queen levitated, high above the money to the flylines. And Tony held out his hands, and his missing thumb was there, twiddling quick as could be, and above him, the money never fell. It only grew thick. He watched it multiply, and he was happy, for he knew that it was sum enough to procure five golden teeth and a six-month supply of Camel Alley opium, high grade. He knew the money was sufficient to buy a black granite headstone and a silver shoe-box coffin, lined in mulberry Egyptian silk.

TEN FUN OF THE NUMBER ONE

July 22, 1910

The moon over the Baltimore wharf was full and low. Abe and Goldie sat on the Frederick Street docks and watched the towboat lamps dance on the water's black chop. He'd already pointed to the tall pilings and told her how he'd earned his scar. Now he aimed a hand in the direction of Locust Point and said, "See those lights way out there? That's where Daddy landed in '77." He shook his head. "Can you imagine that? Alone and twenty years old. Stepped on a boat in Germany and stepped off it right here."

The big water suited Goldie. She had even grown fond of its smell. And though Baltimore's flatness did not likewise fit her fancy, she enjoyed walking the streets, knit close on all sides with tall buildings.

"I believe I'd be seasick most of the way," she said.

He nodded his head. "Stick with trains."

Los Angeles, California, was where they'd soon travel, though Goldie wondered if the East Coast might better suit her than the West. Ben Moon was living temporarily then in Atlantic City, where he'd purchased a saloon and a home on the inlet too. He'd given both to the Baaches upon their arrival and told Al he could tend the business in whatever measure he pleased. Little Donnie played cards at the new saloon under the name Caleb Shook. At night he slept in a ground-floor white iron bed, inside the Maine Avenue home of Al and Sallie Baach. Under the floorboards was a door and under the door was four hundred thousand dollars. Sallie had looked at the money only once. She sat mornings and evenings in a wicker throne on the home's front lawn. She could see the water and the lighthouse both. She could watch Agnes and Ben duck in the high cordgrass and run on the sand. And all the while, as she watched them hide and seek and build castles and knock them down, as she heard them squeal and whistle and mimic the song of the laughing gulls, she bit the tip of her tongue to keep from crying. The children were all she had to beat back the sorrow. The place itself was nothing to her. She'd stay on their account, but such a place was not meant for Sallie. She belonged in the hills, where she suspected her Samuel had returned. Her Daddy's letters told nothing of her youngest—none in Welch had heard a word. Old Man Hood's last letter had read:

I built that home on Hood Hill Plateau in 1851. I meant it to be a meeting ground for the preachers of God's good word. It burned to the ground on July the seventh.

The dirt still smoldered when Oswald Ladd and his Daddy arrived from Virginia. They left inside a day, afraid for their lives. They'd found that Keystone was in an uproar over the death of their mayor. The circuit judge wore hatred in his eyes and the tiny police chief had told them he cared little for their property deed, and they'd do best to clear off before dark. Sallie cried at the words her Daddy had written. She thought often to go and find her Samuel back home, to go too in the ground with the others she'd borne. To go on finally and rest.

Abe and Goldie had stayed five nights at the Maine Avenue home. He'd proposed marriage to her at a boardwalk cafe. She'd smiled then, even lost some of the ache she'd felt since the foul business with Munchy back in Keystone. Still, when Abe left Atlantic City for Baltimore on the eleventh, Goldie had refused to stay at the shore as planned. He went back primarily to line up work for Chesh and Talbert and Rose Cantu, who'd taken to Baltimore right off. When Abe told her it was safer in Atlantic City, Goldie had said, "I'll die at your side just the same as I'll live."

Now they sat where dead fish and chicken-wire bobbed, and the foghorns blew back at the B&O whistles.

He watched her watch the water. He rubbed at her back.

Presently, he felt a rumble in the pier boards beneath him. He turned to see Bushel-Heap Lou McKill walking in their direction, lamp in his grip, another man at his side.

Abe stood to meet them. The man was familiar. A black

fellow, tall and thin. He wore a glass eye where once none had been.

"Fella here come up from Keystone," Bushels said. "Won't say much other than he needs to speak with you."

A fluttering commenced at Goldie's middle.

"You check to see if he came alone?" Abe asked.

"Already backtracked and lit up the crannies."

Together, they walked to the warehouse. The Radiant Moon sign had been painted over. *Coming Soon!* the bricks read, *Chambers Automobiles!*

Inside, the place was emptied, stripped of presses and cutters and long table lines of wrapper assemblage. The four of them stood beneath a single electric bulb tacked to the ceiling in Moon's empty office.

The tall officer from Keystone took an envelope from his pocket and handed it over.

The photograph nearly fell to the floor when Abe opened the letter. He had not yet read its greeting when he saw his brother's face in black and white, the eyes both swollen shut, the lips split and sunken where teeth no longer rooted.

A sound came up from deep inside him and he bent a little at the waist.

Goldie turned away. "Oh Samuel," she said.

The letter was penned in an unfamiliar script. *Abe Baach and Goldie Toothman, you have two days from receipt of this letter to return to Keystone to face the crimes of murdering officer Munchy Briles and Mayor Henry Trent. You shall bring with you what you have stolen. The man on delivery of this letter*

shall not be harmed and shall travel alone before you to advise.
If you fail to surrender within two days' time, Sam Baach will be
hung by the neck until dead. If you surrender within two days'
time, he will be set free.

Abe looked at the glass-eyed man, who shook where
he stood, pointy-shouldered in a white shirt he'd sweated
through.

"Rutherford is whittled down all the way to you?" Abe
said. He'd gotten word from Chicago and New York of what
had happened to the others who'd tracked him. On July
16th, Harold Beavers had ventured alone and drunk to the
office building at 1 Superior Street. It sat across the lane
from the Cathedral of the Holy Name, and before he'd
stepped inside 1 Superior, Harold had looked up at the
spire, two hundred feet above. He'd hesitated, then entered
the squat building through the front door, expecting to see
secretaries and spectacled types with pencils behind their
ears. Instead, he found himself in a smoke-filled lounge of
pitiless men playing pocket billiards. He'd said, "I'm looking
for Phil," and the ones who were bent across the felt had
straightened and stared him down, and the ones leaning at
the wall had put their hands inside their coat. When Harold
Beavers moved his own hand to the small of his back, they
drew down and fired all at once. They were not the timid
kind. They spent their days at 1 Superior Street, headquarters of Dropsy Phil O'Banyon's North Side Gang. The bullet
hole in Harold's manhood had barely scabbed black when
they filled him with fifty more.

Abe studied the tall man's real eye. "I know you," he said. "You're the first fella I met when I came home in April. Believe I gave you a silver dollar."

The man's breathing turned quick. He looked to his right at the giant.

"How's your short friend?" Abe asked him. "One with the titties?"

"Dead," the man answered, but Abe already knew.

When Harold Beavers had sent no word from Chicago for three days, Rufus tasked the short tittied man to New York, for he was wholly unintimidated by a producer's lair. But 57 Great Jones Street was no variety theater. In truth, it was home to Little Naples Saloon, and when the short Keystone officer turned up there, having drunk considerable courage to run his mouth, Paul Vaccarelli himself pulled his piece, and he shot the tittied man through the cartilage of his nose.

The glass-eyed man's tremble had increased and he feared he'd wet his pants. "I'm just a messenger," he managed. He'd been drunk when he agreed to do it. Rutherford had paid him two fifty-dollar notes.

The light bulb was hot above them.

Abe said, "You ought to consider how you align yourself in this life. You tell that to Taffy Reed and the other police too." He folded the letter around the photograph of Sam. He took out his watch. "You tell Rutherford and Rufus Beavers that I will do what's been asked. But I will come alone."

"No," Goldie said. "That's not right." Her voice was quiet but sure.

Abe did not look in her direction. He stared hard at the glass eye and said again, "I'll be traveling alone."

The man started to speak. He'd been given a script which demanded that both of the accused answer for their crimes. A witness had said with certainty that it was Goldie who'd shot Munchy Briles. Now the man could not remember what he'd rehearsed on the train.

Goldie said, "You tell them all that two of us are coming home."

Abe looked where she stood. She wore no expression. He remembered what she'd said on the docks. *I'll die at your side just the same as I'll live.* He winked at her and went on. "Tell them we will come with one man watching to be sure they hold up their end. We'll step off the train when we see Sam step on it, alone."

The man stood there nodding, his tremble subsiding.

Abe left the office and whistled at the head of the stairs.

When he stepped back inside, another man was with him, the kind who took jobs no one else would touch. "One-Eye," Abe said, "this is Anchors. He's going to follow you to the station, ten paces behind the whole way." Anchors wore a scowl. He'd been too long in the sun. Abe went on. "He totes a police revolver, and if he sees any other with you, he'll slap it out and lay you down."

"I come alone," the tall man said, "all the way." It was the truth. Keystone could not spare the men.

Abe believed him.

The light bulb surged. From out on the water, there arose a grinding sound.

Abe called over the man known as Anchors. He slipped him two twenties and whispered in his ear. "Get on that train but don't let him know it. Follow and watch. You can get you a toothbrush on arrival."

Anchors put his hands in his pockets and stepped to the tall man's side.

Abe regarded once more the glass eye, its crude brown paint-job. "Go on," he said. "You can make the ten o'clock if you trot."

The tall man started for the door. He'd nearly made it through when he stopped and spoke without turning. "When do I tell em you'll arrive?" he asked.

Abe worked his jaw. "Tell them we'll be there at sundown on Sunday. Last train in."

Goldie listened to their footfalls on the stairs. There was something in the sound of it that recalled her Daddy.

Bushels was feeling particularly protective by then. He said, "I was ready to go with you the first time Abe, when you came through in April." He'd always liked the young man from West Virginia. "I'll ride in ahead of you, on an earlier train. Lay down some work. We can figure this."

Goldie moved to the long office wall, where she sat down beneath a square hole. It had once housed Ben Moon's safe, and a dusty outline of the big portrait remained.

Abe said, "You still keep up with that counterfeiter?"

Bushels said he did.

"You'll need to call on him."

Goldie made an airy sound and lay her head back on the wall. How tired she had grown of such games.

Bushels looked at her there, and then at Abe, who regarded the folded letter in his hands. "Abe," he said. "We need to wire Mr. Moon. We need to work out a plan."

Abe nodded. He was already thinking on it. The pain in his head was back, but it could not block what he conjured. "I'll stop at the telegraph office on my way to Tony Thumbs'." he said. He hoped the old man would be there. He hoped he wasn't dead.

Before he left Moon's office, Abe sat down next to Goldie on the wall. He told her not to fret. He told her they'd make it out of Keystone yet again, alive and free.

She only shook her head. He kissed her on the temple.

He walked up South Street figuring, talking to himself aloud.

Outside Tony Thumbs' building, he smelled rain. He looked up for night clouds, but there were none. It was only the moon, big as it had been at the Keystone eclipse. The Old Drury's sign was in need of repair. They'd not run a show in months.

Inside, Abe pounded on Tony's locked door.

The old man had taken up opium full time since putting his monkey in the ground. There were days when he stayed eight hours inside the stale, cushioned joint on Camel Alley, when the only words he spoke were his order, "Ten fun of the number one." He grew tired of the walk to and fro, and so he'd bought from the joint's proprietor his own full layout—skewer, lamp, and pipe. He'd not left his bedroom since.

Tony Thumbs would turn eighty-three on August 21st. He felt no need to leave his little spot above the Drury.

He felt no need to answer when a knock came at his door.

But Abe pounded still, and the ringing in his ears built until it broke, and inside the clamor of his shrill mind, a quiet place came forth, like the one he and Jake had once known. And inside the quiet place, he could not hear the pounding of his very own fist, even as he watched it knock. He heard instead the pulse of his blood. He shut his eyes and saw Sam, his empty lips and crushed nose.

His knees nearly gave, but he neither fell nor hit his head. He sat down on his heels and breathed deep. He thought of the last time he'd seen Jake, his purpled neck and motion-less eyes beneath the lids. He thought of Sam's face in the photograph.

There is nothing without family. There is nothing without one, two, three.

Abe needed the old man and his miracle cures.

He stood up and kicked down the door.

THEIR DAY HAD COME

August 21, 1910

At a minute past midnight, Ah Tong tossed the pebble. It was wrapped in a sheet of paper. He'd listened from the alley for Abe's whistle, then come closer to hear what Goldie hummed. When the perimeter guards moved to the jailhouse's opposite side and she still hummed *All clear*, Tong ran up and tossed the pebble through the high window bars.

Abe took it up from the floor just as the officer on hall guard stirred awake. He sat in a spindle-back chair just outside cell one.

"You dozin One-Eye?" Abe said. He held the pebble note in his fist.

The tall man took out his watch. His shift was done. "I'm going home to bed is what I'm doin," he said. He sometimes felt he was living under a curse, one put upon him by Abe back in April, one transmitted by way of that Morgan dollar. He put his fingers in his ears and shut his eyes and waited.

Two minutes later, Taffy Reed followed Rutherford through the main hall door. They nodded to One-Eye as he left, and Rutherford called after him, "Be back here at seven, no later."

Rutherford sat down in the chair that faced Abe's cell. He stared hard at the condemned, who was naked and had dropped flat on his belly.

"Bet you didn't know this here is called a push-up," Abe said. His voice strained as he up-and-downed on his knuckles. "I know the fella who first coined the term."

Taffy stood behind Rutherford with a sack of dried peppers in one hand and a lantern in the other. He watched the fluid motion of the push-up. "I'm going to pickle," he said. On his way past Goldie's cell, he swung his lantern to see. She stood over the drainhole, naked as a jaybird.

On the embalming table, Taffy poured brine from a quart jar into a gallon that was already half full of boiled eggs. He'd left the door cracked to take periodic peeks at Goldie's cell. He'd done so for a week, since the condemned had begun to fight the heat with nudity. They were generally clothed only in the early morning hours.

When Abe finished his forty push-ups, he hopped to his feet and brushed the dirt off his chest. He looked down at himself. "Rutherford," he said. "What about my hog? If I come over and waggle it between the bars, will you brush off the dust for me?"

Rutherford had not shifted posture an inch since he'd sat. "Come on over here," he said. "I'll brush it. Rip it clean off too. Fry it up in back with some purple onion, serve it to your mother."

Abe laughed. "You could serve five or six more than that with it," he said.

Rutherford looked away momentarily. He tried to see Goldie down the hall, but it was too dark at that end. "Five or six?" he said. "I believe that's about how many I'll get to kill when I do find your mother and Daddy, and whoever else has that money."

"That isn't going to happen."

"You won't be here to see it, that's certain." If he pointed his boot toes, he could almost touch the floor. He sighed and sat back. "Less you go ahead and tell me now where the money is. I believe you know this is your very last chance to stay what's comin tomorrow."

Abe went to the straw tick in the corner and lay down and crossed his legs at the ankle.

Rutherford hated the man with such fortitude he could barely keep from shooting him through the bars right then. He wouldn't do it. He'd watch instead as Abe died before a crowd. Rufus Beavers had declared Thursday morning that the pair would be properly hanged as soon as a scaffold was built. He even had a man for the job, a man who'd built the gallows used by Isaac Parker, Rufus' most favorite of judges. By that time, Rufus was drunk every hour of every day. He'd nearly gone mad since the heist and his brother's disappearance, and he'd finally grown weary of Abe and Goldie's trickery and money-baiting. He should have known better than to keep them alive on the promise of four hundred grand. He should have known better, even on that July Sunday sundown, when the two of them had surrendered to Keystone. They hadn't stepped down from the train right off. They'd stood on the coach steps and opened the lid of a four-foot steamer trunk. They'd tipped it forward so Rufus could see the money stacked neat to the top. That's when Rutherford turned Sam Baach loose on the final outbound train. The young man who'd wanted only to come home now wanted only to leave. When it had departed, and they reopened the trunk, beneath the top layer there was nothing but newsprint.

Rutherford spat on the hallway floor. "Rufus may have given up on that money, but I won't ever," he said. "I'll kill everyone you know to get it back."

Abe put his arm beneath his head. A luna moth walked up the wall toward the ceiling. "That isn't going to happen," he said.

"You don't know what I can do." Rutherford stood up and put his face near the red-rusted bars. He lowered his voice and said, "I've killed enough to where I lost count. Easier and easier and easier." He smiled a little. "Even the Keystone Kid, even ole big brains never knew what I done. Always thought I took orders from Trent, from Beavers."

"That's right," Abe said. "You always were superior at takin orders."

Rutherford didn't care to bite his tongue when death for Abe Baach was this nigh. "Wasn't takin orders when I dropped on that guinea from a tree branch," he said. "One ridin into town with your Daddy?" He let it sink in a minute. "That was my first." He smiled at the old bad memories he'd twisted to good. "Vic Moon kept breathing through a broke neck too, had to knock him in the brain box with the butt of my axe." He ruminated a moment at his humane ways. "Could have been Jew Baach on that horse," he said. "Doesn't matter. Point is, nobody told me to do that. I just done it."

Abe sat up on his elbows and looked at the tiny man.

Rutherford kept on. "And that same night, when your Daddy stood in the road with Trent like they was friends, and the Beavers threw them snakes on me from the high porch, I didn't go to no White Sulphur Springs like Trent ordered me to." He shook his head. "Nossir, went to that old slope mine and tossed Vic Moon in there. First of many. And here you and your Daddy always thought it was Trent that didn't ship that body."

Down the hall, Goldie could hear every word.

Taffy Reed had noted the tone in Rutherford's far-off voice. He'd put his ear to the cracked-open door.

"How about we get down to it?" Rutherford said. "How about ole Jake?"

Abe stayed as he was, his arms beneath him tingling.

"People knew him and that Italian wasn't just carpenter buddies." All that Rutherford had kept to himself was blooming from his throat unchecked. "Me and Harold Beavers was on a bender, and we followed them nancies up in the woods." He pointed upward toward nothing in particular and kept on. "I bet Harold he couldn't hit your brother more than two out of three from a hundred yards off." He laughed then. "Fuckin rifle jammed or he'd have took the other one too."

Down the hall, Goldie had quit breathing. She saw, inside the darkness, the white of Taffy's eye as he blinked and aimed his ear on the hall.

Rutherford gripped the iron of Abe's cell door. He said, "Trent never spoke a word on ridding this world of Jake Baach. Jake wasn't no more than a fart on the wind to Henry Trent." He stuck his mouth between two bars. "And hasn't nobody of import taken notice of you bein here neither," he said. "And tomorrow I get to watch you and your woman drop, and there isn't anybody but me left to run this whole place." That very evening at dinner, he'd strangled the life from Rufus Beavers. They were arguing over the money they'd discovered as counterfeit when it escalated. He'd pinned the old man to the floor of Trent's office and watched his eyes pop. He'd rolled Rufus up in a horsehair rug and toted him to the shuttered bootleg slope mine, and there he'd dumped him down the three-hundred-foot hole.

Without a sound, Taffy Reed stepped into the darkened hall and cupped his ear.

"No more Rufus," Rutherford said, "and pretty soon no more Fred Reed."

Abe looked at the man. The lantern by his chair cast him

bigger than he was and his shadow stretched long on the floor.

Rutherford stepped back from the bars. "Taffy!" he hollered. "I'm going home to bed! Come out here and watch this cocksucker!" He left a white-labeled pint of Chokoloskee whiskey by the chair.

On the straw mattress, Abe listened to the main door close, and when it did, he unclenched his fist. He unwrapped the pebble and read Tong's coded note:

Luna in flight
Serpiente tucked tight

Taffy Reed stepped back in the embalming room for his lantern.

He walked past Goldie without swinging it. He set it down by the chair at cell one and took up the whiskey and drank. It nearly choked him. When he'd quit coughing, he said, "I've reconsidered."

Abe stood up. "What's that now?"

"How to align myself," Taffy said.

Abe smiled. "Good," he said. "Set yourself down there. Let's talk a little while." His plan could proceed a little easier now. He could finally use what he'd stashed in his mattress.

Taffy said, "I can likely take out the perimeter guards." He pointed beyond the jail's walls. "You two might slip out before sunup."

"No," Abe said. He procured the notes and fattened folds of paper from betwixt the straw shoots of his foul tick. "The people want a hanging." He pulled on his drawers and stepped to the bars, sliding through to Taffy Reed what he'd accumulated at the behest of the wild notions in his mind. He smiled. His eyes went wide. "The people want a big show," he said.

Taffy swallowed. There was a coldness at the pit of his stomach.

Abe told him to gather himself. "You got work to do," he said.

*

Sleep was not something to be had. In the past, Abe had gone without it for as long as fifty-four hours, maybe more. Still, he did not feel sharp as he walked in a fine suit and shackles to the box wagon waiting at the jail's side door. He could hear the words repeating as he sat down and swayed at the bullwhip crack on horse's rump: *You can sleep when you are dead.*

It was the truth.

The early morning hours of their execution day had played as if a dream. Now noon was close at hand, and as he got his first look at Goldie in near a month—beautiful as she was, straight-backed on her coffin-seat—he thought he might drop where he rocked, sabotaging all that he'd planned.

But she winked at him as they rolled over mud ruts and

through the people crowding the lane. In the rain, she mouthed the words *I love you* and *keep your temper*. And so he did.

And as he sat there between a preacher and a devil-man, rolling past an alley where bent souls shot dice, Abe nodded to Ah Tong, who leaned against the bricks and grinned. He'd dismantled his Punch and Judy booth and was making his way through the crowd, giving signals and watching the box wagons close.

After Independence Day, Tong had hidden himself in Wan's storeroom for a month before venturing onto Keystone's streets. On his first night in the Bottom, he'd stood in the lane and stared at the empty Baach saloon. Across Wyoming, Goldie's beautiful cathouse, where he'd seen a window woman dance, had been burnt to the ground. All that remained was piled ash and two-by-fours bubbled and blacked. It was the same night he'd met Bushel-Heap Lou McKill, who was clumsily tossing a paper wad at the jailhouse window while the outside guard paced his square. Tong had helped the giant man and then together they got drunk, and they discovered the wondrous things folks discover when they sit and visit awhile. It turned out that Tong knew more than the superiority of marionettes over puppets, and when he'd shown his back-palm and his cigar-through-the-nose and the difficult maneuverings of plugging a gun barrel undetected, Bushels had known he could help. "Abe's got a big one brewin," he'd told his new friend.

Now Tong stepped quick from the brick alley wall and fell in behind the surrey at the rear. He had sabotaged Rutherford's tomato-crate speech and plugged the chief's gun barrel too. He'd swayed the mind of his rain-dotted crowd with the tale from his puppets' mouths. And he'd called out his signals to the paid-off jewelry peddlers and the barkers at their tables three-shelled.

Ahead of him, the wagons split the crowd as the procession toward death carried on.

On the hillside to the east, Bushels was in position, peeking now and again from the willow-tree's cover. The crowd had backed up the ridge from the push at leveled plot, and he could hear them laugh and mumble down below. His pocketwatch read two minutes to noon. He leaned into the wide willow's trunk and rested his head on the scrape. He thought of Ben Moon's last telegram, and he hoped that it was the truth.

Near the circled chain link, with his hands in his pockets, a stout man stood eyeballing the gallows wood. It had been some time since he'd leveled and planed such fine timber. He'd enjoyed the elaborate work, particularly when his son had helped him with the latches and the hinges encased inside. He'd not understood at first when Frank brought by the giant Scotsman and the Chinaman who dressed like an Italian. But they told him he could avenge his nephew's death, and time was of the essence, it seemed. So Tilio Dallara had ridden into Keystone Thursday morning, just as they'd told him to do, and he'd presented the forged letter to the drunk judge and his midget friend, and now he looked on, waiting for the show.

He nodded to his son, who stood by the peanut vendor.

Frank Dallara had grown tired of the peanut man's shouts. "Sellin nuts! Hot nuts!" the man called, again and again. Frank had eaten three bags already, hungry and spent as he was from such lantern-light, last-minute work.

Four policemen hopped from the surrey and cleared an entrance at the gallows fence gate.

Taffy Reed undid the ankle cuffs of the Kid and the Queen.

They all climbed the thirteen stairs single file.

On the scaffold stage, Abe listened for the sound of the noon train. None came.

The preacher preached on eternity and time, and Goldie was told to say her piece. But by then, she'd lost a little of her hope, and all those babies in the crowd had frightened her.

Rutherford swayed imperceptibly where he stood. He told Abe to make his speech.

Abe too was losing hope in the plan by then, and so he stalled with reminiscence on his Daddy's saloon. He spotted ole Warts Wickline at the fence, and together they told a tale.

At nine minutes past twelve, the whistle of the westbound noon train came faint on the air. The rain slowed.

When Abe took out from nowhere his deck of playing cards, Rutherford nearly fainted. His skin hummed and a squelching sound arose from his gut.

The dozen eggs he'd eaten were taking their effect, for before the sun had risen, Taffy Reed had used an embalmer's bulb-syringe to inject each one with a careful mixture. The mixture itself had come from the medicine trunk of Tony Thumbs, a final gift for Abe, given on July 22nd, in a foul-smelling room above the Old Drury Theatre. Bushels had kept the trunk locked and hidden at his boardinghouse room in Kimball, and along with it, he kept the old man's batch-book. When chances arose, Tong had tossed paper sleeves through the bars of Abe's cell window. Each powder was named in pencil. He'd wadded batch book recipes and thrown those too. Abe had stashed them all in the rotted spaces of his straw tick, and he'd hoped he might use them somehow. That morning, he'd given them over to Taffy Reed, who worked fast from a torn page of Tony Thumbs' scrawl:

Paralysis without death or the cessation of respiratory function: A half-pint of water to a tablespoon of fart juice. Two teaspoons of curare and a dash each of maypop and opium and valerian too.

Now Rutherford stood on the sweetgum boards and swayed on his feet. The crowd before him seemed to groan and wobble.

Abe split the card deck's seal with his thumbnail and said, "At the end of it, if the law is still behind me, he can by God yank the handle."

Taffy Reed leaned to Rutherford and whispered, "I best put them ankle irons back on." Rutherford nodded, unable to speak, and Taffy knelt before Abe and set to work. He could see that the chief was well on his way. He left the ankle cuffs undone and loosened the wrists all the way.

With his last bit of gumption, Rutherford bent to the nooses where they hung and gathered their lengths in his fist. The tingling in his fingers and toes had reached a burn.

Beside him, Abe roared, "I'll tell the truth before I die, or I'll walk out of hell in kerosene drawers and set the world on fire!"

Some in the crowd were struck by his words, for they'd heard tell of a fire out West. It burnt wild on the wind and swept three states, and it killed the men who fought it. There were those who said it would swallow the country whole. A bald street preacher claimed foreknowledge of the Devil's Broom Fire. He said sinners were reaping what they'd sowed.

Rutherford wobbled, then dropped to his knees. When his face hit the boards, there came from his backside a ragged slap of wind that carried forth without cease for a full fourteen seconds.

Abe said, "Amen," and tossed the deck to Goldie. They played shackled catch as if it were a common game. She winked at him and pulled back the flaps and dropped the wrapper to the boards. The cards wore heavy varnish.

The sun came free of the clouds then, and the people looked skyward, and there was only the north-born sound of the tardy noon train's wheeze. The engine was not yet fully stopped at the station when Ben Moon's men began to jump from inside the empty coal hoppers. They hit the hard dirt beside the railbed and rolled and got to their feet quick. They ran on wrenched ankles, headlong into the people staring dumb at the heavens.

Anchors had gotten the telegram in Baltimore the evening prior, and he'd gathered the men and talked fast. To each he handed cash and a rifle from Moon's stash. They slid them in duffels and hopped the train. Orders were to be in Keystone by noon, and to suppress with drawn guns whatever crowd had gathered there. Now they did just that, shouting "Nobody moves, nobody dies!" at the men on the edges who looked to be pondering the vigilante's way.

At the scaffold Abe hollered, "Unroll your bought confessions and read what it says at the end! Turn over our last living photographs and heed what's written there!" He heard faintly the engine of the airship then, coming in against the westerly wind.

The people read what was printed on their execution souvenirs. *Abe Baach and Goldie Toothman are innocent of murder. Henry Trent and Munchy Briles were killed as they leveled their guns. There is only one murderer on the gallows today, and his name is Rutherford Rutherford. Listen close to what you're told and do not produce any weapon.*

Mr. Tong and the barkers and peddlers drew their guns from the circled perimeter they'd made. They trained them on those they suspected of trouble.

Some had heard the airship engine by then too, particularly those on the hill. The cloud cover was wispy. The rain was no more.

Abe and Goldie stepped from their ankle cuffs and shed the irons from their wrists.

The one-eyed police officer was panicked by then. He drew his revolver slow.

Goldie cocked back a card and let it fly. It sunk in his neck at a pulsing vein and he dropped his gun to the ground.

Ah Tong shouldered his way through the people and stood at the fence, where he tossed a tin bullhorn in a perfect arc into the open hands of Taffy Reed. Taffy put it to his mouth and told the people to listen, and they did. He told them their police chief had killed their judge, that he'd been tossing bodies down Buzzard Branch mineshaft for years. It was the same thing he'd told his Daddy that morning, and now, as he spoke it to the crowd, Fred Reed was up the ridge, prying open the mine's mouth to see.

Some in the crowd were beginning to shout. Others were protesting they knew not what.

Abe took the bullhorn then. "Listen!" he called. Some heeded and some did not. He hollered, "You'll never again pay a monthly consideration!" It drew the attention of all those then living in Keystone. "You're about to see a show you won't ever forget! You have my word we'll astound and delight!" Children asked if they could perch on the shoulders of their daddies. Abe went on, "And if you keep calm and steady, then riches will rain down from above!"

He pointed to the sky, where the airship named *America* was nearly in view.

High above in the gondola basket, Ben Moon stood in a wide stance with binoculars at his eyes. "We need to get east by fifty yards and decrease altitude!" he called to the relay man, who nodded from where he hung from the envelope, then shot into the hull, where he relayed to the elevatorman and the rudderman both. They were low already, just over the canopy on the ridge. "Can he slow this thing down?" Moon asked, but it was too loud up there. No one in the basket could hear him.

Beside Moon was Walter Melvin. His blue scarf whipped behind him. He turned the handle of a moving-picture camera he'd built himself. It was mounted on a tripod he'd bolted to the deck. He aimed it down. "Just marvelous, absolutely marvelous," he said of the mountains and riverbed below. "They said we couldn't fly *America* in here," he shouted. "Well? What say they now?"

Little Donnie crouched at basket's edge, tethered to the guardrail by his belt. He cut the safety tie premature, and the massive rope cargo net unfurled with a whoosh. As wide as the ship, it extended in seconds to its full length of two hundred feet, and its weighted bottom tore off the high limbs of the big willow-tree.

Beneath the tree, Bushels ducked and covered his head, and the branches came down around him. After a moment he stood and came out toward the flat, and he reached up as the cargo net moved on.

The airship *America* was at the mercy of the day's strange wind.

Bushels caught up and grabbed at the rope's thick lengths. He held fast, hooking his arms through the holes. Willow branches twisted throughout, and a sizable limb knocked his head.

The people on the hillside stared as Bushels came, his boots dragging in the dirt and then lifting upon the air. They could not understand what they saw, a giant riding a cargo net to a behemoth silver ship in the sky. A few fell trying to get down the hill, where the others looked up at the vision of flight. *America* was a rigid, bullet-shaped zeppelin, a hundred and fifty feet long, and sixty feet side-to-side. Its shadow played across a vast stretch, and some in the crowd were deathly afraid.

By then, Taffy Reed had drawn his gun and convinced the officers below to put theirs on the ground. He took his place by the lever, his boots on the framed two-by-four edge.

Goldie had let go her cocked cards and told the preacher and stenographer they had better descend the stairs or jump off from where they stood. She glanced up the hillside where Bushels twisted and yanked. She wished Agnes were there. *See*, she'd tell the girl, *some giants are good*.

Rutherford's eyes were open where he lay. He was alive enough to moan and blink.

Abe tossed the bullhorn to Goldie. He bent and cinched the little man's ankles in the noose. Then he stood again on his square, and Goldie stepped to her own. "Behold!" she called through the horn. "The devil drops!" Together, they nodded at Taffy.

When he pulled the lever, the whole scaffold floor unlatched and the hinges creaked as it swung open in two parts. Tilio Dallara had made a masterful box, an anti-gallows where the squares of the condemned remained pedestal-fixed while all other panels fell free. Rutherford dropped through the open middle as a dead man would, snapping straight when the slack went taut. He made the sound of an animal shot but not dead as he swung in full view of the crowd. The encased bottom panels had fallen too, smacked flat and laid out on each side. Only the frame remained. Abe and Goldie stood on their pedestaled squares and looked below at Rutherford. He was upside-down and swaying loose, his arms limp as window meat. And all around his fingers, copperheads and rattlers coiled up and sidewinded both. Some were scared into striking by the thud of the boards and pendulum man above.

Frank Dallara watched close the snakes he'd put in place. Four sacks he'd carried in, each with five inside. Twenty snakes caught in two days' time by his son and the boy they called T.

Up on his square, Abe took to humming the snake-charmer song, and Goldie joined him in a practiced and symphonious perfection.

The people looked on as Rutherford moaned. One rattler

struck out and latched at his wrist. A copperhead struck higher and hung undulating from his head.

There was nothing in this world Rutherford feared more than serpents, and he could not move a muscle as they came.

The women holding their babies aloft now clutched them tight at the chest. A rumble struck up, and some said the show was the devil's work, displayed before the very eyes of God.

Up above, the big ship slowed and circled back. Ben Moon dropped his binoculars from his face and licked his finger and held it in the wind. "Oh hell," he said, "let it go, I guess," and Little Donnie pulled the cord on the cinched king sheet. A hundred thousand dollars in fives, tens, and twenties dropped in a cluster from the basket's side rail. The cluster unbunched and the notes spun in whorls. The wind took them west to a stretch of uncut trees.

The people looked up again, and when they saw what came, they chased the big-faced notes to the woods. At first, only the greedy among them ran after the money, but when it was clear that Abe had spoken the truth, that riches were in fact raining down, every man, woman, and child lit out for those hardwoods, and once there, they shimmied up trunks and tightroped boughs in order to pluck out a bill.

Here and there, a twenty clung to the cargo net that extended so long beneath the ship. Bushels strained and jerked at its bottom still, trying to slow *America* down, trying hard to get himself back to the ground. He managed to come lower and touch his toes to the mud, just as the people all cleared.

They would not even notice the end of the show, so busy were they in the woods.

Abe and Goldie had leapt from their perches on high, careful to clear all serpentine paths. Taffy Reed jumped too, and Abe shook his hand at the fence. "Well done," he told Taffy.

Ah Tong and the barkers and peddlers and riflemen all congregated outside the circled fence. Five or six kept their guns trained on the singular straggling police officer. They watched close the few remaining townspeople—elderly, lame souls who could not run for the trees.

Further hand-shaking had commenced but was cut short in a hurry, as the big net approached twenty yards to the east. Bushels skipped at its bottom and hollered, "Get set!" His arm muscles swelled, intwined at the cargo's holes, his biceps as big around as telegraph poles. His voice was a boom on the wind. "It's time to go!"

Abe and Goldie ran then for the tail of their vessel, and their conspirators smiled and looked on. Up above, the elevatorman and the rudderman had slowed *America* as much as she could be slowed, and Walter Melvin had run out of film. He called to his assistant to fetch another canister.

The wind shifted direction, and the cinders came on, for some men at Cinder Bottom never ceased their making. They worked every Sabbath before the six hundred red-mouthed holes in the mountain.

Bushels hooked Goldie first, locking her forearm in his, and he swung her like nothing over his head. "Keep both hands gripped and both feet on a square," he commanded, "and move up just as quick as you can."

It wouldn't be long before the riverbed bent back, so narrow it was between the stumped high walls. If they didn't reach the basket before the lowland turned, they'd slam dead against the clear-cut cinch.

Abe was next to lock the strongman's arm, and he swung upward just the same as his bride, took hold of the rope's rough hide. A five-dollar note slipped free from a length and hit him square in the forehead before fluttering away. There were willow twigs woven throughout the big net, and they welted his arms like a switch.

Goldie stopped climbing long enough to look down, to make sure her Abe was on. She saw the top of his head beneath a willow-tree limb and the sight of it jolted her bones. It was what she'd seen in a dream thirteen years before, when all the money and the blood was yet to come. But in her dream, Abe hung dead by the willow-tree limb. He'd not once moved. He'd not looked up at her as now.

He smiled from below with the rope in his fists, and he winked at her too. And though their bodies rocked about inside the cindered wind, he would not look away from the Queen. It didn't matter where he looked at her—the dark of her eye or the nape of her neck or the curve of her wrist at the hand—she swelled the blood's forgotten memory and she stirred its music too, and for a thing such as that, a man would gladly die.

He called up to her, "Best view in the natural world."

It tickled her and she laughed despite the task ahead. She even shut her eyes without knowing why, and for a moment, there was not a sound. There was nothing. No beaten ground beneath them and no zeppelin above. Then she heard Abe call out a word from below, and he called it again and again.

Climb.

ACKNOWLEDGMENTS

Deborah Weiner's *Coalfield Jews* was so very helpful in so many ways. Jean Battlo's *A Pictorial History of McDowell County* was also immeasurably valuable, as was all of Battlo's work. I'd like to acknowledge the Archives at the West Virginia Division of Culture and History, particularly the 1897 *Jackson Herald* article covering the last public execution in the state, as it became an important resource for this book's opening chapter. Talmage A. Stanley's *The Poco Field: An American Story of Place* was helpful as well. I suppose I must also acknowledge a strange, ridiculous, and anonymous source, for it indeed provided a sense of time and place and prevailing racist attitudes, and beyond that, it actually became a tangible part of this novel: *Sodom and Gomorrah of Today or the History of Keystone West Virginia*, published in 1912 and authored by "Virginia Lad."

I am neither a poker man nor a magician, and so there are many others I'd like to thank for their guidance. James

McManus' *Cowboys Full* was particularly enlightening, as was the work of Jim Steinmeyer, particularly *The Last Greatest Magician in the World*. And Ricky Jay's *Learned Pigs & Fireproof Women* provided information and inspiration both. David W. Maurer's *The Big Con* was also quite helpful.

I must acknowledge Larry Merchant's "Suddenly Respectable" from *The National Football Lottery*, where I first encountered a version of the bank president tale used in this novel.

I'd like to thank West Virginia University's Eberly College of Arts and Sciences for providing me with a Riggle Fellowship, and I'd also like to thank West Virginia University's Senate Committee on Research and Scholarship for providing a summer grant. Both allowed me time to complete this novel.

Thank you to my marvellous agent, Terra Chalberg. Thank you to Allen Crawford for the beautiful work on this book's cover. My many thanks to everyone at Tin House, where great books are being made. My gratitude goes to Jakob Vala, Meg Cassidy, Nanci McCloskey, Masie Cochran, Lance Cleland, Cheston Knapp, Win McCormack, and my remarkable editor, Tony Perez.

This is a book about the past, when money and people poured into southern West Virginia. Now, McDowell County is a very different place, due in large part to the mechanization of coal mining and to the lack of corporate, public, and governmental concern for people living in places sometimes referred to these days as "sacrifice zones." I would be remiss if I did not acknowledge those who are working to tell the story of today's McDowell County. Rather than listing them all here, I will give the reader a good place to start: hollowdocumentary.com.